BIGFOOT GALAXY: AFTERLIFE

PREVIOUSLY PUBLISHED AS: AFTERLIFE (THE UNDERMOUNTAIN SAGA #2)

ERIC KENT EDSTROM

1

______

READ YOUR CHAPTERS

A chill rain lashed out of slate-gray Nashville skies, needling Danny Michaelson's face as he trudged home from school. Even his high-tech, hooded jacket couldn't keep him dry. He bowed against the headwind and wished he had a car.

Just thinking about his lack of transportation stirred his anger, most of which he directed at Vincent, his mother's boyfriend.

Danny gritted his teeth as a particularly brutal gust blasted him. He didn't need an expensive car, just a few grand for a junker, which would be no biggie since he had fifty thousand rotting in the bank, earned from that TV commercial.

Danny pulled the drawstrings of his hood tighter and vowed to have it out with Mom when he got home.

But what was the point? She'd just say, "We'll discuss it with Vincent." And then Danny would say, "But it's *my* money." And his Mom would frown and give him that raised eyebrow thing that he hated so much, as if he was a seven year old asking for another piece of cake.

In a last ditch effort, Danny would go to his strongest argument. "Em got to spend her money on the Jeep." And his mom would smile and shake her head as though Danny had said something silly. "Your sister is eighteen."

As far as Danny could tell, Em wasn't any more mature than him. After all, if you're going to spend $27,843 on a car, why would you buy a Jeep? They were cool and all, but they weren't very fast.

Danny had all kinds of ideas about how to modify a car. He kept thinking about getting an old Mustang or Camaro. The knowledge from his implant gave him many insights into how internal combustion engines could be made more efficient, and more powerful.

Way more powerful.

But here he was, walking in the rain–car deprived, cold, and wet. He turned onto Woodmont and into the tree-lined lanes of his neighborhood.

He checked the traffic and jaywalked toward his house. As he stepped onto the sidewalk, he noticed a truck drive by, a moving van. A chime of recognition sounded in his head at the sight of it.

He watched it drive past and scanned the license plate. Sure enough, he'd seen it before. He had to hand it to these sneaky gossip reporters. After all, who would suspect a guy driving a moving van?

The only advantage Danny found in being a minor was that reporters couldn't approach him. Yet everywhere he went, it seemed someone with a long-lensed camera hid in a car or behind a bush, waiting to snap his picture. And then some strange article about him would pop up on an Internet news site, or some random blog, or even in a big national magazine.

Danny hadn't realized how big of a sensation his ordeal in the Canadian Rockies had been until he'd returned to school last fall. Students had swarmed him when he walked through the doors, patted his back, and peppered him with questions. The attention disrupted the hallways so much that the principal had waded in, shouting at the students to get to their classes. Then she took Danny aside and asked him all the same questions his friends had asked.

Danny checked the van's license plate number against the list he stored in his implant, the computer-like memory he'd gotten from the tangoga in Antarctica.

The list included the date he'd seen each license plate, the make and model of the car, and the vehicle's color. Each time he suspected a car of scoping him out, he added it to the list. This one had shown up five times in the past three weeks, certainly enough times to justify calling the police. Except he didn't want to draw attention to the situation. Mom had been a bit overprotective since the Canada fiasco. He worried she might cancel his trip the next day to Indianapolis to meet up with Breyona and Wa.

He went into his house, kicked off his soggy shoes, and tossed his jacket onto a wall peg.

"Danny, is that you?" his mom called from the kitchen.

"Yeah." He hefted his backpack and headed up to his room, taking the stairs two at a time. A glance at the alarm clock by his bed told him Breyona wouldn't be home yet. They would video chat later.

He didn't really have any real homework to do, aside from reading for English class. He always completed his math and science work in study hall. It was so ridiculously easy for him. He never got answers wrong thanks to the implant, which not only helped him remember everything, it also gave him knowledge of super-advanced math and science. Stuff humans hadn't even discovered yet.

He pulled out the book his English teacher had assigned, *Frankenstein* by Mary Shelley. He flopped onto his bed and opened the book, but he couldn't get into the story. His mind kept going

back to the moving van. He wondered if Breyona was having problems with the media too.

She never seemed to mind the attention, though. She excelled
at interviews, and the press never said anything negative about her.
Not the way they did about Wa, who they recently caught in the
middle of a prank, one which resulted in his expulsion from his
high school. Danny didn't know all the details, but he didn't think
it was fair. After all, putting a Ronald McDonald on top of the
school didn't really hurt anyone. Though now that Danny thought
about it, Wa's version of the story lacked a lot of specifics.

Danny's pocket vibrated. He pulled out his phone, the one
thing Vincent had allowed him to buy with his TV commercial
money. The phone wasn't very fancy, not like Em's. But human
technology didn't impress Danny anymore. He looked down at it; a
text message had just come from Breyona.

*Running late. Probably won't be home tonight in time to chat.
Read your chapterss. I'll see you tomorrow.*

Danny mashed an angry response into the phone but deleted it
without pressing send. This was the fourth time this week Breyona
had cancelled. She always uncovered some crisis or other with one
of the kids she worked with. And then Danny felt bad because he
knew how desperately they needed her help. But still, he wanted
time with her, even if it was just video chatting.

He tossed the phone aside and sulked. At least he'd see her
tomorrow at his grandma's house in Indianapolis. It would be their
first reunion since shooting the commercial three months back.

A chime sounded on his computer. He smacked the spacebar to
shut it up. The poor old notebook sat there gathering dust, doing
little other than providing video chat and an occasional alarm.
Sometimes he typed out a report for school on it.

He'd set the alarm to remind him to get out his trainer. He dug
the shoebox out from under his bed, threw aside a few swimsuit
issues of *Sports Illustrated*, a little Millennium Falcon model he'd

made two years ago, and a Rubik's Cube with several pieces missing. At the bottom of the box lay the trainer, a tablet computer unlike any ever made by humans. Because it had been made by bigfeet.

A wave of anxiety passed through Danny's gut as he picked it up, a side effect of the implant he'd gotten in Antarctica. Tangoga rules strictly forbade using–or even touching–a trainer. As a human, he found it easy to ignore most tangoga rules, but the stricture on the trainer had seeped into his brain, had created a blind spot where the device was concerned.

He tried to call Shiv on it but didn't get any response. He checked the time and realized that Shiv was still at the daily *werden* observance in Undermountain.

Danny didn't see the point in pursuing his trainer studies without Shiv. His mind turned back to Breyona, and he glanced at a little snapshot of them standing together wearing the jackets the Super Tech Clothing Company had given them for the commercial. Even then, she had seemed kind of distant. So calm, so sedate. He thought about the brief times they'd spent together. She'd been attentive, caring. She'd held his arm and leaned against him as they sat watching the sunset. Her kisses had been passionate, and he'd felt nothing but love and peace when he had been with her. But when he got home, and she returned to Chicago and her work with those kids . . .

He lay back down and picked up *Frankenstein*, determined to read it and forget about Breyona. He would see her in Indianapolis, and then he would know for sure her true feelings.

2

DO SOMETHING

Danny had blasted through two-thirds of the book by the time his mom called him downstairs. Dinner was always one of three things: macaroni and cheese, spaghetti, or sandwiches. That night it was tacos.

He hooked a kitchen chair with his foot and slid it out. "What's the occasion?"

"I saw this recipe on Katie Perilli's show," Mom said. "I thought it would be a healthy change. There's lettuce."

Em sat at the table in front of an empty plate. "I know," she said into her phone. "He was all like, 'I'm God's gift,' and he couldn't even tell we were all laughing at him." She frowned at the meat in the saucepan, which rested on a hot pad in the center of the kitchen table. "He's harmless. He thinks he's a celebrity now." Em looked at Danny as she said this.

Danny filled a taco shell with some of the dry, very well done, ground meat and added a leaf of lettuce and a handful of shredded cheese. "Who's she talking to?" he asked Mom.

"Probably Jenny."

Em pushed her empty plate away. "And what about the whole CIA story? And that he was an extra in the *Lord of the Rings* movies?" She burst out laughing and rolled her eyes.

Danny set down his taco. She could only be talking about one person. "Em? Where did you see Bronson?"

She ignored him.

"What's Bronson doing in Nashville?"

Em gave him annoyed look. "I'm on the phone."

Mom cocked her head to one side. "Why does that name sound familiar?"

Em said goodbye to Jenny, pocketed her phone, and went to the refrigerator.

Danny stared at her. "Well?"

"I ran into him at the mall after school. He's in town with his dad. Something about a car show."

Danny pushed his plate aside. "Why did you talk to him?"

"I didn't want to. I just ran into him at the food court at the mall." Em pulled a bag of celery and a bunch of kale from the fridge and dropped them on the counter. "I guess I'll make a smoothie." She dug the blender out of a cabinet and put some water in the pitcher. "Anyway, I tried to walk away, but he stopped me. He said he had something really important to tell me. I thought he was going to apologize for what he did to Vincent." She shook her head, as if at her own stupidity.

"What did he want?" Danny asked.

Em stuffed the entire bunch of kale into the blender. "He was worried about me. Said Harvin had called, asking where I live."

Harvin was the grizzled old mountaineer who had been their guide on the hike. Bronson had tried to shoot Harvin but accidentally shot Vincent instead. "Why in the world would Harvin call Bronson?"

"I don't know." Em added some frozen raspberries, a couple stalks of celery, and pressed the button. It sounded like she was blending marbles. She shut it off, dipped a finger in, and brought it to her mouth. "Oh my God, that is *so* good."

"It doesn't make any sense," Danny said. "Harvin would never call Bronson in a million years, and even if he had, what does it have to do with you?"

Em gave him a flat stare. "Danny. The Harvin issue is what we call a pretext. Bronson made it up because he wanted to seem important. You know how full of himself he is." She rolled her eyes as she poured a gloopy, green mixture into a tall glass. "He said he was afraid Harvin might try to . . ." She glanced at Mom for second. "You know. Do something to me."

Mom shrugged into a jacket and grabbed her purse. "I know what 'do something' means, honey. I want you to stay away from Bronson . . . and Harvin. Tell me if either of them tries to contact you." She kissed Em on the top of her head and sighed. "I'm working third shift, so I won't be home until late morning. Don't forget to call me when you get to Grandma's house tomorrow."

Em took a long swig of her smoothie. "Okay, Mom."

Danny endured a kiss and waved goodbye. "Harvin's an oddball, but he didn't give off that kind of creepy vibe, did he?"

"No. Mom's just paranoid. And Bronson's making stuff up, as usual."

Danny shook his head and gave the taco another nudge. "Can I have some of your smoothie?"

Em blinked in surprise. "Really?"

"And stick a fork in my eye while you're at it." Danny grabbed a handful of cookies from a bag on the counter and headed back to his room.

He tried to get back into *Frankenstein*. But the whole discussion of Bronson and Harvin had brought up a bunch of bad memories about Undermountain. He needed to talk to Breyona more than ever.

MIND IF I SMOKE

"Wake up, Danny."

Danny rubbed the sleep out of his eyes and glanced at his clock. Six a.m. "What the hell?"

Em stood over him, frowning. "We've got to go get Bronson."

"Huh? Why?"

"Jenny told him about our reunion at Grandma's. He wants to come with."

"No way."

"He knows Wa is coming."

Danny groaned. "Even more reason for him not to come. Wa hates him more than I do." He pulled the covers over his head.

He felt the bed sag as Em sat next to him. She yanked the covers down. "Wa isn't supposed to leave California. He could end up in juvie if he gets caught in Indiana. And you know Bronson will make sure he gets caught."

He pulled a pillow over his eyes. "Bronson's not coming. Besides, you don't go to juvie for putting a Ronald McDonald on the school roof."

"There was more to it than that."

Danny peeked out from under the pillow. "I knew it! Drugs?"

"Maybe," Em bit her lip. Before Danny could say anything more, she raised her hand. "Okay, okay. Yes. But they weren't his."

"How convenient."

"Listen, Danny. Wa may not take too much seriously, but he wouldn't risk his future with me like that. He was just in the wrong place at the wrong time with the wrong people."

Danny closed his eyes and sighed. "You're as full of yourself as Bronson." Not exactly a fair statement, since, unlike Bronson, Em truly was beautiful. She had guys falling all over themselves to impress her. Wa loved Em and would likely do anything to be with her.

"He's your friend, too, Danny. Do you want him to get in trouble?"

"No." Danny heaved himself up and leaned against the headboard. "But why does Bronson even want to come with us? He knows we don't like him."

Em didn't answer right away. She stood and moved to the door. "Do you think it was really a coincidence that I ran into Bronson at the mall?"

"What are you saying? Did you call him?"

Em gave him an are-you-an-idiot look. "No. He's up to something, Danny. God, you can be so thick sometimes. That's the answer to the question of why he wants to go. He's got something up his sleeve, and he's got leverage over us with Wa's issue."

Danny swore, and not under his breath. He looked around his room stupidly, trying to get his brain to wake up.

"Get packed," Em said. "And put on some pants. Your boxers are gaping." As she walked out, Danny noticed she was already dressed, hair perfect.

He pulled on some jeans and a t-shirt before stuffing random bits of clothing into his duffle bag. He considered the trainer for a few moments and decided to take it, thinking Wa and Bre might like a chance to chat with Shiv.

He wet his hair, brushed his teeth, and tossed the brush into his backpack. Em sat waiting at the kitchen table, eating a thimble-sized portion of yogurt. "Took you long enough," she said. "Grab your coat. It's cold out."

It was still dark when they hopped into Em's Jeep. She wrestled with the manual transmission, which Vincent had insisted on because it was cheaper. She eventually popped it into reverse and backed up until they heard a thunk.

"What the hell was that?" she asked.

Danny got out to check. "You killed Mom's deer!" he said. The cement animal lay on its side, four legs broken, one antler snapped off at the head. Em swore then barked at him to get back into the Jeep.

"I've always hated that stupid thing," she said and gunned the vehicle down Woodmont toward Hillsboro Pike.

The endless February rain seemed to seep into everything. Danny shivered and turned up the heat. "Why did we have to leave so early?"

"I want to get to Grandma's before everyone else. We're the hosts."

Em had a point, but he didn't expect Breyona to be on time anyway. "Still, it's not even seven."

"You should drink smoothies. They'll make you a morning person."

"I want people to like me."

Fifteen minutes later, Em turned the Jeep into a hotel parking lot off West End Avenue. Bronson stood outside in a Texas Rangers jacket, holding a sack in one hand. He was big, well over six feet tall, and had the build of an NFL nose guard. Small eyes punctuated his round face, and a permanent smirk turned his mouth down on one side. He tossed a cigarette to the ground as they drove up.

"Back seat, Danny," Bronson said by way of greeting.

"What?"

Em patted Danny's arm. "Just move."

Danny climbed over the armrest into the back seat as Bronson hoisted his bulk into the front. He slammed the door and gave Em a lingering hug, which she returned limply. "It's so sweet of you to offer us gas money, Bronson."

"Yeah. You want me to drive?"

Em showed her teeth, her best effort at a smile. "No. Vincent said the Jeep isn't insured for any other drivers."

Bronson shivered at the mention of Vincent's name. "Let's roll," he said.

As Em drove down the glistening streets toward the freeway, Bronson rummaged through his sack and pulled out a long stick of jerky. He offered a bite to Em, but she gave him a tight shake of her head. If the idiot knew anything about Em, he'd know she did not eat jerky.

The smell of the jerky wafted into the back seat, and Danny discovered he was starving. Bronson didn't offer him any, though.

"Won't your dad wonder where you've gone?" Danny asked, flailing for some way to get Bronson to change his mind.

Bronson inhaled a long, whistling breath through his nose. "Nope. When he found out a girl was coming to pick me up, he gave me a hundred bucks and slapped my back on the way out."

It was hard to tell in the dark Jeep, but Danny thought his sister's face went pale in the rearview. If Bronson wasn't so creepy, Danny would've laughed.

"It's hot in here," Bronson said. He turned the heat off and cracked the window. "Mind if I smoke?"

4

I MIGHT MAKE YOU MY PROJECT

The sky brightened to a dull gray as they drove north on I-65 toward Indianapolis. Sleet chattered on the Jeep's windshield, and Bronson's window whistled and spat bits of ice into Danny's face.

He lay curled on the hard back seat, snuggled deep into his jacket, thankful for its warmth. Once Bronson had fallen asleep, Em flipped on the heat.

Danny sat up and stretched his arm past Bronson to roll up the window. "Why doesn't this piece of junk have power windows?"

"It's not a piece of junk."

The window crank lay just out of reach. He scooched behind Em's seat to get out of the draft. "How far?"

"Twenty miles or so, I think. I've never driven to Grandma's before. Do you know what her address is?"

Danny didn't.

Em dialed her phone. "Hi, Mom," she said in the cheerful voice she always used on Mom. "The deer? Oh no! It was fine when we left."

Bronson woke up with a snort. He rolled the window all the way down and hocked a loogie into the wind.

"We left early," Em said to Mom. "But I forgot to get Grandma's address."

"Who's she talking to?" Bronson asked.

"Shh," Em said, hand over the phone. "Oh, that was Danny. I think his voice is changing."

"What?" Danny said. "My voice–!"

Em cut him off with a look in the rearview.

"Don't *tell* me the address, Mom," Em said, "Text it to me. Good. Thanks."

Em ended the call and shook her head in disgust. "You're both going to get us in trouble. We do not want Mom finding out Bronson is along."

Bronson shrugged and lit up a cigarette. He seemed to have an endless supply in his sack.

Forty minutes later, they pulled up in front of Grandma's tidy, little, suburban house. They piled out and trudged up the sidewalk, past perfectly winterized flowerbeds guarded by a troop of pointy-hatted gnomes. The door opened before they got halfway up the walk, and Grandma's cotton-ball head peeked out. Her piercing blue eyes took them in at a glance. "You're here!"

"I hope we're not too early," Em said.

"Heavens, no. I've been up since four thirty." She gave a laugh, flashing straight white teeth, and winked. "I'm almost ready for lunch."

That sounded good to Danny.

Grandma jabbed a finger at Bronson's cigarette. "Put that horrible thing out. And don't put any butts on my steps, or I'll put yours out there with 'em."

Bronson mumbled something and stubbed the cigarette out on the bottom of his shoe.

Satisfied, Grandma ushered them into the house and planted papery kisses on Danny's cheeks.

The front door opened directly into the living room, which Grandma called the parlor. The house hadn't changed at all during Danny's lifetime. By the door sat the garish, porcelain frog vase serving as an umbrella stand. A blue sofa sat beneath a picture window hung with misty drapes tied back with blue and yellow ribbons. Across from the window was a fireplace. On the mantel stood an old wind-up clock. Family portraits and porcelain birds covered every other available surface.

A set of brass fireplace utensils hung from a stand on the hearth: shovel, poker, broom. Not a speck of ash marred them.

"Now," Grandma said, "who's this smoker you brought with you?" Her eyes accused, judged, and sentenced Bronson as she looked him up and down. Since Grandpa had died of lung cancer, Grandma took all smoking as a personal offense.

"This is Bronson," Em said. "We weren't planning on bringing him, but he happened to be in Nashville. He was on the hike in Canada with us."

Grandma harrumphed and spun toward the kitchen. "I'll fix you something to eat."

Soon the smell of bacon and eggs filled the spotless, little house. Grandma put out her delicate, bluebird-patterned plates, stacked perfectly browned toast on a platter, and poured freshly squeezed orange juice into minuscule glasses.

Danny wondered why his mom never cooked like this. Even Em ate an entire egg and a piece of toast. Bronson didn't even chew, nor did he seem to notice how good the food was. Worst of all, he didn't thank Grandma when he finished.

"I grew up on a pig farm," Grandma said. "But 'til this day, I'd never had one in my kitchen."

Bronson laughed and gave Danny a disgusted look. Danny opened his mouth, a snide on his lips, but Em kicked his leg under the table. "That was wonderful," she said to Grandma. "Thank you so much."

"My pleasure, honey. Now why don't you both get unpacked. I've got some things I need carried up from the basement. I'm sure Bronson can take care of that in a jiffy. If his lungs still work after inhaling all that smoke."

"Aw, come on," Bronson said. "I don't feel like–"

Grandma pinned him to his seat with her eyes and smiled. "I think I might make you my project."

Danny and Em high-tailed it to the Jeep to get their bags, anxious to escape the kitchen. You never, ever, wanted to be Grandma's project.

Bronson wound up retrieving several chairs, two of Grandpa's old army cots, and some boxes of junk that Grandma wanted to sell on eBay.

"These old radios must be worth something," she said.

"Is that what these are?" Bronson asked. "They weigh a ton."

The doorbell rang. Danny's heart quickened as he opened the door, hoping to see Breyona.

But it was just Wa. He stood there, bobbing his head, white earbuds sprouting from his ears. Wa stood only a hand taller than Grandma. He wore all black, as usual. He smiled up at Danny and held his hands out to the side. "Here I am. Where's Em?"

Wa gave Em a tight hug, which Danny thought lasted entirely too long. Em didn't seem to mind.

Wa saw Bronson and flashed a humorless smile. "Bronco! What an unpleasant surprise."

Bronson made a rude gesture. At least he had the presence of mind to make sure it wasn't in Grandma's line of sight.

"This must be Grandma," Wa said. His smile became genuine. He dug in a duffle bag and presented Grandma a long box with a red ribbon around it. "For you, ma'am."

Grandma opened the box and pulled out a red rose. Her blue

eyes shone and even welled up for a moment. She turned to Bronson and pointed to Wa. "You will study this boy's manners and emulate them. Understood?"

Bronson grunted and went outside for a smoke.

Soon they were back around the kitchen table, catching up. Grandma put the rose in a vase and featured it in the center of the table. She also managed to bake brownies while no one was looking, and Danny found room for two or three.

"I need to check bids on some items," Grandma said. "I've got five auctions closing today." She headed to Grandpa's old den where she kept her computer.

Wa smiled as he watched her go. "She's something else. I wish she was my grandma."

"Trust me," Em said. "After that rose stunt, she *is* your grandma."

A look of concern passed over Wa's face. He glanced through the door into the living room then leaned over the table. "Can someone explain why Bronson is here?"

"Blackmail," Danny said.

Em explained, and Wa's face darkened further. "But why did he want to come? He knows we hate his guts."

Em shrugged. "He wouldn't say. Just that he didn't want to be left out."

"He's going to tell on me anyway, Em. He's such a—"

"Hi Bronson," Em said too loudly.

Wa clamped his mouth shut and glanced back. Bronson ambled in, smelling like an ashtray. He lowered himself onto a chair, which creaked under his weight, and blew out a heavy sigh that made his cheeks billow.

Wa gave Bronson a once over, a mischievous glint in his eye. "You sure spend a lot of time out on the front stoop. A stupe on a—"

Em placed a hand on Bronson's arm and asked if he'd like something to drink.

"A beer," he said.

Em poured him a glass of milk and gave him a brownie, which seemed to satisfy him.

Wa shot dirty looks at Bronson, but Bronson didn't notice. His eyes were sliming all over Em as she moved about the kitchen. Danny shuddered.

"What's keeping Breyona?" Wa asked.

Danny glanced up at Grandma's wall clock. "She should be here soon."

But only moments later, his phone chimed.

Running late. Crisis with one of my kids.

Danny shoved the phone back into his pocket and headed for the front door. He needed air, needed to be alone, frustrated that, once again, Breyona had put him second. He cut through the living room, only to be stopped by his tiny grandmother.

"Hold on," she said. "I want to talk to everyone." She poked her head into the kitchen and told the others to assemble in the parlor. Danny clenched and unclenched his fists. He wouldn't walk out while his grandma was talking, wouldn't disrespect her like that. But anger filled him with nervous energy, and he stood impatiently, half-listening and staring out the picture window. A gray rain fell steadily on the quiet street, perfectly matching his mood.

Grandma took position in the middle of the floor, hands on hips. "It's time to set down some ground rules. The girls will share a room. You two," she pointed at Danny and Wa, "will share another. The smoker will sleep in the den on one of the cots."

A moving van drove past, slowed, and backed up. Danny leaned closer to the window and squinted.

Grandma paced up and down like a sergeant. "I'm a light sleeper, and I know every sound this house makes. If I catch a boy in the girls' room or vice versa, there will be severe consequences." Her eyes locked on each of them for a moment so her words might soak in. "Severe."

Danny scanned the list of cars in his implant. He couldn't make out the license plate number of the van from where he stood, but the make and color matched the one he'd seen yesterday after school.

Oh crap, he thought. The media had found them. He turned toward Bronson, accusations forming on his tongue.

"Danny!" Grandma's voice cracked like a whip, and he spun around. "Have you been listening?"

He looked back outside, but the van was gone. "Uh. Yeah. No going into the girls' bedroom."

"Does everyone understand?"

A quiet chorus of "yes ma'ams" sounded. Even Bronson nodded.

Still angry, Danny went to the door. He didn't care about the van at that moment. He just needed to clear his head. His hand had just closed over the knob when the doorbell rang.

YOU'RE TURNING BLUE

Danny froze as a surge of excitement filled him. The doorbell rang again, followed by two sharp knocks.

"Are you going to stand there like a lump, or are you going to open the door?" Grandma asked.

Danny smiled. It had to be Breyona. He turned the knob.

The door smashed into his face and sent him stumbling backward. He tripped over the porcelain frog and landed hard on his back.

A man wearing a black track suit and gas mask barged in. "Okay, so nobody move!"

Another man in a gas mask rushed in and pointed a spray can at Danny.

Grandma stepped forward and kneed Track Suit in the groin. He bent double, swearing in a high-pitched rasp.

"Sit on him, Bronson," Grandma said.

Bronson stood with wide eyes, mouth agape. He didn't move. Danny struggled to his feet, shock making him clumsy and slow.

Wa sidestepped Bronson and swung the fireplace poker at the

spray can guy. The man stepped back and brought up the can. Thick blue mist spewed from the nozzle. Wa swung again, striking the man's forearm. He cried out in pain and hurled vile curses at Wa.

Track Suit fought to straighten himself. "Gas 'em, Jack! Gas 'em!" He shoved Grandma back, and Danny just barely caught her before she toppled.

He backed toward the kitchen, pulling Grandma with him. But she apparently wanted to fight, for she strained forward. "Get out of my house, you rats!"

Jack waved the can back and forth, filling the whole room with a hazy mist. Wa roared and brought the poker down on Jack's wrist. The can fell to the floor and rolled to Danny's feet. He snatched it up.

Jack screamed and clutched his wrist. Em jumped on his back and pummeled his head until they both fell to the floor. Wa swayed, dropped to his knees, and yanked the mask from the man's face. He was middle aged, bearded, and balding. Wa put the shaft of the poker on the guy's neck and pressed him down.

Track Suit lunged for the spray can, but Danny twisted away. The mist reeked of sulfur and made him dizzy. The room slanted to one side, and Danny found himself on the floor.

"Freeze," Grandma shouted, her voice high and crackling with rage, "or I'll shoot your face off."

Danny rolled over to see Grandma pointing Grandpa's old rabbit gun, a .22, at Track Suit. She must have slipped into the pantry where she kept it ready behind the broom and dustpan.

Track Suit laughed. "You gotta be kidding!"

"Try me," she said. "Now get over to that sofa."

Track Suit raised his hands and nodded. "Okay, okay." He took a slow step toward the sofa then ducked low and yanked the barrel of Grandma's rifle. The gun went off, and the bullet smashed Grandma's ugly yellow lamp, throwing the room into gray shadow.

Track Suit wrested the gun away and turned it on Grandma. "Enough of this. Let Jack up."

Danny stood on unsteady legs and found Wa, Em, and Jack knotted together on the floor. Em had her arms and legs wrapped around the man, pinning his elbows to his side. Wa kneeled over him, poker raised to strike.

Jack gasped and kicked.

"Don't make me shoot Granny," Track Suit said.

"Wa, Em!" Danny said. "Let him up."

Wa backed away as Em released Jack. The man struggled to his feet. He held his hand out to Danny. "Give me the can, boy."

Danny tossed it to him.

Grandma had her arms folded across her chest. If she felt any fear, Danny didn't see it in her face or posture. If anything, she looked ready to rip Track Suit's arms off. "You picked the wrong old woman to mug, Bucko."

"Shut up."

Grandma's eyes flashed with indignation, but she didn't say anything more.

"Wait a minute," Track Suit said. His lips moved as he counted the heads in the room. "Where's the black girl?"

Danny breathed a prayer of thanks that Breyona hadn't arrived yet.

"Check the other rooms. The rest of you, sit." He waved the rifle barrel at the sofa.

The four of them sat. Wa and Em were like coiled springs. Danny hoped they wouldn't risk getting shot by doing something rash. "Where did Bronson go?" Wa whispered.

"No talking!" Track Suit shouted. The rifle barrel swung toward them.

Bronson had been standing by the kitchen door. He must have run away. Maybe he was calling the cops. Hope surged in Danny. If he could stall long enough . . .

Jack came back. "She's not in the house."

Track Suit swore. His eyes were unreadable behind the gas mask, but Danny sensed uncertainty in his posture.

And where there was uncertainty, there was opportunity. Danny cleared his throat. "Whatever they're paying you, I'll–"

Both men started laughing before Danny could finish. "Not likely, boy," Track Suit said.

"But my stepfather is wealthy. I'm sure we could work something out. Let me call him." Vincent wasn't technically his stepfather, but he was close enough.

Track Suit ignored him. "I think we better get going," he said to Jack.

"So I can gas 'em now?" Judging from the tone of Jack's voice, this was the part he'd been waiting for.

Track Suit swore again. "Don't be an idiot. Put your mask on first."

Jack strapped his gas mask on and sprayed the mist into their faces. He lingered in front of Em, stared at her until she passed out, head lolling to one side.

Danny felt Wa tense, as though preparing to attack. But just as quickly, the boy relaxed and slumped heavily onto Danny's shoulder.

Danny held his breath for as long as he could, even tried to cover his face with his shirt. He glared at Track Suit, clenched his jaw. But Track Suit just shook his head and chuckled. "You're turning blue."

The needs of Danny's body overcame his resistance, and he gulped air.

IT'S LOADED

Breyona blinked her eyes as she drove on I-65 south from Chicago to Indianapolis. The two hours of meditation she practiced each day did not make up for her lack of sleep. And this day had already been long, getting up early to exercise, finishing her homework, attending school—and then the emergency.

Cold February rain pelted down on her windshield, and the wipers' steady motion seemed to lull her closer and closer to sleep. It didn't help that oncoming headlights glared off the wet highway, forcing her to squint. She hated how it got dark so early this time of year.

Breyona turned her thoughts to the boy she'd saved earlier, Andre. He'd attended some of her outreach meetings.

Andre had always been aloof and quiet. She had tried to draw him out, but he never said more than three words at a time, and he never looked her in the eye.

Earlier that day, Breyona had been in choir class when the principal came looking for her.

His stony expression scared her as he took her aside. "We just got a phone call that one of your kids, Andre Pickens, is holed up in his attic with a .45 to his head."

Breyona closed her eyes. One of her kids. She had been working with at-risk students in the inner city since getting home from the adventure in Canada. She taught meditation, led discussions about the challenges the kids faced, and sometimes provided a shoulder to cry on.

"I know an excellent suicide prevention counselor," she said. She started to look the number up in her phone, but the principal stopped her.

"The boy wants to talk to you. Normally we wouldn't allow a student to get into this kind of situation, but you're different."

A squad car waited outside the school and drove her to Andre's house, lights flashing. It dropped her at a rickety house on a street of homes bunched so close their eaves nearly touched.

A paramedic led her to the attic where a strong man with salt and pepper hair sat in front of the attic door, speaking in low tones. Breyona introduced herself.

The man nodded and held out his hand. "I'm Dr. Brooks. Andre won't let me in. The only thing he's said so far is that he wants to talk to you. I'm very concerned now that I see you. Is it possible that he's got a crush on you or that he's going to demand some sort of promise out of you?"

Breyona didn't know. It was certainly possible. Guys who came to her group sessions tended to fall for her, mistaking her compassion for romantic interest.

She knocked on the door. "Andre? Let me in."

Andre's voice came through the door. "Is that you Breyona?" A moment later, the latch clicked, and the door opened a crack. One big, sad, brown eye peeped out. "Come in. Only you."

Breyona glanced at Dr. Brooks. He shook his head and mouthed, "Not while he has a gun."

Breyona went in anyway. The low-ceilinged attic, barely more than a crawlspace, stretched the whole length of the house.

Andre closed the door and locked it. He was so tall and wide he had to duck and twist to move between the rafters. A bare, dusty light bulb hung from the ceiling, casting harsh light against the cobwebs and beams.

Andre looked from her to the gun in his hand. Breyona wondered whether she should calm him outright and take the gun or talk to him first. She knew from her own experience that being calmed too forcefully could create a lot of resentment. She decided to focus on her own emotions, to settle her own nerves first.

She closed her eyes, took a few deep breaths, and sat on the floor. "Andre, please sit. Let's talk."

She began all of her outreach meetings with those words, and Andre seemed to accept it. He sat on the floor across from her, gun cradled in both hands.

"Take some deep breaths," Breyona said. "Try to clear your mind." She held her hand out, and he took it in his huge, meaty one, which trembled. "Close your eyes."

"You'll take the gun," he said.

"I promise not to take the gun unless you drop it."

He closed his eyes, took a deep breath, and exhaled with a shudder. Breyona watched his tormented face. Deep pains played out there, in trembling lips and trickling tears.

"I don't want to die," he said, "but I don't want to live, either. I'm afraid."

"Why wouldn't you talk to Dr. Brooks?"

"Nobody understands me but you, Breyona. When you look at me, you don't judge me. You're the only one. You're so beautiful, and I know I got no chance with you, and it kills me."

Breyona sighed. Her heart went out to Andre, but she knew she couldn't give him what he really wanted. She loved Danny Michaelson.

"And so you'll kill yourself if you can't have me? I don't believe that, Andre. No one kills themselves for a girl or a boy."

He swallowed. "I'm not stupid. I didn't think you'd fall in love with me. There is nothing about me anyone could love anyway. But I wanted you to see this. I want you to see it because I know you understand. You understand 'cause you always talk about surrendering and letting go. I'm gonna surrender and let go." He tensed and with a robotic motion brought the gun to his temple.

Without thinking, Breyona sent a massive pulse of calm through their connection. The gun clattered to the floor. A moment later, Andre fell back, head striking the rough floorboards.

"Get in here," Breyona said, her voice loud and forceful. The door flew open before her words were out, splinters flying from the doorjamb where the latch had been. Dr. Brooks tumbled in, followed by the paramedics.

"What happened?" Dr. Brooks asked, eyes wide, face gray.

"He passed out. I think he's okay, but he was about to do it."

The counselor eyed her. "You seem too calm."

"Trust me," she said. "I'm about as nervous right now as I've ever been." Which was true, though the fear bubbled on the outside of the calm that she continuously cultivated, a gift she had been given by a hateful bigfoot named Shaggy.

The paramedics tended to Andre. The counselor swept up the gun and inspected it. "It's loaded," he said and sighed. He eyed Breyona again. "I don't know what you did, but you saved his life."

"Can you help him?"

Dr. Brooks looked doubtful. "It depends on his insurance situation. We'll admit him to the hospital. Observe him. We'll see if we can line up some counseling. I doubt his family can afford it." His eyes glanced around the attic meaningfully.

Breyona reached into a pocket and pulled out one of her cards. "If there's a problem with paying for it, please call this number."

Breyona's charitable foundation helped with cases just like

Andre's. Over the past four months, she had raised three hundred thousand dollars, mostly from friends of her parents. She had gotten a single, twenty-five-thousand-dollar donation from a popular hip-hop group called Rhyme Without Reason, whose members had read about her outreach programs.

Breyona blinked and rubbed her eyes, bringing herself back to the highway. A sign for Indianapolis flashed by. Twenty miles. She checked the time on her phone. Four hours late.

Danny would understand. And that's why she loved him.

7

THERE'LL BE REPERCUSSIONS

It was dark by the time Breyona pulled up in front of Grandma's house. It was set back from the street, fronted by a primly manicured lawn. In fact, all the houses on the street appeared to be trim and tidy. Breyona figured the average age in the neighborhood was somewhere north of sixty. She sighed contentedly, thinking it would be a nice escape from the noisy life of Chicago. Except for a single moving van, she hadn't seen a moving car since exiting the freeway.

She reached into the back seat for her umbrella, but it wasn't there. Breyona sighed. Her sister, Lola, had driven the car last, and in typical fashion had lost, or just decided to keep, the umbrella.

Breyona pulled up the hood of her jacket and got out. The rain seemed to intensify as she grabbed her bag from the trunk. She ran past the garden gnomes to the front steps and into the shelter of a slight overhang.

She rang the bell, but no one answered. She checked the number on the side of the house. It was the right place. She rang the bell again and knocked, then tried the handle. The door swung open into a small living room. The air stank of sulfur.

"Hello?" she called.

A man spun in the darkness and raised a gleaming object over his head. Light from the kitchen revealed two figures slumped on the sofa: a white-haired old woman and Em.

Breyona stepped forward and touched the man, dropping him to the ground with numbing calm. She went to Danny's grandmother and shook her. "Are you okay? Wake up."

The woman's eyes fluttered open, but she didn't speak. Breyona went to Em and patted her face. After a moment of confusion, the girl threw her arms around Breyona. "I'm so glad to see you. I'm so glad you're okay."

"What happened?" Breyona asked. "Who is this?" she pointed to the big guy she'd stunned.

Em leaned forward, squinting. "That's Bronson. What the hell happened?"

"That's what I want to know," Grandma said. "Where is Danny? Where is Joachim?"

They split up to search the house. Breyona checked the kitchen and a small den. Em came out from one bedroom and Grandma the other. They checked the basement. They checked the backyard.

"Those SOBs took my grandson," Grandma said. "And that delightful, young Joachim." She'd turned on a light in the living room, and Breyona saw anger and fear in the old woman's eyes. "Call 911, Em. I've got to check something." She marched into the den.

While Em called the police, Breyona knelt by Bronson, who still lay unconscious on the floor. She must have hit him with more calm than she'd intended.

"Girls," Grandma called from the den. "Get in here."

They found Grandma sitting at her desk in front of her computer. An array of small knickknacks stood on a table to one side, each labeled with a date and a price. Above it on a shelf, in a neat row, were a dozen old-time radios, also labeled.

Grandma pointed at the screen. "You need to see this." She pressed play on a video showing her own living room.

"You have a security camera?" Breyona asked.

"An old woman can't be too cautious these days, especially when you've got so much merchandise lying around."

Time code clicked by in the upper right-hand corner as the video showed Grandma standing in the middle of the living room lecturing Danny, Bronson, Wa, and Em. Grandma fast-forwarded to a point when Danny grabbed the doorknob, and the door burst open in his face.

Breyona watched the attack unfold, Wa swinging the poker, Jack spraying gas in the room, and eventually, Track Suit snatching a hunting rifle out of Grandma's hands.

"I should have popped him," the little, white-haired lady said.

A few minutes later, they all lay unconscious on Grandma's blue sofa.

The man in the track suit dug through Danny's pockets. "Where is it?" he said. "It's supposed to be on the boy at all times. Jack, go search the other rooms. We can't leave without the device. Mr. GorVit was very clear about that."

At the mention of GorVit's name, Breyona gasped and met Em's eyes, which were wide with recognition. GorVit was the boss tangoga who had led the assault on Undermountain. Gor had nearly killed Breyona. She rubbed the spot on her neck where one of GorVit's blades had once drawn blood.

"Hush," Grandma said.

Jack left the camera's field of view while Track Suit pulled some zip ties out of a pocket. He yanked Danny off the sofa by his ankles. Breyona winced as Danny's head bounced off the floor.

Track Suit zip-tied Danny's wrists together behind his back. "That ought to hold him."

Jack came back. "I think I found it. It was in his backpack." He held up a shiny, flat object.

Grandma paused the video and squinted at the device in Jack's hands. "What is that?"

Breyona recognized it instantly. Danny's trainer. "I think it's the tablet computer Danny got last summer."

Grandma frowned. "I've never seen one quite like that, and I know my technology." She unpaused the video.

"I can't get it to turn on," Jack said.

"Let me see it." Track Suit snatched it from Jack. He turned it in his hands. "There aren't any buttons on this thing."

"That's what I was saying. Let me–"

"Shut up. We gotta get going." Track Suit stuffed the trainer into the deep, front pocket of his velour pants. He waved at Danny's body on the floor. "Take the boy to the truck."

Jack muttered something inaudible, but he scooped Danny up and carried him out.

Track Suit scanned the room and frowned. His head froze when his eyes fell on Em's limp form. He cocked his head and jutted out his jaw. "Well," he said, "since the black girl isn't here, you'll do."

Just as he had done with Danny, he grabbed Em's ankles and pulled her from the sofa.

Grandma glared at the video and clenched her fists. "There'll be repercussions for that," she said to the screen. "There'll be repercussions."

Em rubbed the back of her head. "No wonder my head hurts. I thought it was the gas they sprayed us with."

On the video, Track Suit knelt next to Em and studied her. "My, my, my," he said and ran a finger along the side of her jaw. "You are a pretty one. What fun. What fun."

Breyona gritted her teeth. It took a force of will to keep herself calm as she remembered a similar situation with a janitor at her school. She took a deep breath. Next to her, Em contracted into herself, hugging her arms and turning away from the screen. Breyona put a comforting arm around her friend and sent a trickle of calm into her.

Track Suit smiled. "I think you'll do nicely, and it's a long trip for our meeting with Mr. GorVit. I think we're going to have a little bit of entertainment, you and me." He grasped the zipper on Em's hoodie.

Bronson strode into view. "Get away from her!" His bright red face betrayed anger and fear. "You get away from her right now."

Track Suit turned around and laughed. "Oh, so the coward boy is back."

Bronson grabbed the poker off the ground and raised it to strike.

Track Suit's eyes shot to Grandma's rifle which leaned against the sofa. But Bronson got to it first.

"You're not taking her."

Track Suit stood and brushed his hands off. "Mr. GorVit was very specific. He wanted to make sure we brought some leverage so that the boy would cooperate. Since the black girl isn't here, his sister will do fine."

"Touch her again, and I'll kill you," Bronson said.

"I don't think Mr. GorVit would like that, and you do not want to be on his list."

Breyona couldn't see Bronson's face in the camera angle, but she could see the tension in his posture. The door opened and Jack came through. "What the–?"

Bronson spun the rifle toward Jack and then back to Track Suit. He backed toward the kitchen. "Get out."

Track Suit raised his hands. "We can't leave without someone the boy cares about. Mr. GorVit was clear about that." He glanced back at the sofa where Grandma lay. "We'll take the old lady."

"No way!" Bronson shifted from foot to foot. His head turned toward Jack and then back to Track Suit. He dipped the gun barrel briefly at Wa's form on the sofa. "Take him. He's Danny's best friend."

Track Suit shook his head sadly and gave a last look at Em. "Oh well, she can wait for another day." Then he bound Wa wrists with a zip tie, and he and Jack carried Wa to the door.

"You'll regret messing with me," Track Suit said as he went out. "Mr. GorVit will be in touch."

Bronson shut the door, then knelt next to Em and dropped the rifle. He put a pillow from the sofa under her head and covered her with one of Grandma's afghans. Then he went to Grandma, shifted her so that she was lying on the sofa, and put an afghan over her too. He picked up the poker and paced the room while cursing and mumbling under his breath.

"This was not supposed to happen," he said. "This was not supposed to happen." He kept saying it. Then the door opened again, and he spun and raised the poker over his head. Breyona came in. She walked straight to him, touched him, and he fell.

Grandma paused the video. "That's a lot to absorb." She squinted at Breyona. "How did you knock that boy down so easily?"

The doorbell rang. Breyona sprang up and went with Em to answer it.

A police officer stood on the stoop. "We had a report of a kidnapping?"

8

ILLEGAL IN SEVENTEEN STATES

Danny lay on his stomach, neck twisted uncomfortably to one side. A rotten egg taste filled his mouth, and crust sealed his eyelids shut. He wanted nothing more than to wipe them clear, but his hands were bound behind him.

He got one eye open, but it was too dark to see anything. Road noise roared all around, and the floor swayed and jolted.

He licked his lips. "Hello?"

He rolled onto his back, managed to lever himself to a sitting position, and then onto his knees. He inched his way forward until he came up against a cold, metal wall. He followed it to a corner and then along another wall to another corner. Now he had a sense of the layout. He started working along the third wall, but his knee hit something soft and he fell forward.

Someone moaned beneath him. "Ow! Get off me." It was Wa.

Danny wriggled and tried to get up, but with his hands bound behind him, he couldn't do it.

"Get off me. Who is that?"

"It's me," Danny said.

"Geez, Danny. I like you, but not like that."

Danny managed to roll over and get back to his knees.

"Where the hell are we?" Wa asked.

"In a truck. A moving van," Danny said. "Em?" he called. "Grandma?" But he knew that he'd covered most of the square footage in the truck. His sister and Grandma weren't there. "We've got to get out of here. The door's this way."

"I can't see anything."

"Follow my voice."

Danny worked his way to the back of the truck. Each time it rolled over a bump or an uneven part of the road, the back door rattled. He twisted his body to get his hands against it, searching for a latch.

"I found something," Wa said. "A handle."

"Pull on it."

"I am. It's locked."

Danny scooched over to his friend, feeling his way with his finger tips. Instead, he found Wa.

"Hey," Wa said, voice pitched high. "That's illegal in seventeen states."

"Sorry." Danny eventually found the handle, a cool, metal bracket screwed to the door. "On three, two, one."

They both pulled, strained, and groaned, but the door didn't move a millimeter.

"I told you, it's locked," Wa said.

Danny grunted and sat back. "Maybe it's better to get this over with."

"What do you mean?"

"Let's just let them take us to Undermountain."

"Undermountain?" Wa said. "This isn't really the bigfoot style, is it? I thought they were totally against violence."

Danny snorted with disgust. "That's what they say. And it means something to some of them, like Grizz and Notchy, but Shaggy will do anything to get what he wants. After we escaped last summer, we should have guessed he would come after us somehow. Besides, technically, these humans he hired are doing the dirty work, not him."

"Maybe," Wa said. "What I don't get is why they only took us. I mean, why leave behind witnesses?"

Danny realized what that might suggest, that maybe these goons had done something to Em and Grandma. "Maybe they're riding in the front," he said, voice weak.

"Do you have your phone?"

"I don't know. Check my pockets."

After a few embarrassing moments of being groped by his friend, they determined that the goons had taken his phone.

"Your turn," Danny said.

"No," Wa said. "I don't have a phone any more. I lost that privilege after–well, never mind." Wa rushed on, changing the subject. "So you think we're being taken to Undermountain. Why now? We've been away for six months. Shaggy knows we haven't said anything about them. We haven't tried to expose the bigfeet to the world."

"It's just out of spite," Danny said. "We beat him. We got away, and he doesn't like that. He's probably been working on this since we left. I bet he found these two idiots through the Internet. They've never met him. The bigfeet probably have billions of dollars in Swiss bank accounts or something. They can wire money to somebody without ever meeting them in person."

"You know," Wa said. "If I hadn't actually been in Undermountain and seen the bigfeet, I would think that was the most ridiculous thing I've ever heard. But you're probably right."

Danny inched his way to the front of the truck and leaned his back against the wall. Uncomfortable, but better than lying on the floor.

"Now all I've got to do," Wa said, "is not think about how bad I need to pee."

JUST WATCH

Breyona sat next to Em in a small office at the police station. Breyona took a sip of tea out of a paper cup and looked up at Detective Bill James, a middle-aged, rotund man with soft eyes.

Grandma had already given her statement. Bronson was next.

James tapped his pen against his notepad. "Okay, Ms. Lewis. Start from the beginning."

"I arrived at about quarter to five, and I went inside. That's where I found Bronson holding a fireplace poker. I didn't recognize him, so I shoved him, and I guess he lost his balance and hit his head. Then I found Mrs. Michaelson and Em on the sofa. We looked everywhere for Danny and Wa. Then Mrs. Michaelson showed us the security video."

James scribbled some notes. "Okay, we've watched the tape. The man in the Track Suit mentions a Mr. GorVit. Do you know who that is?"

Breyona threw a nervous look at Em. Danny's sister nodded. They'd agreed to tell the truth about GorVit and the bigfeet. Now that Danny and Wa had been kidnapped, there was no reason to keep secrets. They owed the bigfeet nothing.

"Yes. GorVit held me prisoner when we were lost in Canada last summer."

The investigator raised an eyebrow. "I thought you were lost in caves."

"We lied."

James leaned back and rubbed his face. "Why didn't you say this at the time?"

"We couldn't," Breyona said. "It's complicated."

"Take your time."

"I think it might be easier to show you something first." She nodded to Em, who pulled out her phone and turned it for the detective to see.

Breyona cleared her throat. "Em took this video last summer while we were on the excursion."

"What is it?"

"Just watch."

Em pressed play. Shaky video showed a huge, furry creature carrying the limp figure of Breyona in its arms. The creature's legs and shoulders were massive, muscular, and completely covered with black fur. The head had shorter fur and ears that stood up on each side. It turned for a moment to show its profile, revealing a bear-like snout and a wide, green eye that flashed in the sunlight.

James pursed his lips and squinted at Em, then Breyona. "What is this? Why are you showing me this?"

The video stopped. Em replayed it while Breyona added commentary.

"This is a bigfoot. We called him Grizz. He saved us from an attack and then took us to a cave where we met others like him. They invited us to see their city—which is under the mountains. We decided to go with them, but once we got there, they told us we could never leave because they wanted to keep their existence secret."

James looked away, but he waggled the pen between his fingers. Breyona could tell he wasn't buying any of it. She charged forward with the story anyway.

"But it got worse because at the time, the bigfeet were at war with some other creatures called tangoga. GorVit is the leader of some of the tangoga. It's a long story, but GorVit ended up holding me at knifepoint. He nearly killed me. But we all escaped, and that's when we came out on the side of the mountain and called for help. While waiting for the helicopter to pick us up, we decided not to tell anyone about the bigfeet because, well, they're pretty advanced technologically, and we agreed that humans can't have that knowledge because we would make weapons out of it and kill ourselves."

Em smiled weakly. "That's the short version."

Detective James threw his pen on top of his notepad and looked at them with weary eyes. "Bigfoot. Cities under mountains." He sighed, and his face grew dark. "Your brother has been kidnapped, and you are making up stories. I don't understand this, unless you are somehow complicit in his disappearance. That . . . or you're on drugs."

Breyona resisted the temptation to reach out and calm the man. She thought he might see it as an attack. She did the best she could to maintain her own calm.

This had been the problem all along. No one would ever believe the story about bigfeet without proof.

"The video is real," Breyona said.

James held his hands up, exasperated. "It's fake. It's obviously fake, like a bad, viral YouTube video. I don't know why you bothered making this or why you're choosing now to show it to me, but it's not helping."

Breyona started to insist again, but James held up a finger. "Hold on." He pulled out his phone and dialed a number. "Yeah, this is James. We need to get someone in here to do an alcohol-drug test on a couple of subjects. Also, is Packard around? I need her to do a psych eval."

Breyona and Em showed the video five more times, but no one took it seriously. In fact, the more they insisted it was real, the angrier everyone got. In the end, Breyona had to calm the psychologist, a Ms. Packard, who got so upset she started screaming at Em and nearly threw the phone across the room.

Realizing the police weren't going to be much help, Breyona suggested that the gas they'd been exposed to had given her a terrible headache. Packard latched onto that as an explanation for the girls' wild story.

"Clearly a psychedelic hallucination caused by some agent in the gas," Packard told James. "We'll need to bring them back tomorrow, once the effects wear off."

James nodded, though he didn't look convinced. "Let's talk to the boy."

Breyona and Em found Grandma in a waiting area. She sat in a folding chair, posture erect, chin high, hands folded primly in her lap. As still as a statute . . . or a grenade.

When Breyona met the old woman's eyes, she knew the pin had been pulled.

10

THREE HUNDRED THOUSAND FOLLOWERS

They drove back to Grandma's house in tense silence, except for the whistle of Bronson's breath going in and out of his nose. He did speak once, suggesting they stop to get a hamburger. Em gave him a look of such contempt even he picked up on it. He mumbled something about having brownies instead.

Grandma looked straight ahead the whole way, and when they got to her house, she marched to the front door and unlocked it with movements of military precision. Only after the feisty woman had dropped her purse onto the kitchen table did she turn her bright blue eyes on Breyona and Em. "What in the Sam Hill is going on?" she demanded. "Why would you tell tall tales when Danny and Joachim are missing?"

"We told the truth," Em said. She brought out the phone and showed the video of Grizz carrying Breyona. Grandma frowned at it. "The police said that video was a fake. They said you got it off of YouTube." She squinted at Em's eyes, scrutinized the girl's face. "Maybe you *are* on drugs."

"We're not," Breyona said. "Trust me."

Grandma's eyes flashed. "I don't know you, girl. I'm going to let your parents deal with the both of you." She looked at the old clock on the mantel. "Paulette and Vincent will be here in an hour or two, Em. You'll go home with them. Breyona, did you call your parents like I told you?"

"Yes, ma'am," Breyona said. It wasn't a lie exactly. She'd left a message.

Grandma turned to Bronson. "And what did you tell the police?"

Bronson scratched at his carpet of red hair and frowned. "I told them what I told you. I don't know anything. They kept asking the same questions. I don't know who GorVit is. I didn't know what to do."

"You should have shot them both," Grandma said.

Bronson opened the fridge and peered in. "My dad said I shouldn't shoot anyone again. For a while." He pulled out the milk carton and closed the door. A frown creased his doughy face. "I tried to do the right thing."

Grandma slumped into one of the kitchen chairs and covered her face. "First my son, then my husband, and now my grandson; it's too much for an old woman to bear. I'm going to go lie down." She stood and tottered down the hall.

Bronson grabbed the brownie tin off the counter and pried off the lid.

Breyona closed her eyes and took a few deep breaths. "It's up to us to save Danny," she said.

Em sat at the kitchen table, absently twirling a lock of her hair around her pinky. "We don't even know where those guys took him."

"GorVit is a prisoner in Undermountain. Where else would he take Danny? He obviously wants revenge for what Danny did to his army."

Bronson swallowed a brownie whole. "You guys really are insane," he said.

Em glowered at him. He shrugged and dug out another brownie.

Breyona ignored Bronson. If GorVit had taken Danny and Wa to Undermountain, there wasn't much she could do about it. . . . Unless she could contact Shiv or Grizz. But the goons had taken Danny's trainer.

Em rubbed her elbows. "What are we going to do? No one believes our story. The more we tell the truth, the more trouble we're going to get into." She glanced down at her phone. "You-Tube," she said in disgust. "They should have just checked YouTube. They would have found right away that this video is not up there. Maybe I *should* upload it, expose the bigfeet to the whole world."

Breyona inhaled sharply. An idea gelled in her mind. "YouTube! I need to use your grandma's computer."

"I was kidding about putting it on YouTube," Em said.

"No, that's not what I mean. Let's go." Breyona headed to the den. Em followed behind, but Bronson settled in on the living room sofa, brownie tin in one hand, remote control in the other.

Breyona sat in front of the computer. "GorVit held me prisoner in a cave for a little while," she said. "He was hiding from the bigfeet, who were searching everywhere for him once Danny blew his cover. He brought in a bunch of computers. He had CNN going on one of them. He said the People like to keep up with what's happening in the world."

"What does this have to do with Danny?" Em asked.

"I bet the bigfeet have been following our activities online very closely since we left, in case we try to expose them."

Em smiled when she caught on. "Like uploading a video of them to YouTube. But how are you going to use that to get in contact with them?"

"Twitter."

Breyona logged into her account.

"You have three hundred thousand followers," Em said, amazed.

"I've been on TV a lot recently. News stories about my outreach programs." She thought about what to type, trying to think up something that would get the attention of the bigfeet right away.

"I've got it," she said and typed in the Footese word *donovthosameezu*. "Now we wait."

Breyona focused on her breathing to keep her nerves at bay while she stared at the screen and waited for a response.

"I never considered that they were following what I was doing online," Em said. "But I suppose they can monitor everything on the Internet."

They sat and watched the tweets roll by, many from various celebrities and musicians that Breyona followed. Then a tweet with the word *donovthosameezu* came back from a user called @BigfootGrizz.

Em let out her breath. "That's not a very subtle username."

"Grizz wants us to know it's him," Breyona said. A second later, another message came through. It simply said, "video chat."

Breyona loaded the video chat program and logged into her account. Moments later a call came in. Despite all that had happened to her in Undermountain, she felt a flush of affection for the face that appeared.

Grizz stared at her with his wide, green eyes. "Donovthosameezu, Breyona," he said and held his hands palm out toward her.

She responded in kind before rushing into her story. "Danny and Wa have been kidnapped, and GorVit is behind it."

It was usually difficult reading bigfoot facial expressions, but not this time. His eyes widened in shock, and he covered his ears with his hands. "GorVit escaped from Undermountain a month ago," he said.

Em swore.

Breyona took another deep breath. "Do you have any idea where GorVit went?"

"No," Grizz said. "We didn't even realize they were gone until Shiv requested to speak with them."

"The guys who took Danny and Wa made sure they had his trainer too. They knew what they were looking for."

"Let me see if I can track it." Grizz looked down, obviously studying his own trainer. "It's over the Atlantic Ocean." He raised his eyes and blinked. "This is very troubling."

"Troubling," Em said, voice raising. "That's all you have to say?"

"Quiet, Em. You'll wake up your grandma," Breyona said, then looked at Grizz. "Can you tell where he's going?"

Grizz raised his hands in a shrug. "If he's on an airplane, he could be headed anywhere in southern Europe or even northern Africa." He paused. "We'll know when the signal stops moving. In the meantime, I think you should come back to Undermountain."

It was Breyona's turn to be indignant. "Are you crazy? Shaggy is the head of the council now. If we come back, he'll never let us go. Besides, if Danny is headed across the Atlantic, the Canadian Rockies are in the wrong direction."

"If you need to cross the Atlantic, it will be much faster to come to Undermountain first."

He had a point. The bigfeet had teleportation hubs in all of their settlements, and Breyona knew that there were at least five on Earth, though she couldn't remember their locations offhand.

"I will speak to councilor Filinesama, whom you know as Notchy," Grizz said. "I am positive I can get his word that the council will allow you to leave whenever you want."

"But Shaggy will just ignore it," Em said, "like he ignores the Oath."

"He cannot."

"I don't know . . ." But inside she did know. What choice did they really have? If they wanted to save Danny, they would have to trust the bigfeet.

"I should get Grandma," Em said. "You should speak with her and convince her you exist. Then you can talk to the police. No one believes us. We even showed them video of you."

Grizz leaned back, eyes wide. "I didn't know you had any video. I thought the council had confiscated your cameras."

Em waved her phone. "I'm an expert at concealing this thing."

Grizz sighed and scratched an ear. "It doesn't matter. You know I can't speak to your grandmother. The People must keep our existence secret. The council explained all of this to you."

Em started to object, but Breyona interrupted her. "Wait a second, Em. If you convince your grandma, she'll insist on coming with us. Is Undermountain a place you want to take her? She's old, and we're likely to end up confronting GorVit."

Em folded her arms, but she didn't argue. "How are we going to get back in?"

Grizz's expression softened. "I assume you have access to one of your GPS devices," he said. "I will send you coordinates. We have a convenient opening reasonably close to a main roadway."

A message containing GPS coordinates came through on the computer. Breyona clicked the numbers, and a map website opened with a little pin marking the spot.

"That'll take a day of nonstop driving," Em said.

"We'll leave immediately," Breyona said, "before Grandma wakes up."

"And before my mom and Vincent get here. But I have to leave a note so they'll know we're okay." She tore a sticky off a pad next to Grandma's computer and scrawled a note. Breyona read it over her shoulder.

Mom, Breyona and I have gone to get Danny and Wa. Don't worry. We know some people who can help us. I'll call you when I can.

Em stuck the note to Grandma's computer screen and nodded to Breyona. "Let's go."

They grabbed their bags and slipped out of the house.

"We'll take my Jeep," Em said. "From the map it looks like we may have to drive on some pretty rough roads." Breyona opened the passenger door and pushed the seat forward to throw her bag in the back. A large figure sat there, staring at her with a blank expression.

Breyona jumped, and Em shrieked.

"It's just Bronson," Breyona said, catching her breath. She frowned at him. "Get out of there."

He didn't move. "You're not going anywhere without me. If you know where Danny is, I'm coming to help you save him."

"Since when have you ever cared about Danny?" Em said. "You let them take him, and you told them to take Wa. Get out."

Bronson crossed his arms and leaned his head back as if he was going to go to sleep. Breyona considered calming him into a stupor and dragging his body out, but she knew Bronson. He'd end up accusing her of assault.

"Let's just go," she said. "I don't want to waste any more time."

Em swore, but she didn't argue.

"Where are we going exactly?" Bronson asked.

Em fired up the engine and slammed the Jeep into gear. "Canada."

"Crap. My dad says they're practically commies up there."

11

A VILE, BUT APPROPRIATE, CURSE

Danny rolled onto an elbow. Realizing his hands were free, he sat up and rubbed his wrists. Wa sat nearby, bruised and dirty.

"Where are we?" Danny asked.

Wa shrugged. "The last thing I remember was being stabbed with a syringe and thrown in a crate."

"Yeah, I remember that too." Danny felt like he'd been out for days. Hazy memories swirled up, of his ears popping and stomach turning in the turbulence of an airplane flight.

He groaned and put a hand to his head. Pain emanated from the center of his brain, a side effect of either the drugs Track Suit had injected into him or simple dehydration. He thought it might be the latter since thirst squeezed his throat so hard he could barely swallow. He ran a tongue around his dry mouth and made a face.

He got to his feet and looked around the small, dark room. It smelled dry and musty, like a museum attic. A light fixture of bigfoot design hung from a hook in one corner. A rough wooden door on crude hinges stood in one wall. "I didn't know Under-mountain had any wooden doors," Danny said.

A clatter came from behind the door. It swung open, and blinding light glared through, silhouetting the familiar shape of a tangoga.

Danny squinted and held up his hands against the light. "Tell Shaggy he can go–"

One of the tangoga's heads cut him off with a squawk. "Follow me."

Danny's blood turned to ice. He knew that voice.

Apparently Wa did too. "GorVit."

"Ah, I'm touched that you remember me," said Gor with mock sweetness. Then his voice turned cold with menace. "Now follow me."

Each of the tangoga's two heads sat atop its own sinuous, swan-like neck. Its four spidery legs ended in sharp points that clicked on the stone floor. A red shirt covered most of the torso, signifying GorVit's position as a boss. In truth, he stood much higher in the tangoga hierarchy than that, being one of the eight *frellk* that ruled the entire society.

GorVit wore a boss armpack, providing them with two mechanical arms ending in claws and two more that ended in wicked blades. Gor waved the knives with the agitated motions of a cat's tail.

"Follow us, or else," Vit said.

"Shut up, Vit," Gor said. He was the primary head, the one in charge. Vit cowered at the remark and threw a narrow gaze of hate back at Danny.

GorVit turned their back on Danny and left the room. Danny saw a narrow hallway beyond. Two gunner tangoga stood guard, each holding guns in their steel claws.

"I don't think we're in Undermountain," Wa said.

A gunner clattered in and motioned to the door with one of

their guns. Danny didn't see what choice he had, so he followed GorVit down a narrow hallway carved with what looked like Egyptian hieroglyphs. All of the surfaces appeared to be stone.

GorVit led them into a grand hall. Hieroglyphs and huge painted murals covered the walls, lit by harsh work lights. One mural depicted a boat carrying a man and woman of obvious importance; each wore a fabulous headdress. The man held a golden sphere in one hand and a scepter in the other. The woman sat behind and below him, holding two children on her lap.

Dust swirled in the air. Danny coughed and breathed through his teeth in a vain effort to filter out some of the particles. He sneezed hard, making the pain in his head flash to new levels of intensity.

"I need water," he said.

GorVit did not look back. A knife arm merely pointed to the far corner. A dark heap lay there. As Danny drew near, he saw a two-liter water bottle in front of a pile of rags. He grabbed the bottle and took a long swallow before passing it to Wa. He looked down at the pile and recognized a stripe on one of the rags.

"That's Track Suit's track suit," Wa said.

"No." Danny took a step back. "That *is* Track Suit. Or what's left of him." Mingled among the strips of fabric were bits of bloody flesh. And there, sticking out of what once had been a velour pant leg, was a foot, still in its sneaker.

Danny swore and looked away, only to find GorVit standing over him.

"I see you found one of my minions," Gor said. "His usefulness came to an abrupt end, as you can see. He was even more delicious than the other one." The tangoga grew thoughtful for a moment and held up a claw. "But now that I think about it, perhaps that idiot still has one more use. For he serves as an example of what will happen to this young man if you fail me." Gor pointed a blade at Wa, who tried to back away but bumped into a gunner tangoga, one of seven posted around the room. It grabbed Wa's shoulders and pushed him back toward the entryway.

GorVit guided Danny to the center of the room, where a low granite plinth stood on a circular dais. As GorVit stalked toward it, Danny noticed a huge, desiccated skeleton lying off to one side, obviously the bones of a bigfoot.

On the plinth, perched atop a slender stand, stood a golden sphere. The same one depicted in the mural.

GorVit shoved Danny toward it. "You will use the People's device to solve the puzzle of the Spheroid. You have fifteen minutes."

Danny stared at the object. "I don't even know what this thing is. What does it do?"

"It is the Spheroid of the Asht, given to the People by Voo himself. He warned that it contains terrible, destructive knowledge. That means the Spheroid holds the design for a weapon. A weapon so tremendous not even the People can be trusted with the knowledge of it."

The tangoga pressed close. Gor's head hovered just over Danny's right shoulder, Vit's over his left. Their hot breath ruffled his hair. "I mean to have that knowledge," Gor said.

Danny fought to keep his legs from shaking. He shrugged in an attempt to feign disinterest. "I can't help you. I don't know how this thing works."

GorVit pointed a blade at Danny's trainer, which sat on the floor at the base of the plinth. "As I said, use the People's device to figure it out. I'd do it myself, but some rules–" Gor broke off and turned away angrily.

Flashes of hope and anxiety hit Danny at the same time. His stomach soured. His skin went cold at the thought of touching the trainer. But he knew he could use it to contact Grizz for help.

He picked it up and swallowed hard, resisted the urge to throw it across the room. The revulsion seemed to be getting worse. He could only imagine how hard it would be for an actual tangoga, who were forbidden to even touch a trainer.

Danny glanced back toward the tangoga gunners congregating near the entryway. "Wa, are you okay?" he called.

"Yeah," Wa said from somewhere behind the gunners. "When you get done saving my life, come check out this cool mummy back here."

"You now have fourteen minutes," Gor said and turned to head back toward the other tangoga. His bladed arms swished with menace. "But take your time. I enjoy carving up humans almost as much as splitting *gleenshev*."

Danny asked the trainer to contact Grizz. He waited. And waited. A cartoonish icon popped up of a bigfoot covering its ears with its hands. "I'm sorry," the trainer said. "The terrestrial communication system is experiencing an outage at this moment. Please try again later."

A lot of good that would do, Danny thought. He glanced around the room, searching for the signal jammer GorVit must have brought.

"Thirteen minutes," Gor said.

Danny swore and turned to inspect the Spheroid. It was about the size of a basketball. Five rings, stacked one on top of the other, circled the sphere. Each bore a series of Footese symbols.

The fact that GorVit and his gunners had moved to the very back of the chamber didn't inspire much confidence about the safety of the device. Danny reached out and brushed the surface with his fingers, half afraid it might explode on contact. But it didn't.

The rings appeared to be set in channels, as though meant to spin. At a touch, the top one turned, clicking into place every few degrees. He aimed the trainer's camera at the Spheroid.

An image of the artifact appeared on the trainer's screen, along with a text blurb. The bigfeet had brought the object to earth thousands of years before. It had been given to them by the Asht, who admonished the People to keep it safe.

"I didn't know the People had been here that long," Danny said, somewhat awed by the idea.

The text blurb contained a link to a simulation of the Spheroid. He clicked it. Sure enough, a three dimensional version of the device popped up. He could even spin the rings. But he didn't need a simulation; he needed an answer.

"What is the solution?" he asked the trainer.

"Unknown."

He asked the trainer to analyze the symbols for commonalities, but it came back with nothing. The lack of results surprised Danny because the trainer usually excelled at pattern detection.

"Eleven minutes," Gor called from the back of the room.

Danny tucked the trainer into the back of his jeans, relieved to have it out of his hands. He stared at the Spheroid and tried to focus his thoughts.

GorVit squawked. "What are you doing, boy? I told you to use the device to solve the Spheroid. I went to a lot of trouble to get you and that horrible thing to Egypt."

Danny's head snapped around. "We're really in Egypt?" All along he'd thought GorVit had brought him to a museum somewhere, which didn't really make sense considering the bigfoot skeleton.

"It doesn't matter where we are," Wa said. "Try to stay on task!"

Danny walked around the plinth, examining the Spheroid from all sides, looking for some indication of how it worked. "I think it's a combination lock."

"It took you four minutes to figure that out?" Gor asked, disgusted. "Use the device."

"It doesn't look good for you," Vit said to Wa with a cackle. "Or your friend."

"Shut up, Vit," Danny said. Wa and Gor echoed him.

Danny positioned himself in front of the Spheroid and studied the top ring. He turned it to every possible position. As it clicked, he logged each symbol into a table in his head, the same way he stored license plate numbers. He quickly memorized the symbols from the remaining four rings, then sat and closed his eyes.

"Use the device," Gor shouted, "or I'm going to cut this boy."

Wa yelped.

Danny shot up and turned back toward GorVit. Wa stood looking at the floor behind him and rubbing his backside.

"I'm okay," Wa said. "I just tripped over a disgusting beetle statue."

Danny sighed and tried to slow his racing heart. "Just stand still. I can't concentrate with you screaming all the time."

"Nine minutes," Gor called.

Danny did his best thinking while in motion. He started pacing, first around the plinth and then from the plinth to the walls, every so often glancing at the bigfoot skeleton.

He visualized all the symbols as if they were projected on a screen in front of his eyes, a technique he used during tests when recalling books he'd read.

It seemed obvious that he must align one symbol from each ring in a column. He visualized the symbols in rows, one for each ring on the Spheroid.

He paced back and forth, mentally arranging the symbols into groups. Some were animals, some were plants, some were planets, some were constellations, and some didn't fit any category. None of the groupings felt right.

"Um, Danny," Wa said from across the room. "You might want to hurry up."

Danny ignored him. Pressure wasn't going to make him think any faster. He focused on the array of symbols. Something about them made the back of his mind itch.

"How much time?" he asked.

"Eight minutes," Gor said.

Danny cursed and stalked toward the tangoga boss. "You're lying. How are you keeping track of time?"

Vit squawked, offended, but Gor told Vit to shut up and turned his pale eyes on Danny. "It's a simple trick if you know how to use your implant. Oh, now you've only got seven minutes."

Danny gritted his teeth and headed back to the Spheroid. "Let Wa come up. I need his help."

Gor conferred with Vit for a moment, then pushed Wa forward. Wa ran to meet Danny by the Spheroid. "What do you need me to do?"

"I was lying," Danny said, voice low. "I just wanted you away from GorVit. I don't trust them to wait until the time is up to start cutting you."

"How can you say that so calmly?" Wa threw a nervous glance at GorVit, who had stayed back with the gunners near the entryway.

Danny blinked. "I'm sorry. I'm just trying to solve this puzzle."

"I haven't seen you do anything," Wa groused. "All you've been doing is staring into space and pacing."

"It's hard to explain, but I'm working on it." He pointed at one of the rings on the Spheroid. "These symbols all relate to each other in some way, but I'm having trouble figuring out how."

"Six minutes," Gor said.

Danny sat on the raised platform of the altar and closed his eyes. Wa frantically spun rings on the Spheroid.

Gor called out. "Your chances of solving it randomly are nil."

Wa mumbled a vile, but appropriate, curse.

Danny arranged and rearranged the array of symbols in his mind—according to rhyme, according to an approximation of alphabetical order, even though Footese didn't quite work that way. He tried arranging them based upon concepts again—animals together, plants together, but those distinctions weren't really valid since they imposed human concepts on top of Footese language.

He looked at the distribution of symbols from a statistical standpoint, trying to find a trend in them, some hidden relationship based upon how the figures were drawn with curves and strokes. Nothing gelled.

"Five minutes."

Danny's eyes flashed open. "No way," he shouted to Gor.

"Never mind," Wa said. "Keep working. GorVit's coming."

"Start looking for an escape route," Danny whispered.

"Do you think that I've been sitting here doing nothing?" Wa hissed. "There is no escape route unless we can grow wings."

The click of GorVit's steps grew louder as he clattered forward on his pointed legs. He scissored his blades together, delighting in the unnerving effect it had on both humans.

Danny jumped up and stared at the Spheroid. Something about the symbols scratched at his brain, insisted that he pay attention to it.

He closed his eyes and tried a trick Breyona had taught him to clear his mind. He'd never mastered the skill, finding it tedious and frustrating because he could never stop thinking. Desperate for a breakthrough, he took deep breaths to calm his nerves. He tried not to think about the problem, tried to let his thoughts wander, tried to block out the sound of GorVit's feet, Wa's curses, and the pounding of his own heart. He breathed in and out, angry, furious at GorVit for putting him in this position, livid that the bigfeet had lost the Spheroid and hadn't done anything to recover it.

He took more deep breaths and let go of all the anger. The array of symbols floated in his mind's eye.

His attention fell on one symbol in particular, a pictograph of a small animal, kind of like a cat, but with an elongated anteater snout. The symbol also served as a letter in the Footese alphabet, although the alphabet had seven different orders. This particular symbol could be the first letter, the fifteenth letter, the thirty-seventh letter, or the one hundred and second letter.

"Two minutes."

It occurred to Danny that the symbol was used as a constant in Footese physics.

"The speed of light," Danny said, breath going out of him at the realization.

"What?" Wa asked.

"This is physics."

In a flash, the symbols reoriented in Danny's mind. Many of them were a simple code for numbers based upon their positions in the five alphabets. But another smaller set of symbols were mathematical constants and variables used in teleportation physics.

"No wonder the tangoga couldn't solve it," Danny said. "They don't know anything about teleportation."

He pushed Wa's hands off the Spheroid. "The rings limit the solutions. I don't entirely understand the point of this, but it's almost like the combination is a coordinate system."

"But it's wrong," he said. "Teleportation doesn't work that way. . . ."

"Can you solve it or not?" Wa asked, voice pitched high with panic.

"One minute," Gor said. He stood just below the dais now, his tangoga gunners at his back. "Looks like your friend will soon need an armpack of his own."

Danny snapped the top two rings into place and then the bottom two. He studied the symbols that remained in the center ring. "It seems kind of arbitrary." He clicked it. Nothing happened. He clicked another one. Nothing happened. He spun it around and around looking at the symbols again, trying to find a connection.

"Why would one of them be right and others be–?" The ring snapped into place. A high keening whistle emanated from the Spheroid.

"Uh, it's not a bomb is it?" Wa said. "You said something about a weapon."

GorVit backed away and barked at his gunners. They fled to the back of the room, shrieking at one another in panic.

Danny didn't think the Spheroid would explode, and he said as much to Wa. "No bomb would have a detonation system like this . . . unless it was meant for a suicide bomber.

"That's reassuring."

"This is about teleportation, not explosions."

A hidden hatch on the very top of the Spheroid irised open. A slender, golden stalk rose from it. Atop the stalk sat a tiny glowing bulb, no bigger than a marble. Its light phased from red to violet to orange to white. It flashed a broad beam of light onto the back wall of the chamber, opposite the entrance, illuminating it with a patch of brightness. The projection fluctuated through many colors before resolving into a picture of a jungle with a violet-blue sky overhead.

"It's a video projector," Wa said. His voice broke into a relieved laugh. "You've got to be kidding me."

"Is it safe?" Gor asked from across the room.

"No," Danny said, pretending to be terrified. "It's ticking. I think it's going to blow."

Catching Danny's scheme, Wa gasped and covered his mouth. "Oh my God," he said, exaggerating wildly. "We're all gonna die!"

The tangoga gunners shrieked and fought to escape through the entryway.

Danny stepped off the dais toward the projection. The detail was insanely fine, beyond high definition. The trees swayed in a light breeze.

GorVit shouted orders for his gunners to resume their posts. He marched through the room, waving his blades. "What is that? What is that picture?"

Danny backed closer to the projection. Wa followed, eyes flashing first to the picture then to GorVit's knives.

Gor started to rush forward faster. He shouted an order to his gunners. They spread out to block any chance of Danny and Wa running past, not that it would have mattered. Tangoga were incredibly fast and their bullets faster.

"Is that all it does?" Gor asked. "A picture projection? Where is the weapon? Where is it, boy?"

"It doesn't have any weapon," Danny shouted. "It . . ." A breeze ruffled Danny's hair.

"Do you smell that?" Wa asked.

Danny looked back to the projection. Fresh air wafted over him, heavy with moisture and a floral scent. He glanced at Wa, and an instant understanding flashed between them.

"Run," Danny said.

Together they turned on their heels, sprinted toward the wall, and threw themselves through the projection. They landed hard, stumbling over each other. They didn't wait to get their bearings. They stood and ran into the rich, green foliage of a strange, alien jungle.

12

DID IT PUNCTURE ANYTHING IMPORTANT?

Danny's breath came in short heaves as he pushed his way into the jungle. His foot caught on roots hidden among the low foliage that covered the ground, and he fell hard. Wa helped him to his feet. "Come on. GorVit's behind us." They pushed into a thicket of fuzzy stalks, keeping low so fewer of the finger-like branches could snag them.

The hack and slash of GorVit's knives slicing through the vegetation pursued them. Shrieks of his gunners sounded to the left and right.

A canopy of strange trees arched overhead, their limbs heavy with thick violet fronds as circular and concave as umbrellas. What beams of sunlight cut through seemed to swirl in the damp air. Dank and sweet smells wafted from trumpet-like blossoms. Their heady perfume made Danny sneeze.

GorVit shrieked and threatened the boys and his own gunners alike. But Danny and Wa's smaller forms allowed them to squeeze their way between thick stalks that GorVit had to chop down. They kept low and pushed forward.

"Where are we going?" Wa asked.

"Straight," Danny said. He had no idea where he was. The plants didn't look like anything he'd ever seen. He scanned his implant for matches and came up with nothing.

The sounds of GorVit's pursuit faded somewhat, though Danny didn't feel any safer. A tangoga's sense of smell was much keener than a human's, and he worried GorVit would be able to track them the way the tangeg had once tracked Danny and his friends in the Canadian Rockies.

"Try not to bend the stalks," Danny said. "Try not to even touch them."

"Are you serious?" Wa stopped and pointed to the nearly impenetrable vegetation.

"I said *try*. I think we can go slower now."

"Maybe we should double back," Wa said, but a shriek and rustle behind them killed that idea. They continued ahead.

Danny's shirt clung to his body, and sweat stung his eyes. Despite their slower pace, his breath felt labored. "I think this planet has less oxygen than we're used to."

A particularly dense thicket of thorny stems barred their way, each stalk as thick as Danny's arm. Six meters overhead, the plants bent under the weight of strange purple gourds, several of which lay on the ground, cracked open and oozing clear, sticky goo.

The sound of pursuit grew louder. "We've got to get through this," Danny said. He found a spot on the stalks with fewer thorns and pried them apart. He managed to poke one arm through and then his head, but thorns snagged his shirt and tore long scrapes on his neck and arms.

GorVit shrieked something to his gunners. The rustle of the vegetation came from several directions.

"They're closing in," Wa said.

Danny gritted his teeth and shoved himself through the thicket, not caring about the stabs of pain or the sticky goo that coated his shoes.

He finally pulled free of the thicket and backed away. Though it looked like a barrier, he knew that GorVit's blades would make short work of it.

Wa appeared, blood dampening his cheeks and arms from numerous scrapes and scratches. "Stop!" Wa said. His eyes focused on the ground behind Danny.

Danny looked back to find his heels at the edge of a sheer drop. He cursed, fell to his knees, and crawled away from the precipice.

Gor shouted from just behind the thicket. "They went through here." More slashes and crashes sounded as the tangoga cut their way toward him.

"Now what?" Wa asked. He stood with his toes over the edge. The cliff overlooked the most magnificent vista Danny had ever seen. Far, far below lay a broad plain of grass that stretched for kilometers before rising to another cliff in the distance. A silvery river cut the valley in half.

Directly below Danny, the cliff dropped hundreds of meters into a fringe of jungle bordering the grasslands. Vines and stubby trees grew from cracks in the rock of the cliff face.

"We have to go down," Wa said. He eased himself onto a nearby tree that leaned over the edge in its search for sunlight. The trunk bowed under his weight. Just watching his friend hanging out there made Danny's stomach turn.

Heights never bothered Wa, who regularly risked his neck doing insane parkour tricks back home. Danny had seen a number of Wa's YouTubes and had long ago decided his friend had a death wish.

The thicket behind him rattled with the impacts of GorVit's knives. "I can smell your breath," Gor said. "I'm not done with you yet."

Wa eased himself further out on the overhanging tree toward

another smaller one growing from the cliff face. He was headed toward a thick patch of vines to climb down.

Danny decided he'd rather fall to his death than let Gor slice him apart like Track Suit. Swearing, he followed Wa. The tree dipped under his weight, and Wa cried out. "Wait a second! Let me get off this one."

Wa dropped to the trunk below him, which grew nearly perpendicular from the cliff. The trunk bent so far over Danny feared it would either snap or the roots would come loose. But the tree held, and the bowing trunk neatly delivered Wa to the patch of vines.

The tree snapped back after Wa left it.

Purple gourds fell from the thicket behind Danny, and sun glinted from steel blades. A bit of GorVit's red shirt showed through the stalks.

Danny worked his way onto the trunk, letting it sag under his weight. He eyed the tree growing from the cliff face below. He pulled himself farther along the trunk, and it sagged more.

GorVit burst from the thicket. Both heads shrieked with glee when they spotted Danny. The tangoga leaped forward and brought their blades down onto the trunk of Danny's tree. Four rapid blows sent wet chunks of wood flying, weakening the trunk until it split.

Danny flung his arms out to catch the tree below him, felt it slap hard against his face. He clutched at the trunk and wrapped his legs around it. Disoriented he looked to his right and found Wa next to him, clutching vines.

"Grab on," Wa said. He pulled Danny close and helped him place a hand on a vine.

"Let go with your legs."

"I'll fall."

"Only if you let go with your hand."

Overhead, GorVit shrieked with rage. "Gunners! Gunners! To us! To us!"

"Let go, Danny. We're sitting ducks."

Danny managed to wrap the vine around his wrist. He released the tree, and swung down. The vine pulled away from the cliff slightly, but it held, nearly wrenching his shoulder from its socket.

Sweat poured into his eyes, blinding him. Just as well. He didn't really want to see what lay below or above.

Wa had already started down the vines like an old time sailor climbing down the ratlines. The vines did form a sort of web, providing many hand and foot holds. Danny managed to get his wrist unwrapped and took a couple breaths to steady his nerves. His limbs felt heavy and numb from fear, but he started down.

"There's more trees down here," Wa called. "We need to get out of the line of fire."

Danny wiped his face against his upper arm, trying to clear his eyes of sweat. When he looked up, GorVit stood directly overhead, a gunner to each side. Gor shrieked at them, ordering them forward. But the gunners held back, apparently as terrified of the drop as Danny.

He picked up his pace, no longer caring about finding the perfect hand holds. A thicker vine lay on his left. It seemed to stand out from the cliff, and he noticed it wasn't twined with any others. He lunged for it and slid down like a firefighter, bypassing Wa.

He plunged into darkness as the trees grew thicker. Branches stung his legs like the lashes of a whip. His hands burned as he tightened his grip on the vine to slow his fall. The vine suddenly wound among a bunch of others, causing him to lose his hold. His sliding descent became a free fall.

Branches stung his face, and he grasped wildly for anything to stop his plummet. A fat tree trunk folded him like a taco, forcing the breath from his lungs and cracking something in his side. Pain flared, sending flashes of white across his vision.

He hung over the tree trunk, mouth gaping, body straining to pull in even one breath. Fear of falling, fear of GorVit, fear of fear—it all collapsed into nothing as his body fought for air.

"Danny!"

Leaves dislodged by his fall helicoptered all around him in a rain of green, violet, and yellow. Inches from his head, on a thin twig, a tiny, bulging-eyed creature with yellow feathers and gossamer wings stared at him.

His chest and abdomen convulsed, and his vision darkened. A single thought formed in his head.

This is what it's like to die.

Something took hold of his shirt collar and lifted his head. The motion took pressure off his diaphragm, and air sucked into his lungs, the sweetest breath he'd ever taken. Even the pain in his side, which felt like the teeth of a saw blade running across his ribs, couldn't take away the ecstasy of breath.

"That was off the chain," Wa said. "God, I wish I had video of that."

Danny took more breaths and managed to get his hands on the trunk to pull himself up. "I think I broke a rib or two," he said.

Wa sucked air between his teeth. "I hate it when that happens."

Danny couldn't help but laugh, which sent new jolts through his side.

"I think we lost GorVit," Wa said. He squatted on a tree trunk next to Danny's and peered up. "The trees are pretty thick here. There's no way they can see us now."

That fact did not stop the gunners from sending wild shots at them. The gunshots sounded like firecrackers, but the bullets tore through leaves and limbs far from the boys' perch.

"Can you climb?" Wa asked. "We can go limb to limb the rest of the way."

Danny didn't see what choice he had. He sat up, wincing at the pain in his side, and nodded.

Like a monkey, Wa swung to a lower tree and dropped out of view. "Come on, Danny. It's not that hard."

Danny carefully lowered himself, trying not to glance down. He descended from tree to tree, thankful that they grew so thickly. Even if he fell again, he figured the trees would stop him before he picked up too much momentum.

The problem was breathing. If the thin, humid air had made it difficult before, his injury made it twice as hard. Every inhalation brought tears to his eyes, and he had to stop and regain his breath on each new tree trunk.

After what felt like an hour, Danny stopped, breathless and soaked. "Wa! How much farther?"

"You're almost there," Wa called. "There's something you need to see."

Danny put in one last effort and a few minutes later stood on firm ground. He turned around, and what little breath he had went out of him. He'd thought he'd reached the base of the cliff, but now saw he was only halfway down.

He stood on a rocky outcrop. Below, a breeze played over the plain of grass, making it wave and swirl in blues and greens. Far off to his left, the valley ended in a tall cliff where a waterfall, at least a kilometer high, plunged into a cloud of mist. And there, at the base of the waterfall, stood a city protected by a gleaming, white wall.

"It looks ancient," Danny said. Apart from the main city, but still behind the white wall, lay an open area, dotted with evenly spaced shapes. In the center stood an enormous, golden pyramid. Sunlight glanced off its peak. "Where the hell are we?"

"Kansas?" Wa suggested.

Danny pressed his hands to his side and gently probed with his fingers. An electric shock told him which rib he'd broken.

"Did it puncture anything important?" Wa asked, concern in his voice.

Danny didn't think so, or he'd already be dead. Not that it

mattered at the moment. The nearest help would be in the city, many kilometers away. Not to mention hundreds of meters below.

Wa pointed to the side. "While I was waiting for you, I poked around a little. The good news is there are some stairs over here."

Sure enough, stairs hewn into the rock descended from above to the little outcrop they stood on. "I guess we took the hard way," Danny said.

"The steps don't just stop here." Wa strode to the edge and whistled. "It's just like going into the Grand Canyon on a donkey. Easy as a walk in the mall."

Danny crept forward and peeked over the edge. A narrow stairway, hard against the cliff, led down. He followed it with his eyes and saw that it switched back several times before disappearing into the jungle below. "Let's just go before I freeze up."

Wa led the way, and Danny pressed his shoulder hard against the cliff face and tried not to look down.

"Hey," Wa said. "The gravity here feels the same. Maybe we're still on Earth after all."

"No," Danny said, "look at the sky."

"Yeah, it is kinda weird."

Weird wasn't the word for it. High, wispy clouds of pink floated overhead, and a huge orange sun raged in a violet-blue sky.

Danny scanned his implant for some sort of reference, some idea of where they were. Many possible worlds appeared that had suns that were this large, that had violet skies, but he found nothing conclusive. Nothing in his memory banks spoke of a city with a golden pyramid. There were many planets with pyramids, but none that matched this particular one. Not with this city, not with this waterfall.

Danny and Wa switched back several times, once coming to a narrowing in the stairs where erosion had worn it away to nothing. Danny had to cling to vines to work his way across to where the steps resumed. Wa didn't think anything of it, and he didn't hold close to the cliff when he crossed.

Wa occasionally tossed rocks over the edge to watch them fall. One time he sent down a small boulder the size of his head. When it landed among the vegetation, a flock of white birds lifted into the air, squawking and swooping. They had long beaks like spears.

"Cut it out," Danny said. "Those things might attack."

"Good point." Wa picked up another rock but kept it in his hand.

The path led down among the trees, and they found themselves deep in the jungle at the base of the cliff. The canopy of leaves made it so dark the underbrush didn't grow as thickly. A paved but largely overgrown pathway led through the trees.

Danny hadn't heard any shrieks from GorVit or the gunners since his fall. He hoped Gor would give up and return through the portal. But if the Spheroid truly contained some terrible weapon, it was probably in the city. GorVit would reason that out as easily as Danny had.

They hadn't gone far when a tremendous hooting sound came from somewhere ahead. The hair on Danny's arms raised. His gut told him that whatever animal had made the noise had to be very large.

Danny and Wa continued cautiously, peering between the trees, trying to get a glimpse of what had made the sound. They emerged from the tree line onto the grassy plain.

The blades of grass were thick and springy and came in shades of green and blue. Tassels topped some like cattails. Others tapered to heavy lobes, split here and there to show milky white fluff inside. A humid breeze crossed the plain, stirring the grass and making it flash from green to blue, like a tangoga's feathers.

The path ended abruptly where the grass began. Danny couldn't see the city, though he knew it lay somewhere to his left. How far away, he had no clue.

He glanced up at the cliff they'd descended, amazed and somewhat sickened by the height.

"GorVit's going to find the stairs," Danny said. "And when he gets down here, he'll have an advantage through this grass. We've got to get to the city first, talk to whoever lives there, and make sure that the weapon doesn't end up in GorVit's claws."

"Okay," Wa said, not sounding particularly convinced. "But don't you think we should just focus on getting home? If GorVit does get down here, it would make more sense to take the stairs back up and go through the portal. Then you can turn off the Spheroid and trap him here."

Danny glanced back at the cliff. His legs felt like lead weights; his breath came in painful gasps. His tongue had long forgotten the few gulps of water he'd taken from Track Suit's bottle back in Egypt.

Before Danny could begin to explain, Wa nodded. "You'd never make it, would you?"

"No."

"Then let's cut straight to the river we saw. Then we can follow the river to the city."

Just the mention of the river got Danny's feet moving. He thought he'd dive into it and drink the whole thing.

Armed with a plan, they started through the grass. Swarms of bugs jumped away from them in waves with every step, but none of them landed on Danny.

To keep their orientation, they headed for a prominent peak on the far cliffs. The hooting came again from behind them and they stopped to look back. A crash sounded, like a large limb breaking off a tree. Leaves in the canopy swayed side to side.

"I'd love to never see or hear that again," Wa said, his voice unsteady.

They pushed forward with renewed energy but hadn't gone five more steps when they found themselves surrounded.

13

TESTING A THEORY

Breyona cast nervous glances at the rearview as she drove Em's Jeep into Canada. She'd taken the wheel right before reaching the border so that she would be in a position to convince the border guard to let them through.

The hardest part had been coming up with a reason to touch the guy. He asked for their IDs, and she handed up a bit of random paper. The officer frowned at it, but at the slightest brush of their fingertips, she sent peace and trust into him.

He smiled, eyelids heavy. His mouth opened, but he didn't say anything.

"I'm going to go now," Breyona said.

He didn't say anything, just nodded. The barrier arm lifted, and he waved her forward. Em blew out her breath. Bronson swore.

Three hours later, heavy snow fell from gray skies as Breyona turned Em's jeep onto a logging road off Route 59, somewhere near Banff National Park. Bronson snored loudly in the back seat. Em sat in the passenger seat, head against the window, also asleep.

Winter in Canada made Chicago's seem mild by comparison. Breyona cranked the heater up another notch and glanced down at the GPS on Em's phone. According to the coordinates Grizz had provided, they had only a few more miles to go up the logging road. After that, they'd have to get out and hike.

They didn't have much in the way of supplies because Bronson hadn't been willing to pay for anything other than a couple of meals. He'd complained loudly about that and made it clear a debt had been incurred. Knowing Bronson, he didn't want it paid back in cash.

Hopefully, once Bronson saw Undermountain, he'd forget all about the lousy twenty-five bucks he'd spent.

Breyona was thankful for the Jeep. Its high clearance and knobby tires easily pushed through the layer of snow on the road. Breyona couldn't go fast, but she kept going forward, following the bends, twists, and steep climbs as they wound deeper and deeper into the mountains.

At the top of a rise, the road ran out. Em's phone lost its signal a second later. The GPS app still worked, but it couldn't download any more map data. From here on out, they were just a flashing blue dot on an endless field of gray.

"Okay, we're here," Breyona said.

Em's eyes popped open, and she reached back to punch Bronson's leg. "Wake up."

He came to and swore. He pretty much swore in response to everything, which told Breyona a lot about Bronson's mind.

They got out and collected the few things they had been able to buy along the way. They'd drained Breyona's debit card to buy boots for herself and Em, a light backpack with a few granola bars, and some bottles of water.

"I don't see a path," Bronson said. "How do you know where we're going?"

Breyona dug the compass out of her jacket pocket, a slight wave of guilt touching her conscience. They'd stolen it from the same outfitter where they'd purchased the other supplies.

"As long as we go due west from here," Breyona said, "we should find the rock formation Grizz told us about."

The way was easy despite the shin-deep snow. Wind cut through Breyona's light jacket, sending shivers through her body. She picked up the pace to stay warm.

Bronson trailed behind, grumbling about how they were going to get lost, frozen, eaten by wolves or bears, fall off a cliff, or starve to death. She decided not to point out that all the bears were hibernating.

After a few minutes more of Bronson's complaining, Breyona waited for him to catch up and touched him lightly on the shoulder. She gave him a light pulse of calm, and he fell silent.

"Thank you," Em said. "I didn't know how much more I could take of that."

They continued through a stand of pines. The snow muffled their steps, and the stillness gave the world an eerie feel, as if they were the first humans ever to tread this ground. Breyona knew she would have enjoyed it if Danny and Wa hadn't been missing. She took deep breaths of the sharp, clean air and centered herself in calm.

Em touched Breyona's elbow and leaned close. "Should we try to prepare Bronson one last time?"

Breyona considered it. They'd explained the bigfeet and Undermountain to him, but he'd laughed and called them liars.

"What's the point?" Breyona asked. "The only way he'll ever believe us is to see one of them."

Em shrugged. "I guess you're right. I just don't want him to ruin everything for us."

"I don't see what he can do, besides be obnoxious."

They came to the base of a cliff. Nearby, a huge boulder balanced impossibly on top of another, as though stacked by giants.

Breyona stopped. "This has got to be it."

"I don't see any bigfeet," Bronson said. "Let's go back to the Jeep."

"Grizz?" Breyona called. "We're here."

Silence answered her. She scanned the cliff, the boulder, the trees.

"Hello?" Em shouted. The snow seemed to absorb her voice.

Breyona approached the cliff. "The entrance has to be a cave or something."

"Should we go around?" Em asked. "Maybe there's–"

Small rocks skittered down. A boulder rolled aside, exposing a black maw in the face of the cliff. Bright green eyes peered out of the darkness and stared at them for a moment. And then a familiar figure stepped out.

Grizz stood eight feet tall. Long black fur covered his limbs, though it was shorter at the neck and head. He wore his usual long tunic and short pants. The clothes didn't conceal his thick musculature. If Breyona hadn't known him for the kind, gentle bigfoot that he was, she would have been terrified.

He held out his hands. "*Donovthosameezu.*"

Em and Breyona returned the greeting and rushed to embrace the bigfoot. He crouched and wrapped them both in his great, warm arms. His soft, silky fur tickled Breyona's nose.

"I've missed you," Grizz said.

A thump sounded behind Breyona. She turned to see Bronson lying face down in the snow. She looked at Em who smiled and shrugged.

Grizz's eyes flashed to Bronson. "I didn't know you were bringing a guest."

"I'm sorry, Grizz," Breyona said. "We had no choice. He wouldn't let us come without him."

Grizz nodded and motioned someone else from the cave to come forward, another bigfoot. Breyona recognized him immediately. Ty had helped her when they had first come into the cave last summer. He stepped forward, easily scooped up Bronson, and started back to the cave entrance.

They filed in, and Grizz muscled the boulder back into place. Red lights from Ty's and Grizz's trainers lit the way as they walked down rough tunnels, which soon opened into a large cavern. Another bigfoot stood waiting, this one a defender dressed in blue armor.

"Before we go any further," Breyona said, "I want your word that we're going to be allowed to leave."

"You have it," Grizz said, "and you also have Filinesama's word."

Breyona remembered Filinesama, one of the members on the Council of the Strict. Danny had named him Notchy for the notch torn in one of his ears.

"And Shaggy won't override that?" she asked.

"He cannot. When a council member gives his word, only a full conclave may override it."

Realizing that they didn't have any other choice, Breyona nodded in agreement. They soon came to a huge, cylindrical shaft plunging deep into the mountain core. She knew it led down to the teleportation atrium and eventually all the way to the city of Undermountain.

Em balked and backed away. "You're not going to make us parachute. Are you?"

Grizz stopped and blinked. "It would be much faster. Otherwise we've got to walk all the way to the atrium before we can get to an elevator."

Em started to argue, but Breyona put a light hand on her arm. "I can make it so you don't even know it's happening."

Em's eyes went wide as she caught on. Breyona was offering to calm her head into oblivion.

The three bigfeet donned small parachute backpacks and Em nodded to Breyona.

Breyona placed a hand on her friend's head and sent a heavy dose of calm into her. Em's eyes rolled up, and she fell limp into the defender's arms. Bronson was still out.

"Let's do it," Breyona said to Grizz. He picked her up, and stepped to the edge. The shaft looked bottomless.

Breyona breathed deeply, observing the fear that threatened to shatter her calm. She smiled at the fear, keeping it outside her protective shell of calm.

With no ceremony or hesitation, Grizz jumped.

Breyona had apparently hit Em with more calm than she'd intended. The girl didn't come to until they were speeding through the city on a monorail train. Huge earthscrapers towered high overhead, lit up like Christmas trees. The heat of the deep earth made the air muggy. It gave the atmosphere a heavy quality, and the city lights made the ever-present haze glow.

"We're almost to the temple," Breyona said. "Look at Bronson."

Em turned to see the big boy staring out the window, face pale, mouth agape. He repeated the same swear word every few seconds, coloring it with shades of meaning ranging from awe to fear.

The monorail came to a stop at the temple.

Bronson repeated his favorite curse again and stared up at the massive bas-relief over the entryway. It depicted bigfeet bowing before the sun. Above it stood the temple's square central tower, which appeared to be made from nothing but massive glass panels of varying sizes, the smallest standing ten stories high.

They entered the temple and came into the Hall of Statues. The huge hologram of Voo the Asht King sat majestically, staring at all who entered, his face so terribly scarred and ravaged that Breyona had no idea what he might have looked like.

Ty picked Bronson off the floor, where he'd collapsed from the fright of seeing the hologram move.

Breyona had spent plenty of time in the temple, though most of it in the meditation wards. They passed many white-robed acolytes as they strode the grand halls before taking a side passage into some living quarters, an area new to Breyona.

Grizz knocked once on a plain door. It opened into a room comfortably furnished with rugs, cushions, and a large divan, upon which sat an ancient bigfoot so thin he seemed to be mere bones.

His fur had gone white, not like a yeti, but silvery-white like the fine hair of a very old woman. He sat cross-legged with his eyes closed, deep in meditation.

Grizz motioned for Breyona and Em to sit on the floor. Ty brought Bronson in and laid him on a cushion. The large boy moaned and rubbed his head, then sat up and swore.

After a few moments, the ancient bigfoot opened his eyes and held out his hands. "*Donovthosameezu.*"

Em and Breyona returned the greeting, as did Grizz and Ty.

"I am Luonesema. You may call me Luon. I'm going to help you find Danny and Joachim."

The door opened and closed behind Breyona, but she kept her focus on the old bigfoot. "Where are they?"

The response came from behind her. "Egypt. Most likely."

She turned to find a dark-haired human boy of seventeen gazing placidly back at her. He wore acolyte's robes and held his hands folded before him, cradling a trainer.

"Shiv!" Em leapt up and hugged him. He accepted the embrace, smiling slightly. His dark eyes, which always looked sad, seemed to sparkle in the low light of the room.

He greeted Breyona with a quick *donovthosameezu* and then returned her hug. As they touched, she felt a wash of calm rush toward her. Reflexively she swept it aside, barely restraining herself from returning the favor.

Shiv's eyes widened momentarily. "Interesting."

"Why would you try to calm me?"

Shiv glanced furtively at Luon, then back to Breyona. "Just testing a theory." Before Breyona could ask, he rushed on, almost business-like. "I was sorry to hear about Danny and Wa. I hope we can help you find them." His eyes fell on Bronson, and he frowned. "What's he doing here?"

Bronson stood in the middle of the room, jaw slack, face pale. He pointed at Shiv and made unintelligible sounds. Breyona touched Bronson's shoulder and trickled calm into him. He relaxed and slumped to the floor.

"As you can see, Shiv is not dead," Breyona said. "But we don't have time to get into it right now." She turned back to Luon. "Now, let's talk about where GorVit took Danny and Wa."

14

THE SPHEROID

Luon sat in calm silence, taking time to look each of the humans in the eye. Breyona breathed deeply, clearing her thoughts and setting aside the extreme urgency that prickled her skin. She knew the ways of the Strict. Any attempt to prod Luon would result in a longer period of silence.

By and by, Luon spoke. "Acolyte Shiv has been investigating the disappearance of the rebel tangoga, GorVit. Wherever they went, your friends are likely with them." He nodded for Shiv to proceed with his report.

Shiv cleared his throat and held up his trainer. "I did some discreet investigation in the tangoga sub-city. During GorVit's captivity, the People unwisely allowed the rebel boss to roam free down there. The People didn't think Gor had means of escape. We discovered a few tangoga who were somewhat loyal to GorVit. Gor did not have their detonation codes, but he did have leverage over them. Evidence of minor breaches in procedure. That kind of thing. These tangoga became his sources of information and messengers.

"We still don't know exactly how GorVit got to the atrium

unobserved, but it's clear they teleported away. As you may know, tangoga aren't supposed to be able to issue teleportation commands themselves."

Em snorted. "Gor's a rogue. What does he care about rules and procedure?"

Shiv conceded the point with a nod. "Yet I wondered how a tangoga could ignore such a fundamental prohibition. So I interrogated many tangoga. They had difficulty explaining their own behavior. I did find one individual who proved to be an excellent case study." Shiv went to the door and spoke to someone in the hall. He stepped aside to admit a tangoga with only one head.

Em's eyes widened in recognition. "Tog?"

The tangoga slouched in, head held low. He kept his eyes down and found a place in the shadows.

Em approached the poor creature, hands out to console him. "Tog," she said, eyes glistening, "you lost Yip."

Tog gave a guttural moan and looked away in shame. "I'm a useless single-head now."

Em tried to pat Tog, but he shied away. "Where are the arms Danny gave you?" Em asked.

Breyona remembered Danny's story about giving TogYip a boss armpack, which had two claws and two arms with blades. But Tog was wearing the standard issue armpack with two arms.

Tog slumped and looked at one of his steel claws. "The People stripped Danny's gift from me."

Shiv approached Tog, studied him the way he might a particularly intriguing puzzle. "But the People aren't in charge of you, are they? Danny changed your detonation code, so technically you report to him. Right?"

Shiv didn't wait for Tog's answer. He turned to Breyona. "Tog is an excellent example of the challenges the tangoga face. Tog reports to Danny, but tangoga rules clearly state that tangoga are servants of the People. So when the People instructed him to remove his boss arms, he did it. When they ordered him to return to the sub-city to be assigned a new job, he went. But the tangoga in the sub-city did not accept him, even though it was a direct order from Filinesama himself. Because of his . . . condition." Shiv smiled and shrugged. "The complications do not end there. For Tog violates an even more significant rule by continuing to live."

Breyona felt a bit lost. "What's wrong with living?"

"As a single-head, his duty is to submit himself for euthanasia."

Tog squawked and lowered his head even further. "My shame knows no limit."

Breyona wanted to offer Tog some relief, but before she could act, Grizz calmed him. Not enough to knock him out, but enough to stop his feathers from ruffling and legs from trembling.

"That's awful!" Em said. She moved to stand in front of Tog, daring someone to hurt him.

Shiv held up a finger. "But the point is he hasn't submitted himself for euthanasia. This leads us to the question of why?"

Tog straightened, taking on a demeanor of defiance. "And I will not until Danny is safe."

"Tog has determined that his duty to protect Danny supersedes his duty as a single-head to kill himself."

"Don't call him that," Em said, frowning. "Can't you see it hurts his feelings?"

Shiv smiled and gave a little shrug. "Sorry. Really, it's not important except to show that tangoga can violate some rules and procedures if more important rules and procedures supersede them. My theory is that GorVit marches to orders of such importance that he can skirt a few of the fundamental rules, including the prohibition against teleportation and the big one from Voo."

"The treaty," Breyona said, catching Shiv's point.

"Yes," Luon said. "Voo ended the war between the People and the tangoga. He instructed the tangoga to serve us, and taught us the Oath."

Shiv beamed with the self-satisfaction of someone who had solved a very complex math problem. "GorVit can use teleportation without the People's assistance because he serves an order even higher than the treaty."

Breyona took several deep breaths to quell her impatience. "So how does this lead to Danny being in Egypt?"

Shiv turned to Luon and waited. The ancient bigfoot had closed his eyes. He did not open them when he began to speak. "Thousands of years ago the People and the tangoga were at war. We don't remember why, and we don't know for how long, but what we do know is that one day an Asht named Voo woke from a long sleep. Voo was horrified to see the tangoga and the People fighting, and he issued a command that the tangoga should serve the People and that the People should take an oath to do no harm. It was a simple thing for the tangoga, for they are programmed to obey the Asht. But for the People it was a much harder task to accomplish."

"Wait a minute." Breyona said. "Why was it so easy for the tangoga? What do you mean they were programmed to obey the Asht? I thought they served the People."

"It's obvious, isn't it?" Luon asked. "The Asht, not the People, created the tangoga, raised them from the tangeg. You didn't think the tangoga evolved from tangeg and magically had a metallic implant appear in their brains, did you?"

"I never thought about it," Breyona said. "But why did the Asht want to make talking tangeg?"

"For servants," Luon said. "At least that's what we think."

"I had the same question," Shiv said. "It seems strange to go to the effort of uplifting an animal to become a servant, especially one that doesn't even have arms. If you look at the structure of the tangoga armpacks, it shows that the Asht had incredible facility with mechanical appendages. It makes me wonder why they didn't just use androids."

"Yes," Luon said, "it is very curious. And the trainer is silent on the subject, which in itself is extremely unusual."

"We can only surmise," Shiv continued, "that there was some problem using androids and that they found greater success uplifting the tangeg to be their servants. When Voo came back from his long sleep—whatever that means—he commanded the tangoga to serve the People, and because of their programming, it was impossible for them to do anything other than obey."

"And yet," Breyona said, "now there is an uprising, a rebellion. How is that possible?"

Luon chuckled and scratched an ear. "You've hit upon the million dollar question, as your kind says. We have no idea, although it has to originate at the highest level, since GorVit are one of the *frellk*, one of the top eight in the tangoga hierarchy.

"GorVit and three others, whose names we do not know, report to a tangoga leader called the Octz. None of the People have ever met the Octz, nor know exactly where they live, although it is presumed to be on Tangoga Prime.

"Even now, war rages on Ig. Neither the People nor the tangoga seem to be able to gain the advantage. The People have fewer numbers, but more effective defenses, allowing us to withstand assault after assault. The tangoga have large numbers, for they can they have an unlimited supply of tangeg to raise. Still, Ig is split between rebel tangoga territory and that held by the People. Similar battles rage on other planets, and the tangoga presumed loyal won't raise a claw to help us."

Tog said something under his breath.

"What was that Tog?" Breyona asked.

"I was just saying that it isn't our job to defend the People against rebel tangoga. I was among their number for a long time until Danny took charge of me. All I was ever told was that the People had oppressed the tangoga for too long."

Luon scowled at Tog, and the pitiful tangoga lowered his head and looked away.

"So where is Danny?" Breyona said.

"I'm getting to it," Luon replied. "But you need to understand the context for the rest to make sense." He took several long breaths before continuing. "At the time of the treaty, Voo entrusted us with an artifact we call the Spheroid of the Asht."

Shiv showed a picture of it on his trainer. The object was a golden sphere with five rings, each etched with intricate symbols.

Luon cast a glance at Shiv's trainer then leaned close to Breyona. "Voo said that the Spheroid contains terrible, terrible knowledge. A weapon of unbelievable destruction, or so we presume. We were told that if the Spheroid fell into tangoga claws, and if they could open it, all would be lost."

"Do you know what's inside?" Breyona asked.

"Of course not," Luon said, offended. "We were also instructed not to open it. When we first arrived on Earth several thousand years ago, we naturally settled close to the seat of civilization. The most advanced at the time was burgeoning in Egypt."

Breyona's jaw dropped, shocked that the bigfeet had been on Earth so long.

"One day a few of the People were on the surface—perhaps a bit carelessly in retrospect—when they came across a young human. To keep the secret of our existence, the People realized the human must never be allowed return to his kind. So they invited him to their hidden settlement."

"That sounds familiar," Em said, scowling.

Luon ignored the comment. "This human lived among us for many, many years. At the time, the Spheroid was kept in a small shrine. The human became enamored with it, assuming it was the source of our power. We explained that we treated it with such respect because it had been entrusted to us by the Asht. Of course, the human interpreted this to mean we'd received it directly from the gods. To be honest, we didn't truly understand human psychology very well, else we would have forbidden him access to the shrine.

"The care of the Spheroid was given to a small sect among the Strict. Among those was an individual named Choolenama.

"Choolenama struck up a friendship with the human, and one day the human, Choolenama, and the Spheroid disappeared. It was a terrible oversight on our part not to see how desperate Choolenama was to know what was inside the Spheroid. That he could abandon his Oath and betray the People is still appalling to us."

Luon's eyes narrowed in irritation, as if the betrayal had only just occurred. He took a breath and sighed. "We know that the Spheroid is still somewhere in Egypt, for there were many natural passages leading from our settlement under the Sahara into the Egyptian city of Amarna. And this is where the story intersects human history."

Luon looked to Shiv, who held up his trainer to show them a picture of an Egyptian painting. He pointed to a large human figure wearing a headdress.

"It's King Tut," Bronson said.

Shiv glared at Bronson. "No. This is Akhenaten," Shiv said. "He was the human who lived among the People and who befriended Choolenama. Years after he returned to his people, he succeeded Amenhotep III as pharaoh. One of his first acts was to change the religion of Egypt, which at the time worshipped many gods. In their place, he declared a single god, Aten. "He pointed to an Egyptian depiction of the sun. "This represents Aten. It is also the Spheroid."

"You're kidding me," Breyona said.

"I am not kidding you," Shiv said calmly. "Akhenaten reigned for many years, but when he died, his successor moved the seat of government back to Thebes, and the worship of Aten disappeared, and so did the Spheroid." Shiv set the trainer down and rubbed his hands together, smiling. "This is a revolutionary understanding of ancient Egypt by the way. No Egyptologist has any clue, since they don't know the existence of the People, let alone the Spheroid. If an archeologist had discovered the Spheroid, it would have been one of the largest archeological discoveries—no, *the* largest discovery of any kind, ever, in the history of the human race."

Breyona was sick of the history lesson. Only one thing mattered. "So you're saying GorVit went after the Spheroid."

"Yes," Luon said. "Not only that, but we believe he's discovered it."

"What does this have to do with Danny?" Breyona asked impatiently. "I still don't see the connection between the Spheroid and Danny and Wa."

"If GorVit found the Spheroid," Luon said, "they certainly will not know how to activate it. But Danny is unique because he has the tangoga implant *and* he can use the trainer. GorVit believes that with the aid of the trainer, Danny will be able to activate the Spheroid."

"So why did they want Wa?" Em asked.

"That's easy," Bronson said. "Leverage."

"And how do you know that?" Shiv asked.

"Because the guy in the track suit said so when he was going to take her." Bronson nodded at Em. "They wanted Breyona, but she wasn't there. Then they wanted to take Em, but they were going to do stuff to her, and I wouldn't allow it. Better it happen to Wa than to her."

Em glared at Bronson, but Breyona focused on the issue at hand. "So we can reasonably assume that Danny and Wa were taken to Egypt. How are we going to get there and rescue him?"

"The old settlement beneath the Sahara still has a functional teleportation atrium," Luon said. "GorVit's tangoga were likely not subtle in their search. They should have left evidence behind. And as I mentioned before, the settlement connects with ancient Amarna via underground passageways."

A white-robed acolyte swept in and whispered something to Luon. "It seems that the council has learned of your presence in the city. Hanameesovenama requires your presence in the Hall of the Strict."

Breyona closed her eyes and took many deep breaths to retain her calm. Hanameesovenama was Shaggy, the bigfoot who had kept her prisoner. His aggressive use of calming had inadvertently awakened the ability in her. He'd used her as a test subject to demonstrate how easily humans could be subjugated, part of his plan to make First Contact with the human race and take over the governing of Earth.

"Let's get this over with," she said. "I want to leave for the Sahara settlement within the hour."

She followed Luon, Shiv, and Grizz toward the Hall of the Strict. Behind her, Em tried to explain to Bronson to keep his mouth shut.

Tog stayed behind, forgotten.

15

I AM NOT A CHILD

"This is unexpected," Wa said.

A dozen bigfeet surrounded Danny and Wa, having emerged from the grass like fuzzy ghosts. They wore skins over their shoulders and carried spears, which would have been jousting lances for a man.

These bigfeet seemed broader than the ones from Undermountain, stronger, maybe even slightly taller. And where the bigfeet of Undermountain kept their fur combed, straight, and unadorned, these wore braids and ornate knots tied into the fur of their arms, chests, and legs.

One stepped forward, its fur the color of rich chocolate, but striped with highlights of blond and russet. It carried a massive wooden club, spiked with black thorns.

"What are you godlings doing out of the city?" it demanded in Footese.

Danny held his hands out in the ritual greeting. "*Donovthosameezu.*"

The chocolate bigfoot tilted its head to one side and barked a laugh. "I am not afraid of you, godling," he said, as if taking the meaning of *donovthosameezu* literally. As if Danny had the power to hurt him but had decided not to use it. Which would be hilarious given the size and strength difference between them.

"I'm glad we found you," Danny said. "Take me to your Strict."

"Found us?" the bigfoot said, laughing again. "We found you. Not difficult since you tramp around as loud as horgodons." It stepped close and squinted down at Danny. Then it waved forward its comrades. "Bring sacks. We'll eat these godlings and take their power."

"Uh oh," Danny said. He grabbed Wa's arm and started to back toward the trees but found that more bigfeet stood behind them. They held very large sacks made from hideous, scaly skin.

Another bigfoot emerged. "Show me these godlings."

This bigfoot had light, almost blond, fur. Intricate braids wound along his arms and legs. Decorative beads of shell and stone were tied into his fur. Several massive necklaces, also of stones and shells, lay over his shoulders.

He turned on the one holding the spiked club. "Karkoh, you have the brains of a *fwalldurn*! Do you realize how angry the queen would be if we ate her godlings? We must take them back to Mother. She will know what to do."

Wa nudged Danny's arm. "What's going on?"

Danny started to summarize, but the blond bigfoot noticed their exchange and cocked his head at them. "What language is that?"

"Uh, secret, godling language," Danny said in Footese, then rushed on, "Who is Mother? Who are you? What is this planet?"

The bigfoot squatted next to Danny, sniffed the air, and grunted in obvious disgust. Danny realized he was pretty ripe.

"I'm Jostosh," the bigfoot said. "Mother is Mother. The old gods named this world Hoo. So it is and will ever be until the day the sin of the meezu is redeemed." He stood and marched away. The bigfeet with the sacks herded Danny and Wa after him.

"What did he say?" Wa asked.

"A bunch of stuff that made absolutely no sense. The planet's name is Hoo."

"Who?"

"Yes."

"What?"

"The name of the planet is Hoo." Danny caught onto Wa's joke then. Despite himself, he snickered, which sent delightful stabs of pain through his side.

"Maybe they can fix your rib," Wa said.

Danny hoped so, but these bigfeet didn't seem to be very high-tech. "Actually, they were talking about eating us."

Wa gaped for a second before laughing. "I suppose I deserved that. Good one, Danny."

"I'm not joking, I–"

"Search them for weapons," Karkoh said as he strode past them. "I won't have any harm come to Mother. If they resist, put them in the sacks." He loped ahead to catch up to Jostosh.

A bigfoot poked its fingers along Danny's chest, back, and up his pant legs. It pulled Danny's trainer from where it was tucked in his jeans and passed it to another bigfoot who rushed ahead to hand it to Jostosh.

When the bigfoot found nothing else, it grunted and pushed Danny forward.

"What's going on?" Wa asked again.

"They're taking us to someone called Mother. I assume she's their chief. These bigfeet don't seem to follow the Oath. I'm not sure what's going on, but they keep calling us godlings."

"Godlings? Is that like a miniature god?"

Danny shrugged.

"Ask them for some water."

Danny looked around for the least menacing of the bunch and decided Jostosh fit the bill. At least he'd saved them from being stuffed into sacks. He caught up to the bigfoot and asked for water.

The bigfoot blinked at Danny's request and then handed a huge water skin to him. Wa had to help hold it up so Danny could drink. They took turns, though the water tasted like the inside of a pig's colon.

Danny didn't care. It was wet.

He decided to pump Jostosh for a bit more information. "Is Mother one of the Strict?"

Jostosh looked at Danny and bared his teeth. "Mother is often strict with us."

"Have you heard of the Oath?"

"What Oath?"

Danny didn't see any point in explaining the bigfoot oath to a bigfoot.

Jostosh squinted at Danny. "Perhaps you are not godlings of the Golden City. Else you would know more of the meezu."

Danny realized Jostosh was referring to all the bigfeet as meezu. Very strange since *meezu* sort of meant "child" in Footese. *Donovthosameezu* literally meant, "I am not a child." Which figuratively meant, "I mean you no harm."

They skirted the jungle for at least an hour before coming to an area where the jungle had been stripped away. The grass now led right up to the cliff. Above it, hewn into the cliff face, stood the meezu dwellings. Wooden ladders led up to the first level.

As they neared the foot of the cliff, Jostosh looked back at the grassy plain. "I had hoped for better on this, my last hunt." He tossed his spear down and motioned for Danny to climb. "We will take you to Mother, and then there will be a feast."

Before Wa could ask, Danny translated.

Wa started up the ladder. "Let's just hope we're not the main course."

16

DANCE OF DESHUK

By the time they'd ascended to the top level of the dwellings, they'd gained at least one hundred meters of elevation. Danny stood breathless at the top and surveyed his surroundings. They stood on a plaza of smooth bedrock open to the sky. It projected from the cliff face, forming a roof for the dwellings below. The plaza continued into the cliff, where a great overhang arched above the back half. In the deep shadows, dark openings penetrated farther into the rock.

Jostosh lead them across the plaza and into a cool passageway that opened into a natural cavern gleaming with crystalline formations on the walls and ceiling. Shafts in the walls brought in just enough daylight to ignite the crystals with dazzling sparkles.

Jostosh approached a mountain of furs and cushions piled against the far wall and prostrated himself. "Mother, I bring you two godlings."

The mound of furs shifted, and two eyes appeared. Danny realized that only a few of the furs were from dead animals. Most of it belonged to a living bigfoot. The largest, most obese bigfoot he'd ever seen. It lifted a log-thick arm, and furry fingers beckoned him forward.

"It looks like a beanbag chair with arms and legs," Wa said.

The typical bear-like snout barely protruded from the pillowy folds of Mother's face. "Godlings, my son? I hope you didn't steal them from the city."

"No, Mother," said Jostosh. "We found them wandering the plain. We watched them descend the cliff by way of the stairs."

Mother's eyes squinted, or at least Danny thought they did. They got smaller anyway. "The portal of Aten?"

Jostosh growled at Danny. "Mother asked you a question."

"Oh." He made a half-bow because he thought he should show some deference. "I don't know what Aten is, but we did come through a portal. We used the Spheroid of the Asht."

Mother made another motion with her fingers. A meezu rushed to place a bucket in her hand. She slurped from it, draining a gallon of something in one go. The moment she set the bucket down the meezu swept in to refill it.

"The Asht," she said. "You speak of the old gods. Even the queen knows little of them."

"Can you take us to the city with the pyramid?" Danny asked.

Jostosh hissed at him. Apparently one wasn't supposed to ask questions.

Mother continued to squint at Danny. "This is a unique opportunity to study godlings close up. We always assumed the queen of the Golden City lived alone. But she looks like you, about your size. Did you bring any magical artifacts with you?"

"They had just this." Jostosh placed Danny's trainer in Mother's mitten hands.

"It's a trainer," Danny said.

She turned it around to face him. The device's familiar menu system glowed in the dim light. "You will show me how to use this artifact. If I'm satisfied, I will take you to the Golden City. If not . . ." She licked her chops and looked Danny up and down.

"There's nothing to it," he said. "You just tell it what you want."

Mother thought for a moment and addressed the trainer. "Make me a god."

The trainer's voice came back, "I cannot do that."

Mother seemed to shrug. "It was worth a try. What is the secret to the queen's power?"

The trainer responded with a general statement about monarchies, with examples of previous human queens.

Mother tossed the trainer aside. "This isn't useful at all."

She turned her eyes from Danny to Wa and seemed to come to a decision.

"The timing of your arrival is good, for we are to present a new Chosen to serve the queen. Tonight we shall feast, and nearly as well as the queen herself, I'll warrant. The females shall dance."

She waved a dismissal and lifted the bucket for another long slurp. "Take them away and prepare them." With that, Jostosh guided them out of the chamber and back into the sweltering heat.

Danny swallowed and looked up at Jostosh. "You're not going to eat us are you?"

The meezu's expression grew thoughtful, as if he were considering the best way to cook them. "I doubt it."

Jostosh pointed to a shady spot on the far side of the plaza. "Wait there. Do not wander."

They didn't have to wait long before Jostosh returned, followed by the same meezu who'd attended to Mother. Jostosh handed Danny's trainer back. "Mother fears reprisals from the queen if she keeps this." Danny swallowed against the panic that made his throat go dry. He took the trainer, doing his best to conceal how his hands trembled. He tucked the device into his jeans and took a deep breath.

The attendant placed a tray on the ground next to Danny and

lifted a woven cover to expose a basket of strange fruits and two buckets of water. Danny snatched up a hard blue fruit wondering how he'd ever bite through the thick rind." He pointed to the blade on Jostosh's belt. For the bigfoot it would be a hunting knife, for Danny a small machete. "Can I borrow that for a second?

"What for?"

"To cut open this fruit. I don't think I'll be able to eat it otherwise."

Jostosh and the attendant burst into growls, but Danny recognized it for laughter. The attendant laughed so hard it had to sit down and cover its ears. Every time it looked up at Danny, it collapsed into more convulsions.

"It's not food," Jostosh said, after a long effort to control himself. He dropped the fruit into a bucket, and it started to foam. "This is to wash yourselves. Your odor offends our noses."

Even though he'd had no way of knowing what the fruit was for, Danny felt his face go hot. To compensate he kept his voice even and asked if they could have some food.

Jostosh sent the attendant off. He grew serious. "Tonight is a great celebration among the meezu. You must cleanse your bodies, or Mother will assign someone to do it for you."

Danny could tell by Wa's antsy movements he was dying to know what was going on. Instead of explaining, Danny stripped off his clothes and began washing up, laughing at Wa's shock.

The cool water felt good in the heat. Danny looked down at his cuts and bruises, clicking his tongue at the blue-black splotch on his side. Once he felt clean, he used the rest of the sudsy water on his clothes, which were stained with grime, sweat, and gourd goo.

He let the sun dry him, then lay down in the shade. The attendant brought a platter laden with a familiar meat.

"*Gleenshev!*" Wa said, digging in with gusto. "I'm glad it's cooked and sliced, though."

Gleenshev was a meaty plant that grew on ground vines. When raw, it looked just like a giant eyeball. The bigfeet of Undermountain considered it a great delicacy.

Danny ate his fill and leaned back to rest. "Odd that they'd have *gleenshev* here. My implant has no record of this planet existing, so how did it get here?"

Wa lay back with a groan. "Who cares? Maybe it's from here originally."

"Maybe."

The two boys dozed comfortably in the shade for the last few hours of daylight. Danny woke with a start when a great pounding sounded all around him. He shot up, though he winced at the pain in his side. Meezu sat all over the plaza, many beating huge drums wedged between their knees. The tones reverberated in the overhang, which acted as a natural amplifier. Many seconds later faint echoes returned, bounced from the cliffs across the valley.

The cadence built, and the rhythms became more complex. Every drum had a slightly different tone; some were pitched high, some so low they barely registered to Danny's ears but vibrated in his chest. After a time, he noticed an intricate melody emerge, and the faint echoes he'd heard before wove themselves into the composition.

Jostosh came to sit next to them.

"Where's your drum?" Danny asked.

Jostosh scratched an ear. "Not tonight. Not ever again."

Danny wanted to ask him more, but Jostosh gave off a clear vibe that he didn't want to talk.

More bigfeet ascended from the dwellings, many bearing great logs, which they dumped in a pile in the middle of the plaza and set alight. Mother emerged from a dark passage at the back. Danny stared as she waddled with the help of several attendants. She was nearly as wide as she was tall. Her feet emerged just below the sagging folds of her fat. More attendants swept out, placing cushions and furs for her to rest upon.

Mother plopped down and did not move again.

A procession of more bigfeet came out, taking positions all around Mother. Jostosh watched them with keen interest.

"Who are they?" Danny asked.

"The females. We rarely get to see them."

Danny studied the females, but he couldn't see any difference between them and the males. He remembered Grizz telling him that there were no females in Undermountain. "Why are they kept apart?"

Jostosh blinked at Danny, perplexed, as though Danny asked why the wind blew. He looked away and did not answer.

A perfectly clear night settled in as cool air swept down the valley, but the great bonfire kept the chill away.

Overhead, a crisp canopy of stars twinkled in constellations Danny had never seen, nor recognized from his implant. A few stars shone so brightly they had to be planets. A pinpoint of light sped across the sky. "A satellite," Danny said.

"It is a chariot of the old gods," said Jostosh. "With no driver, it will circle in the heavens until time runs out."

Stones were pulled up from the plaza to reveal deep pits. The meezu built fires in them and roasted strange meats, which sent up delicious scents. Soon Danny was burning his fingers on a chunk of something Jostosh called skopa. It had the texture of a football but tasted like chicken.

After everyone had eaten his or her fill, the drumming resumed. Mother called out names, and females stood and stepped to the middle of the plaza, where they began a strange dance, hopping up and down. It struck Danny as silly at first, but the steps became more intricate as the meezu lunged and dipped to the beat of the drums. They began to swing their arms in wide arcs. Groups formed and flung their smallest member through the air. These fliers turned somersaults and landed and rolled, then sprung up to repeat the stunt.

"It's *deshuk*," Wa said.

Danny had never seen a *deshuk* game in real life, but Breyona had told him about it. He'd seen the ancient fighting form during GorVit's siege on Undermountain. But that had been desperate, with no sense of rhythm or art to it. This reminded him of the tai chi his mother had practiced for three months—beautiful yet fraught with barely contained violence.

"Yes," Jostosh said. "It's the dance of *deshuk*, taught to us long ago by the old gods, the Asht."

"So you remember the Asht?" Danny asked.

"Of course not. They abandoned us many thousands of years ago. But we served them here for countless years before that. Before we committed the great sin, and they punished us by leaving."

"What did you do?" Wa asked.

Jostosh picked at the remainder of his food, flicking hunks of char aside. "We don't know. But we once lived in the city. Whatever the act was, it offended the Asht so greatly they cast us out and abandoned the city to the tangoga. And none of us was allowed in until the queen appeared. Tomorrow I will submit myself into her service, if she'll have me."

"There are tangoga in the city?" Danny asked, excited.

"Of course. They served the Asht long before we did. But legend says the Asht were not satisfied with the tangoga. They wanted servants they could relate to."

"A tangoga called GorVit forced me to open the portal," Danny said. "Gor and several gunners are out there somewhere."

"Unusual for a tangoga to be outside the city," Jostosh said. "I can't explain it. But I shall ask tomorrow once I'm presented as a Chosen."

"What did you do to get chosen?"

"I met the two requirements: I am male, and I have mastered my aggression. There are few like me in the dwellings. Mother keeps the best as consorts. As her son, I cannot serve in that role, so naturally I will be offered as a Chosen."

"Is it that hard to pass through *grot*?" Danny asked, remembering a conversation he'd had with Grizz. A bigfoot's youth was marked by such extraordinary violence that they didn't even begin counting themselves as alive until they'd gotten through a rite of passage called *grot*. Danny's implant held little information about it. "Don't you have someone to help you? Like to calm your head when you get out of control?"

Jostosh drew back his lips to expose sharp teeth. "I have no idea what you're talking about." His statement wasn't a request for Danny to clarify, though. "The females are also vicious when young, but they gain control quicker, easier. More than half of the males fail to contain it, and they are banished to the jungles to fight the horgodons. Most are never seen again, and if they are, they're hardly more than animals. Those of us who stay are expected to spend our short lives hunting and mating." A wistful note entered his voice at that. He gazed across the plaza where the females danced. After a moment, he tossed the last bit of his food aside. "Then there are the few like me who are chosen to serve the Queen of the Golden City. It is a rare and great honor." Despite his statement, he spoke with sadness.

They watched the *deshuk* dance as more and more females joined in. The drumming built to a crescendo then stopped. The dancers collapsed with heaving breaths. The last echoes returned then faded, leaving the dwellings in stark silence beneath the starry sky.

The meezu dispersed. Jostosh took his leave, instructing Danny and Wa to remain on the plaza. One of Mother's attendants left them some furry skins for warmth.

In minutes, the plaza lay empty except for the two boys and the dying embers of the fire.

"Should we make a run for it?" Wa asked. "Go to the city now?"

Danny considered it but shook his head. "There's no point. Besides, who knows what's out there in the grass. I'd rather have the meezu with us for protection."

Danny stared up into the starry sky, wondering where he was, and hoping that GorVit hadn't already entered the city, hadn't found the horrible weapon it held.

Wa snuggled into his furs and sighed. "If you forget about GorVit and his gunners, and the unknown terrible weapon he's after, and the fact that we have no way to get home, and that we're surrounded by bigfeet with spears and clubs, this is pretty cool."

17

THEY'RE BUT CHILDREN

Breyona remembered the Hall of the Strict very well. As large as a high school gymnasium, it stood mostly empty. A cone of light shone onto a dais where three white-robed bigfeet sat in meditation. To the right sat Notchy, a pudgy, tan bigfoot with a notched ear. His real name was Filinesama. If humans had an ally in Undermountain besides Grizz, he was it.

To the left sat Terrenora, a bigfoot Breyona vaguely remembered meeting once before. The thin, ashen-furred bigfoot eyed the humans as they entered, giving off an obvious air of disapproval.

As the leader of the council, Shaggy sat in the middle position. Ridiculous poofs of fur stuck out of his collar and sleeves. His mouth bent down in a permanent scowl. He kept his eyes closed, apparently deep in meditation.

Luon guided them to the foot of the dais where he instructed them to take seats on the hard, stone floor. Something in Shaggy's demeanor told her he was aware of her presence, a stiffening in his posture, perhaps.

Breyona stood at the foot of the dais. Em took a position to her left, and Bronson hung back, somewhere out of sight behind her. Shiv, Luon, and Grizz sat cross-legged off to the right.

Breyona refused to sit, refused to lower herself before Shaggy. She stared straight ahead and took many deep breaths to keep her center of calm.

After a long silence, Shaggy opened his eyes part way. "So my acolyte returns."

Breyona met his gaze. "The tangoga GorVit has kidnapped Danny. He wants him to use his trainer for the—"

"I am aware of the circumstances."

"Then why haven't you sent someone after them? Do you want GorVit to have the Spheroid?"

A rumble sounded in the back of Shaggy's throat. "There is no use sending defenders when we know that GorVit cannot activate the Spheroid."

"And how do you know that?" Breyona demanded.

"The fact that GorVit seeks Danny's assistance with the Spheroid shows that Gor has failed to solve it. Gor has the misapprehension that the trainer holds the secret to activating it. I am absolutely certain it does not. The Spheroid was never solved by the People, so it will never be solved by a tangoga, and certainly not a human."

Luon leaned forward, eyes ablaze. "You forget Choolenama."

Shaggy scoffed. "Your Choolenama theory is nothing but speculation. I quite doubt he had any better idea of how to activate the device than you do. Choolenama went mad."

Breyona took a deep breath before speaking. Shaggy possessed a singular ability to irritate her. "We'll go after Danny and Wa ourselves."

"Just wait a minute," Em said. She held one hand clenched into a tight fist at her side; the other pointed an accusatory finger at Shaggy. "This is your fault. Danny and Breyona handed GorVit to you on a silver platter. All you had to do was hold them here. How is it even possible that he got away without any of you knowing? It's completely irresponsible, and all of you should be ashamed of yourselves." She put her fists on her hips and managed to frown down at Shaggy even though he sat above her.

"Forget the council, Em," Breyona said. "They won't do anything for us. Let's go find Danny and Wa." She turned and headed for the exit, but several acolytes positioned themselves in front of the door to block her. A low voice spoke behind her.

"Impressive. Most impressive."

She turned to find Terrenora on his feet, hands clasped before him. He swept down from the dais and came toward her with soft steps. "The human acolyte remains so calm. I understand now what you were saying earlier, Hanameesovenama."

Breyona's skin crawled at the idea that Shaggy had been discussing her with another council member.

"So what do you say, Terrenora?" Shaggy asked.

Terrenora stood over her, eyes squinting out of his gaunt face. Breyona braced herself to be calmed, but the bigfoot didn't lift a hand. Instead, he spun and returned to his position on the dais. "I vote yea."

"And I vote yea, of course," Shaggy said.

Breyona relaxed. It had all been one of Shaggy's twisted tests. Somehow she had passed, and now he would send defenders to find Danny.

"And I say nay," Notchy said.

Breyona stopped mid step, shocked. Even Shiv looked surprised. Breyona had always thought Notchy was on their side.

Em tensed next to her. Breyona could almost sense the shouts rising inside the girl, but Grizz interrupted the outburst before it started.

"Something is going on here," Grizz said, softly.

"I know what's going on," Em said. "They're going to let Gor kill my brother and Wa."

"That's not it. I don't think the vote was about sending help, was it?" The question was directed at Shaggy, but the council leader ignored it.

He'd turned to face Notchy. "I suppose you intend to evoke *okchen*?" he asked in a half growl.

Notchy chuckled and nodded. "A full vote of the conclave is necessary in matters of this import. Furthermore, I propose the humans each get a vote in the conclave."

Shaggy's low and booming laugh echoed in the great hall. "That's ridiculous. Why don't we ask the tangoga if they want to follow procedure? You know very well the humans will resist. They're but children."

Notchy chuckled again. "But we're making history here, Hanameesovenama. Not since the treaty have we made First Contact with a planet-bound species."

"First Contact?" Breyona asked. "What's going on?"

The councilors were too preoccupied with their silly staring contest to bother answering her. Shaggy stewed for a while longer, adjusting his posture in agitation. "Very well," he said to Notchy. "It is true that I head the council in the most historic time since Voo brought us to the Oath. I'll allow these children to vote, but their consensus shall count for a single vote in the conclave."

"Shall we summon the conclave then?" Notchy asked.

"No," Shaggy said in a self-satisfied voice. "I think everyone needs time to consider the import of the vote. We shall hold the vote in three days."

"Three days!" Em cried.

Breyona barely kept her calm. "But we have to go now. Danny and Wa are in danger now."

"Then go," Shaggy said.

With that, he stood, nodded curtly to Notchy and Terrenora, and swept out of the Hall of the Strict. Terrenora leapt up to follow after. That left Notchy sitting on the dais, eyes closed, breathing deeply in the silence. Em stared after Shaggy and Terrenora, jaw clenched. Grizz looked at his hands and shook his head sadly. Luon also had his eyes closed in meditation.

Breyona sighed, found the center of her calm. "So this meeting was all about First Contact. Shaggy was never going to help Danny."

"Yes." Notchy said. "Hanameesovenama was very excited to show you off to Terrenora. He forced my hand to invoke *okchen*."

"And how will the conclave vote?" Breyona asked. "Does it even matter if we get one vote?"

Notchy chuckled. "It will be a close thing. Hanameesovenama is very confident, but I am not sure how solid his votes are. I mean to use the next three days to turn some to your favor."

"But we don't have three days," Em said.

"You don't all have to stay."

Bronson cleared his throat. "I have no intention of going after this GorVit character. I'll stay here and vote, and then I want to go home."

Notchy pointed at Shiv. "And my young acolyte will stay as well. He has nothing to offer you in your pursuit of GorVit."

Breyona relaxed. "That's good. They can vote while the rest of us go after the boys."

Grizz stood and bowed to Notchy. "With your permission, I'd like to go with them."

Notchy chuckled and nodded his approval.

Breyona smiled at Grizz gratefully. She wished all the bigfeet were more like him. "Thank you."

Grizz looked away and rubbed an ear. "You should not thank me for fulfilling my obligations. I can't help but think I'm responsible for all of this. If it weren't for me, you'd never have come to Undermountain in the first place. You wouldn't be tangled up in these problems."

Breyona placed a hand on Grizz's arm. "You saved us from the tangeg that day in the mountains. And don't say you were just following the Oath. Shaggy would have used the same oath to justify letting us die there. You are *good*. You care."

Grizz's wide, green eyes regarded her for a long moment. Of all the bigfeet, he offered the most human-like expressions. She saw tenderness and kindness in his face.

"Ah Grizz, this is a fine lesson," said Notchy. "Hanameesove-nama thinks of these humans as mere children." He nodded at Breyona. "But this one has summarized my teachings beautifully. The Oath does not make one good. The actions of individuals make the Oath good."

Grizz bowed to Notchy then turned to offer the same honor to Breyona. He straightened and motioned to the door. "Come. We have much to prepare before we leave. Your old apartment is available. I will have food and supplies brought up."

Breyona and Em said goodbye to Shiv, who had to return to his room in the temple. Em's eyebrows knitted together, and she kept glancing back at the dais as they left the Hall.

"What's the matter?" Breyona asked.

Em sighed. "I don't know. I guess I don't understand the bigfeet. They have all this amazing technology. It's obvious they could destroy the rebel tangoga if they'd just put their Oath on pause for half a second. They could take out GorVit so easily."

Grizz overheard and turned a sad eye on Em. "That's not how the Oath works. One doesn't break it for convenience."

Em threw up her hands. "If the Oath lets your enemies kill you, then it's already broken."

"The Oath is not the problem," Breyona said. She laughed sadly to herself. "The problem is that the tangoga and the People are only human."

Em frowned and threw up her hands. "I don't get it."

"I do," Grizz said. "I do."

18

NEFERNEFERNEFER

Danny gazed up at the ivory colored city wall. Twenty meters up, the crenellations of gold that gave the city its name glinted in the morning sunlight.

Wa tapped his fingers together nervously. "It doesn't look like anyone's home."

"Be patient," Jostosh said. He wore ceremonial skins, sun bleached and ornamented with shells and beads. "They've been watching our approach."

"Who has?"

Jostosh didn't answer. He looked up at the wall as if it were the object of a holy pilgrimage. Danny supposed it was.

Wa rubbed his head and glanced back at the grassy plain. "We're pretty exposed out here. If GorVit shows up with those tangoga of his, we'll be toast."

Jostosh patted Wa's shoulder. "The queen will protect us."

Two massive doors, cross-banded with steel, sealed the city. Hundreds of meezu had gathered before it and lowered themselves in supplication. More assembled behind them, carrying their great drums, which they beat in a slow march.

A team of meezu bore Mother forward on a palanquin, which they set at the base of the door. Attendants helped her to her feet. She squinted at the assembled meezu and raised her flabby arms. "NeferNeferNefer!" she cried.

The rumbling voices of the meezu called the response. "Nefer-NeferNefer!"

Mother repeated the cry. The crowd echoed her, and the drums started to pick up speed. Soon the meezu were all bellowing a continuous chant of "NeferNeferNefer."

After each recitation, Mother let loose a terrible, warbling shriek.

"I don't care for the melody," Wa said, "but it's got a good beat."

The chant continued, growing more frantic with every passing minute. The meezu swayed and clapped their hands in time with the drums. More voices joined Mother's shrieks. Several females leapt up and flung themselves about in a *deshuk* dance, as though possessed with wild spirits.

Mother shook her hands and turned her eyes to the sky. "Aye-eeee *nostabenzu!*"

The meezu answered with a final guttural "aye-ooh!"

The drums cut off, and the last echoes faded.

Danny didn't know what the meezu expected to happen next, but their anticipation lay thick in the silent air.

A tiny figure appeared at the top of the gate.

"Is that a tangoga?" Wa asked.

Danny squinted up at the unmistakable form. Its two heads peered down at him, and its amplified voice called out. "Present your Chosen."

Jostosh stepped forward and raised his arms. He uttered a long ceremonial phrase, then knelt and lowered his head to the ground.

Mother raised her arms and shouted up. "I present Jostosh, a tame male, intelligent and dedicated. He would have made a good mate, but we sacrifice him to the Queen of the Golden City."

The tangoga squawked an order, and the gates began to grind open, shaking the earth as they moved.

Moments later the tangoga appeared at the door, flanked by two meezu dressed in narrow skirts and headdresses. They carried staves, each topped with a golden circle and cross.

Mother stepped forward and nodded her head, the closest she could approximate a bow. "I also present to you these godlings, whom we found astray in the wild. We return them to the Queen of the Golden City!" She waved at Danny and Wa with a flourish that made her whole body wriggle.

The tangoga wore a white cape cinched around both necks. It flowed over the creature's hindquarters and dragged on the ground. A jeweled scarab broach secured the cape on the left neck, a simpler broach held the cape around the right neck. The cape left the torso exposed, which bore minuscule feathers that rippled in waves of gray, blue, and teal. But instead of the standard steel armpack, this tangoga wore golden arms, the claws delicate and thin. A more refined version than Danny had seen before.

The eyes of the left head bore into Danny for a moment, then shifted to Jostosh. "On behalf of the queen, we accept Jostosh among the Chosen."

A golden claw came up and beckoned to Danny and Wa. "Be welcome in the city, humans. You're arrival is most unexpected, but I hope the queen will find you diverting."

Danny didn't move. "Who's hierarchy do you belong to?" he asked. "The Octz or the Glutz?"

"That's none of your business. I am SulKit, the primary on this planet."

"Are you with the rogues who attacked Undermountain?" Danny demanded. "Is GorVit in there?" He pointed through the gate.

Mother's eyes narrowed, obviously displeased with Danny's interrogation of their host.

"I know nothing of rogues or Undermountain," Sul said. "Nor of this GorVit. Please come in. We will present you to the queen."

Danny didn't trust SulKit, but he didn't see any other choice. If a terrible weapon existed on this planet, it had to be in the city. Why else would the Spheroid open a portal so near to it?

He shared a shrug with Wa and cautiously stepped past the tangoga and into the city.

Wa scratched his head. "Is it just me or are those bigfeet dressed like Egyptians?"

"I noticed that too," Danny said, eying the two meezu in head-dresses.

"These are the priests of the queen," Sul said. "They are the oldest among the Chosen. They require you to be purified before your audience with the queen." Sul emphasized *purified* like it was some sort of joke.

They followed the priests and the tangoga into a great plaza on the other side of the gate. Several more meezu stood guard with huge axes in their furry fists. Beyond the plaza, lay plantings of flowers, grassy parks, and copses of trees. A wide thoroughfare led past grand fountains and through a series of open-air courtyards enclosed by columns crowned with carved palm fronds.

Tall, flat-roofed, wooden structures stood here and there. Living quarters for the meezu, according to Sul.

"Where is everyone?" Danny asked.

The city looked and felt empty. Almost all of the structures were monuments, temples, or parks. No one walked the streets.

"The population of meezu is held constant at thirty," Sul said.

"And how many tangoga?" Danny asked.

"A few."

"What planet are we on?"

"Hoo," Sul said.

Danny had been hoping Sul would provide a name his implant recognized. He rescanned his implant for info about Hoo and came up blank.

They strode down the thoroughfare. To their right ran the river, which coursed along a deep channel through the heart of the city. On the other side of the river, rising above the roof of a temple, was the tip of the golden pyramid.

Ahead, a palace bisected the thoroughfare, which sloped slightly upward. Beyond the palace, the falls poured down the cliff face, sending up a scintillating, golden mist.

They came to a wide stairway guarded by two enormous, carved humanoid figures, their bodies distorted with sagging bellies and droopy ears.

Danny wiped the sweat from his eyes. The white paving stones seemed to magnify the sun's heat. He wondered how the bigfeet could stand it, covered with fur as they were. He didn't have long to consider, for they entered an open-air temple. The priests stopped before a wide pit in the floor and began to chant. Other meezu stepped forward with armfuls of flowers, bushels of fruits, and bundles of long, black sticks that looked like giant bug legs.

The priests waved their staves over the offering then pointed to the pit. The meezu cast in the offering, and the priests finished their chant.

A priest step toward Danny and dipped his finger into a pot. It came out dripping with black oil. The priest pressed his finger to Danny's forehead and uttered a prayer before doing the same to Wa. It left a large black smudge between Wa's eyes.

"Come," the priest said. "You may now enter the presence of the great NeferNeferNefer."

They skirted the pit and continued out the back of the temple, into the palace, and up a long stairway. Danny puffed and wiped sweat from his forehead. His sleeve came away smudged with black ceremonial oil.

Danny climbed the last few steps and found himself in a grand room. More meezu priests formed ranks to each side. Massive columns, colorfully painted in reds, blues, and yellows, supported a high ceiling. Straight ahead, mounted on the back wall, was an enormous golden disc, its surface etched with many of the same symbols Danny had seen on the Spheroid.

Stairs climbed to a raised platform, on which stood a golden throne positioned directly beneath the disc. Sitting there, arrayed in white, face serene and cool, sat the Queen of the Golden City.

"Holy cow," Wa said. "She's a human."

The priests led Danny and Wa toward her until they came to the foot of the stairs. The queen stared down at them, expression unreadable. She was the most beautiful girl Danny had ever seen. Except maybe for Breyona, he reminded himself.

The queen wore a crisp, white wrap, cinched at the waist with a wide belt of intricately linked gold rings. A broad necklace of sparkling jewels hung around her neck. Short sleeves capped her shoulders, leaving bare her long, elegant arms. Cuffs of etched gold encircled each of her biceps. She held a scepter in her right hand. It bore the same cross and circle that topped the priests' staves. Her headdress stood up and back from her head, wider at the top and tapering in a way to enhance her neck.

The queen stood and descended, graceful as a swan on water. Her black eyes locked onto Danny.

Two huge meezu guards paced beside her. They carried bronze swords longer than Danny's entire body. The blades curved and widened toward the tip.

A voice behind him barked, "Kneel before the Queen of the Golden City." Danny turned to find one of the two white-robed meezu priests looming over him. Before Danny could comply, a staff pressed on his shoulder, pushing him to his knees. To his left Wa knelt under the same forceful inducement. Mother, panting and wheezing from the climb, struggled down to her knees as well.

The queen touched Mother's head with her scepter. "The blessing of Aten be upon you." She glanced at SulKit. "Provide Mother medicines and delicacies."

Mother kissed the queen's sandaled foot. "Thank you, Great Queen. Thank you. You're generosity is known wherever words are spoken."

The queen gave a noncommittal hum. She turned her attention back to Danny and Wa. Danny looked up into her eyes. He found himself at a loss for words, stunned by her beauty. And her youth. She couldn't be much older than he was.

Wa cleared his throat. "Are you Cleopatra or something?"

The queen shifted her gaze to Wa, clearly irritated. "What language is that?" she demanded in Footese. "Are you a thieving Hyksat?"

"You are from Earth," Danny said in Footese. From her blank stare, he realized the English word for Earth meant nothing to her. "You are from the land of pyramids, the great desert. The Sphinx."

"Yes. Many lives ago."

"Who are you?"

"In my first life, I was the favored wife of Akhenaten, Pharaoh of Egypt, anointed of Aten. In these lives I am the Queen of the Golden City, guardian of the faith, and goddess of the meezu. I am Nefertiti."

Wa coughed. "Did she just say Nefertiti?"

"Shut up, Wa."

The queen raised an eyebrow at Wa. "Are his manners always so base?"

"Pretty much," Danny said. He licked his lips and eyed the guards and their great swords. "Listen. We came through the portal. We used the Spheroid."

"Of course you did. I've been waiting for you."

"For me?" She couldn't mean him in particular.

"And a long wait it has been."

She glanced at Wa then back to Danny. An uncertain look flashed in her eyes, but she lifted her chin up a hair higher and turned to the tangoga. "Prepare them!" She turned to go.

"Wait!" Danny said. "I need to talk to you. There's another tangoga out in the jungle. They want something inside the city. A weapon."

She didn't answer. She strode back up the stairs and disappeared behind the throne.

"What did she mean by 'prepare them?'" Danny asked Sul.

SulKit came forward and waited for them to stand. "Follow us. You must be washed and dressed for the feast. Rooms have been made ready for you."

19

HOOK ME UP WITH TEXAS

Breyona stared out at the city of Undermountain from the top floor window of the earthscraper. The view took her breath away despite the barren spots where collapsed buildings had been cleared away.

Em said she'd lived in this same apartment while being held prisoner the summer before. Breyona turned to study the space, remembering the spare meditation cell she'd been confined to. She supposed there were different degrees of prison life. Where her cell had only gray stone walls, a cot, and a light, the living area in this luxurious apartment sported a huge sofa and a long dining table. And food whenever you wanted it.

Em and Grizz sorted through supplies strewn across the table, preparing for the departure to the Sahara settlement.

Tangoga from the sub-city had managed to find or fabricate backpacks sized for humans. They had also manufactured clothing identical to what Em and Breyona had arrived in.

Grizz stuffed apples into a satchel. "I hope it's enough," he said. "I don't know how long we're going to be gone."

Breyona couldn't believe how much food Grizz meant to take. It looked to be enough for twenty people, but then she supposed bigfeet ate a lot.

Em folded clothes and stuffed them into a backpack. "You realize if you bigfeet ever do make First Contact, one of the technologies we're going to want most is your ability to make custom clothing so quickly."

Breyona shouldered her pack. She hadn't wasted any time folding. She'd just stuffed in everything she thought she might need.

The elevator door in the foyer slid open and out stepped Tog. The poor creature shuffled in with his head held low. He had changed into his boss armpack. Over one of his arms, he carried a satchel very similar to the one Grizz was packing with food.

Grizz eyed the tangoga. "What's the meaning of this?"

Tog held his head a little higher. "I mean to help rescue Danny. He is my boss."

Grizz scratched an ear. "I don't think that's a good idea. You'll just get in the way. Besides, you can't control those blades."

"I've been practicing," Tog said. He waved the blades around in circles briefly. "I'm quite skilled with them now."

Breyona remembered TogYip's confrontation with GorVit. TogYip had rushed GorVit and fought them blade to blade. The altercation resulted in Yip's injury and eventual death. Breyona felt pity for the poor creature.

Grizz stopped packing and approached Tog. "I can't be responsible for you. It will be hard enough to protect these two humans. "

Tog's feathers ruffled as he turned toward the elevator. "Hanameesovenama was right," he said, voice raspy with anger.

"Why were you talking to Shaggy?" Breyona asked. "What did he want?"

"He had an assignment for me, something to do with the boy you call Bronson. But I told him I was going with you to rescue Danny. He told me you'd never let me go."

"When was this?" Breyona asked. Nothing good would come from Shaggy talking to Bronson.

"It happened shortly after your meeting with the council. I was passing among the galleries in the temple, and that's where I found Hanameesovenama speaking with Bronson."

"Did you hear what he said?" Em asked. She'd stopped folding clothes and stared at Tog with worry on her face.

"All I heard was Bronson saying, 'Can you guarantee that?'"

A static of nervousness danced around Breyona's center of calm. "What did he want a guarantee about?"

"I don't know. I didn't hear that part. That's when they saw me. Hanameesovenama sent Bronson away and asked me to help him. I told him I was going to go after Danny. He laughed at me and said it was a waste of time. He said he would assign me a job helping Bronson after you turned me down."

Breyona met Grizz's wide, green eyes. "You know what this means, don't you?"

"The vote," Grizz said.

Em swore. "When I find that big, stupid–"

Grizz waved his furry hands, cutting her off. "We must keep our emotions in check and think this through. Clearly Hanameesovenama has made some sort of bargain with Bronson to secure his vote in the conclave."

"And with Shiv being the only other human voting," Breyona said, "they'll cancel each other out. I've got to talk to Bronson. If Shaggy is cutting a deal with him, he must believe the vote will be very close."

"But we've got to go find Danny and Wa," Em said.

Breyona bit her lip, torn between her personal desire to go after Danny and the threat of the First Contact vote. "It won't take that long. I'll straighten Bronson out, and then we can go." She turned to Tog. "Do you know where Bronson is right now?"

"I believe he stayed at the temple," Tog said.

They scooped up their packs and followed Tog into the elevator. After a monorail ride, they entered the Temple of the Strict. Tog led them to a room in the acolytes' quarters. Not one of the cells in the meditation wards, but a nice room with cushions and wall hangings. Bronson sat at a table, stuffing his face with a chicken wing.

He looked up at them and stopped mid-chew. "You're still here?"

"We were just about to leave," Breyona said. "But Tog says you've made some sort of bargain with Hanameesovenama."

Bronson swallowed. "I don't know what you're talking about."

Breyona knew Bronson well enough to believe nothing he said. "What does he want you to do? What is he giving you for your vote?"

It looked like he was going to try to play stupid for a minute, but then he dropped his chicken wing on a plate and leaned back, smiling. "He's giving me Texas."

"What do you mean he's giving you Texas?"

"You're looking at the People's ambassador to Texas. I'll be like the governor there, which is really going to be more like being the king once Hanameesovenama comes out from under this mountain."

Em started around the table, fists raised. Grizz caught her and held her back.

Breyona laughed without humor. "You have no idea what you're talking about."

"Laugh all you want Breyona, but he said once I'm done with my training I'll be one of the most important humans in existence." He jabbed his chest with his thumb. "Because I'll be the first."

Breyona had heard that before. Shaggy had said the same thing to her last summer. "Do you even know what your training is going to be like?"

"Yeah. I've got to do some meditation, and I've got to take an oath, and then he's pretty much going to hook me up with Texas."

Breyona stepped close to him, an icy anger gripping her mind. He leaned away from her, but she put her face close to his. "He will lock you in a cell, where you will eat nothing but gray mush. You'll meditate all day, every day, except when Shaggy lectures you on the Oath. If you displease him—and believe me, you will—he will calm your head senseless, until you can't tell up from down. Before you know it, you'll be wagging your tail and fetching for him. And when you're all done, and he's made First Contact, he's going to renege on his promise, and you'll be just another insignificant acolyte among the billions of others on this planet."

A tiny muscle under Bronson's left eye twitched. He looked away.

"Let's just go," Em said. "We've got to get Danny and Wa."

The icy feeling that had taken hold of Breyona spread to her heart. She closed her eyes and took a few calming breaths. She distanced herself from her fears about Danny, from her longing to see him. She faced the truth. "I have to stay," she said. "I have to be here to vote."

A smile played on Bronson's lips, which didn't make sense to Breyona. If she stayed, she would cast the deciding vote to stop Shaggy's plans. But Bronson was stupid that way.

"I have to stay," she said again. "I don't want to, but I have to." She looked at Em, hoping that maybe Em would change her mind and offer to stay in Breyona's place. But Breyona knew that wasn't going to happen. Not only was Em in love with Wa, she was very protective of her brother, despite their bickering. Breyona was just Danny's long distance girlfriend.

Grizz heaved a great sigh and twisted an ear between his fingers. "You're doing a great thing Breyona. Danny will be very proud of you."

"Go," she said. "Go now."

Em gave Breyona a quick hug and left the room. Grizz nodded respectfully and then he, too, went out.

Breyona spun on Bronson. She had thought she was done with hatred. She thought that she had overcome all of her negative emotions, but she hadn't. In fact, what she wanted to do in that moment was harm Bronson. Severely.

Something in her face must have scared him. He stood and tried to back away, toppling the chair behind him.

An incredible pressure built in Breyona's head, making it throb. Her vision went gray. She took another step toward him.

He held up his hands. "Ah, that hurts!"

Breyona gasped. She wasn't even touching him.

The pressure fizzed from her brain, leaving her dizzy and breathless. She rubbed her elbows, desperate to shake the strange, electrical tingling that coursed through her body. Sweat sprouted on her forehead. She closed her eyes and took deep breaths until she rose above the anger and let it go.

Tears trickled down her cheeks, and she turned away from the stricken boy. "I'm sorry," she said as she stumbled through the door. "I'm sorry about everything."

20

HOW MANY GOATS?

"I'll wear the shirt, but not that," Danny said for the third time. He stood naked and dripping wet in the middle of his luxurious suite in Nefertiti's palace. A small puddle had formed on the tile floor beneath him.

The meezu priest ignored him and pointed to the costume lying on the bed. It consisted of white shirt and a short, narrow, blue skirt. Danny had no intention of wearing a skirt. Ever.

Except his real clothes had gone missing while he'd been soaking in the enormous copper tub the meezu had prepared for him.

He put on the shirt, but it barely covered his belly button. At least the bruise on his side was gone. The tangoga had healed Danny's rib with a quick pass of a small device called a *vahng*.

"I want my clothes back."

The meezu priest flexed his grip on his staff. "You must prepare for your audience with the queen."

"I already had an audience. This is dinner. How formal do we need to be? There're only three humans on the whole planet."

SulKit clattered in. "Oh my. Why aren't you dressed?"

Danny expressed his concerns about the costume.

Sul squawked and said something about useless meezu and their superstitions. "I'll see you get your clothes back, but it won't be until later. You'd best don this for now."

"What part of 'no' don't you understand?"

Sul blinked. "Very well. Clothing is optional, I'm sure."

Danny folded his arms. "Fine. I'm not going."

The meezu hissed and gaped. "But the queen *commands* your presence."

Danny turned on the priest, but SulKit slid between them. "In the interest of harmony, please reconsider. Can you explain why the clothing provided is objectionable?"

"I can't wear a skirt!"

Sul took up the garment in question and held it between his delicate golden claws. "I think it will fit."

"That's not the issue. I'm not going to go traipsing around in a skirt. If Wa saw me wearing it, I'd never hear the end of–"

Wa strode in, wearing shirt and skirt. He held up a hand to shield his eyes. "God, Danny. I don't want to see that. Put on your dress and let's go eat."

Danny snatched the skirt from SulKit and pulled it on. A second later, the priest wrapped a belt around Danny's waist and cinched it tight. "You can look now, Wa. But if you say one word–"

"Nice legs!"

The priest seemed antsy, shifting his weight from foot to foot and tapping his great staff on the floor with impatience. "Please. The queen waits."

They followed the priest out of the suite and into a long gallery. A balcony overlooked the plaza in front of the palace. The sun stood low, washing the monuments and gardens in gold. A slight breeze ruffled Danny's hair, heavy with the scent of flowers.

Wa sighed. "If you were a girl, and I wasn't in a skirt, this would be romantic."

Danny turned on SulKit who clattered along behind them. "Who decided to make this girl a queen?"

"She declared it upon her arrival," Sul said, as if that were a rational explanation.

"And you believed her? I don't know why you put up with it."

Sul eyed the meezu and sidled closer to Danny. "We choose to humor her, for now. For many ages we lived here alone, awaiting the Asht's return. We did not expect this alien to come to us, but the Asht were clear in their instructions. Any extraterrestrial species who come to the city are to be admitted. Our hospitality procedures instruct us to 'spare no expense for the comfort and pleasure of guests'."

Sul waved his golden claws, shooing away the thoughts in his head. "She wears me out with her orders and demands. But we obey her, as that is what is required. Fortunately, we were able to position the meezu such that they do most of the difficult labor, like her construction projects."

"So you have to treat me and Wa the same way?"

The tangoga glanced at him. "Technically, yes. However, Nefertiti's power here is real. The meezu will do her bidding—or die trying. In the end, she will likely turn them on you, and you will die."

"How can you be certain of that?"

"Over the years she's sent them after us tangoga, even her favorites. When you live with someone a few thousand years, you're bound to have a killing or two."

"A few thousand years? How can she have lived that long?"

"It's a matter of hospitality."

Danny wanted to ask more questions, but the priest guided him and Wa into a dining hall. Elaborately painted columns supported the high ceiling. Braziers burned in the corners, and oil lanterns hung from hooks on the walls.

"Stand there," the priest said, pointing to a spot in the middle of the floor.

SulKit clattered to a corner and went still, golden claws clasped before him. Behind the columns stood several meezu guards with their massive swords and axes. They fixed their eyes on Danny and did not blink.

A parade of meezu priests strode in, elaborately costumed in Egyptian-inspired garb. They chanted a continuous round of "NeferNeferNefer," and one tossed flower petals to the floor.

Nefer glided in behind them, dressed in a long, flowing gown of pale yellow. She sat at a small table with a single chair. A tangoga clattered in, placing a tray of food before her.

Danny's stomach rumbled as the warm, spicy smells of food wafted to his nose.

The meezu priests ceased their chanting and stood perfectly still. The only sound in the great chamber came from the clack of Nefer's dishes. She picked at her food, taking delicate bites, ignoring the presence of all around her.

After a long drink from a golden goblet, she raised her eyes to meet Danny's. "Would you like some food?"

Danny took a step forward, but in an instant two guards stood between him and the table.

Nefer's laugh chilled Danny. "I asked you a question. I did not make an offer."

Danny clenched his jaw.

"Well?" Nefer asked.

The guards shifted and tightened their grips on their weapons.

"Yes," Danny said, "we are very hungry."

"Hungry enough to do what?"

Danny blinked, confused by the question. "Um, I don't know. What do you want us to do?"

Nefertiti stood and parted the guards, giving them an annoyed glance. "My meezu worry over nothing."

She approached Wa and gazed down at him. She stood a full hand taller than him. Her dark eyes openly inspected Wa, traveling up and down his body. She walked around him, trailing a finger along his shoulders, and passed behind Danny until she came around to face him. She stood close enough that he could smell the fruit on her breath.

She tilted her eyes up to meet his. This close, he discovered her skin bore no makeup aside from the little she wore around her eyes. Her face was as smooth, rich, and clear as . . . Danny didn't know what. She smelled of strange perfumes, exotic and spicy.

"How many years have you?" she asked.

"Sixteen . . . and a half." His voice sounded very high in his own ears.

With a flash of insanely long lashes, she broke eye contact and walked back to her table. She sat and waved at Wa. "The short one may leave. Provide him a feast."

A tangoga stepped forward. "Follow us," it said to Wa.

Wa shrugged. "No habla footese, ese."

Danny coughed. "He said for you to follow him. He's going to give you dinner."

"Oh. Good." Wa smiled and elbowed Danny before leaving. He cocked his head toward Nefer. "She's almost as hot as your sister."

Danny watched Wa leave and felt suddenly very vulnerable without his friend by his side. Wa had gotten Danny out of more than one sticky situation.

Nefertiti clapped her hands, and a meezu brought out another chair, which he placed opposite hers. She invited Danny to sit and eat.

For a moment, his hunger warred with his indignation, but as usual, his hunger won. He barely waited for the tangoga to set its tray in front of him before digging in. He didn't taste the first bites as he gobbled down bits of this and that, mostly fruit and chunks of the same chewy black meat the meezu had fed him.

Nefer watched him, lips pursed. "What did that boy say to you before he left?"

"He said you were almost as beautiful as my sister."

Nefer frowned at this. "Is she your wife?"

Danny choked and coughed until a guard stepped forward and smacked his back. "What? My sister?"

His appetite disappeared as horrific images of Em popped into his head. The more he tried not to think about them, the more vivid they became. "No! What made you ask that? That's disgusting!"

Nefer shrugged and took a sip from her goblet. She ran a ringed finger around the rim and locked eyes with him, smiling. "I assume you come from a powerful family for Aten to have sent you to me. If an alliance cannot be forged by marrying outside one's family, it is wise to concentrate your power by marrying within." She said all this matter-of-factly, as if she were discussing a trade between base-ball teams.

Danny snatched up a goblet and took a long swig of a warm, syrupy liquid. A moment later, he coughed and choked as a delayed spicy heat kicked in, like the habanero pepper he'd eaten on a dare in sixth grade.

He pushed the goblet away. Tears streamed from his eyes. "What was that?"

"*Veenshup*. The meezu harvest the berries in the jungle and make this delicious wine from it."

"Wine?"

Danny's mom had let him have an occasional sip of wine, but he didn't remember it tasting like pepper spray.

"I seem to recall having the same reaction the first few dozen times I tried it," she said absently. "Tell me about your family."

Minutes passed as Danny suffered. He wiped tears from his eyes and repeatedly blew his nose into a cloth napkin.

Nefer pointed to a tiny dish of yellow relish. "That helps ease the worst of it."

He kicked the whole dish back. Instant coolness washed through his mouth and throat. "Why didn't you tell me sooner?"

"Because I wanted to watch you. How a man deals with pain says much about his character. Now, I asked you a question. Tell me about your family."

Danny thought about how to explain it. "My mother cares for the sick."

Nefer nodded in appreciation. "Altruism is honorable. And your father?"

"My father died when I was young."

"Pity. What lands did he possess? How many goats? How many wives?"

"Um. He sort of had two wives, though the second one wasn't technically a wife. As far as I know, he never had any goats. He owned a double-wide outside of Nashville for a while. But that was before I was born."

"What wealth did he have then?"

"None. He was broke all the time. At least that's what my mom says."

A look of uncertainty passed over Nefer's face. "Why would Aten send me a peasant?"

"I don't know who Aten is, but I didn't want to come here at all. A tangoga named GorVit forced me use the Spheroid. He threatened to cut off Wa's hands if I didn't figure it out."

"Dark tidings. How can it be that the name of Aten is not known, or that strange tangoga trample the old world? No tangoga were in my lands when I left. I first saw them when I came here. And why would a tangoga need your assistance with the Spheroid? You must be a god, for no mortal could solve that wizard's device. I had the assistance of a meezu called Choolenama."

Danny considered his answer. "I studied with the meezu in the, uh . . . old world. GorVit didn't know what the Spheroid was or what it did. All Gor said was that a great weapon was hidden inside it."

Nefertiti's eyebrows scrunched together, and she sneered skeptically. "A weapon? I have been here a long time. The only weapons you'll find are those I've had forged for my guards, or those the meezu and horgodons fashion from sticks and bones." The sides of her mouth turned down in a particularly pretty way. "The tangoga have projectile throwers they refuse to share with me, but I assume this GorVit already possesses those."

"You should be prepared," Danny said. "Gor will come to the city soon in search of the weapon."

"I'm not concerned. The wall will keep them out."

Nefer stood and walked around the table, dragging her chair behind her. A meezu stepped forward to assist, but she waved him away. She placed the chair next to Danny's and sat.

"Nothing enters the city without my permission," she said, then took up a bit of fruit and held it to Danny's mouth. "Try it," she said. "It's sweet."

Danny felt his eyes cross as he looked at her slender fingers. He bit into the fruit. Juicy sweetness like a peach filled his mouth and dribbled down his chin.

"Aten moves in mysterious ways," Nefer said, voice low. Her hand went to his leg, just below the hem of his skirt. Danny coughed and stood quickly. His knee banged on the table, and the pain brought him right back to his seat.

"So there isn't a weapon here?" he asked in a rush.

"I answered that already." Nefer moved her hand to Danny's arm and squeezed his biceps. "Are you a warrior that you are so concerned about this weapon?"

Danny laughed nervously. "No."

He stood, slowly this time, thinking it might be better to leave before she got much friendlier.

Nefertiti clamped her lips together in frustration. But then she slunk up to him. "If you are not a warrior, why has Aten sent you to me?" She curled her arms around his neck.

Danny's mouth went dry. He closed his eyes and tried to picture Breyona. Nefertiti's fingers toyed with the hair on the back of his head. He opened his eyes to find hers mere inches away, heavy-lidded.

He met her dark gaze and swallowed hard. "Aten didn't send me. I told you about the tangoga–"

Nefer put a finger to his lips. "I am to be the mother of the race of man in this world. Aten sent you to be the father." Her body pressed against his, warm and supple. Hot tingles filled his brain and body.

She stepped back and disengaged her arms. "And yet," she said with a frown of disapproval, "a commoner? This does not please me. Tomorrow we shall go on a hunt. You will show me your skill with a spear and prove you are worthy."

Danny couldn't think straight, couldn't see straight. He wanted nothing more than to sweep Nefer into his arms, though he knew it was wrong. He turned away so that he wouldn't have to see her.

"I'm *not* worthy," he said. He thought of Breyona and how crushed she'd be if she knew the course of his thoughts at that moment. If she knew how close he'd come to kissing Nefer. Deep in his heart, he knew he wouldn't have stopped there. Just like his father. The realization shamed him.

He spun on the queen, angry with her for tempting him. "I wasn't sent here for you. All I want is to find the weapon, destroy it, and go home."

A throaty laugh bubbled out of Nefer. "What *you* want?" She stepped close to him again. "What you want is of no concern to me. I have waited many, many lifetimes for you. I care only for what I want. And I have but two desires."

Danny backed away from her. "I think I'll go back to my room now." He turned and headed for the door.

"Don't you want to know what they are?" she called. "My desires?"

"No."

As Danny approached the tall, open entrance, her voice followed him, hot with anger. "I order you to return to your rooms!"

Danny came out of the dining hall and stopped, unsure of which way to go. Fortunately SulKit appeared behind him. "Follow me," Sul said.

They walked in silence. Or nearly so. The tangoga's sharp legs ticked softly on the stone walkway. After a minute, Sul cleared his throat. "Are you mad? You must correct your conduct, else the queen may have you executed just to teach you a lesson."

Danny dismissed the warning with a grunt. "She'll have bigger worries soon. GorVit will not be nice about getting into the city. The walls might hold, but maybe not."

The tangoga scoffed. "This GorVit would need an army to breach our walls, and even then, they'd have a terrible time of it." SulKit tapped golden fingers together. "But I'm perplexed at the idea of a rogue tangoga. Was their download scrambled? Perhaps they have a faulty implant. It's been known to happen . . . from time to time."

Danny wondered at that. Had all the rogue tangoga been caused by a single faulty implant in GorVit or the Octz? It made as much sense as anything else, given what he knew about the creatures.

SulKit seemed unconcerned. "I shall speak with GorVit when they arrive. I'm confident the conflict is entirely a misunderstanding."

"Maybe, but I don't know what it's about. The tangoga are supposed to serve the meezu, and the rest of the meezu in the galaxy are strictly non-violent, so I doubt they started it."

SulKit stopped in mid stride. "The meezu? Nonviolent? Perhaps you *are* mad."

"I'm not talking about the ones here," Danny said. He waved a finger at the stars above. "I'm talking about the other meezu out in the galaxy. They all take an oath to do no harm."

Sul stared at him blankly, and then conferred with Kit who squawked noncommittally.

"We have been cut off for a long time," Sul said, "unaware of the many happenings in the galaxy. I'm distressed by your assertion that we tangoga must serve the meezu. It seems . . . backward."

SulKit dropped Danny at the entrance to his rooms. "I recommend you get some sleep. There will be much danger tomorrow on the hunt."

Danny laughed and rubbed the back of his neck. "I'm not going hunting. I've got to find the weapon and get out of here."

Sul blinked and tilted his head. "Tomorrow evening, assuming you still live, reflect back on this moment and draw what lesson from it you can."

Without further comment, the tangoga clattered away.

21

HE SAVED OUR NECKS

Breyona looked down at the trainer and asked it to contact Shiv. She waited with her eyes closed, breathing deeply. A few moments later Shiv's face stared back at her, his voice coming through the tiny speaker. "Hello Breyona."

"I was wondering if you would be able to show me around the city, what's left of it. When I was here last time, I didn't get to see very much."

He bit the inside of his cheek and looked away. "I'm kind of busy right now. You know, I am part of Notchy's school."

"Oh," Breyona said, "I'm sorry to have bothered you."

"No, no, it's no bother. Maybe some other time." Shiv's eyebrows drew together. "I should get back to my studies."

"Okay. I'll see you later."

His image disappeared, and Breyona frowned at the trainer's blank screen. Shiv had always been a bit aloof, off in his own world. He saw himself as a scholar, and he cared about nothing more than learning. Still, Breyona was surprised he didn't want to spend more time with other humans. After all, he had been alone for many months in Undermountain with just the bigfeet and a tangoga for company.

Not content to sit around waiting for word from Em, or for the conclave to begin, Breyona headed into the city. She made her way to a monorail platform and boarded the first train to stop. A gray bigfoot sat nearby. It shot furtive glances at her when it thought she wasn't looking.

"*Donovthosameezu,*" she said, holding up both hands.

The bigfoot replied in kind.

"Is there anything in this city that I should make sure to see? I've already been to the temple and the *deshuk* stadium."

The bigfoot raised its hands in a shrug. "You could visit the sculpture garden. It wasn't damaged in the catastrophe." He gave her directions, even volunteered to accompany her.

She politely declined. "I think I can find it."

The sculpture garden lay directly beneath one of the wide, arching rock formations that led from the central city into an outer district. Lights shone down from high above, highlighting the stone sculptures. Most were massive, abstract constructions in odd geometric shapes. An immense obelisk in the center reminded her of the Washington Monument in DC. But instead of the pyramid at the top, it was crowned with a sphere. Intricate geometric carvings decorated all four sides of the column.

As she approached, she noticed that it was hewn from the bedrock. Raised beds of greenery surrounded the sculptures. She sat on the lip of one of these plantings and looked into the city proper. The damage Danny caused using the detchain on the tangoga army was focused there. Huge swaths, once covered with buildings, lay completely empty. Except in one lonely spot where a new tower sprouted. She headed toward it, curious to see bigfoot construction.

The building shot high overhead, its top a ragged crown of steel girders and cranes. A safety fence kept her away, but she saw bigfeet and tangoga moving about inside. Something struck her as strange, though.

A bigfoot strode toward one of the entry doors and ducked low to go through. When she compared the space between floors to the other buildings, it became obvious that the scale of the new building was smaller.

It was sized for humans.

That meant Shaggy had decided on First Contact long before Breyona had returned to Undermountain. He wouldn't be investing resources into building human habitations otherwise.

Her eyes unfocused as she pictured thousands of humans filing into Undermountain. They would be locked in these horrible buildings to be brainwashed, calmed into oblivion until they gave up their will.

She maintained her calm through sheer discipline as she marched to a monorail line and headed to the Temple. She needed to know if Notchy had made any progress with the other members of the conclave.

When she arrived at the Temple of the Strict, she didn't know where to look. She was about to call him on her trainer when she saw Tog. "Can you take me to Notchy?"

"Of course."

As they walked through the halls, Tog cast curious glances at her. "Why didn't you go after Danny?"

"I had to stay here and vote against First Contact."

Tog considered this for a moment. "When Danny was here, all he talked about was finding you, rescuing you. I find it curious that his loyalty is not reciprocated."

Tog's words hit Breyona like a punch to the gut. "It's complicated."

Tog didn't seem convinced. "There were days, back when I had two heads, when I was sick and tired of Yip. He was an idiot, but he was also part of me, and now that he's gone . . . I don't feel complete. Is that how you feel without Danny?"

Breyona didn't answer. She took a few deep breaths and continued walking. It was none of Tog's business how she felt.

"I wish I had been allowed to go after Danny," Tog said mournfully. "He saved our necks."

"I'm sorry, Tog," she said. A spark of anger flared in her then. "This situation isn't fair to either of us."

Tog stopped before a door. "You can go on in."

As Breyona stepped past Tog, she lightly touched his torso with her hand, passing the smallest amounts of calm and compassion she could. Just enough for him to feel better. His head stood a little higher, and he gave a swift nod before clattering away.

22

NO BETTER THAN SHAGGY

Notchy's room reminded Breyona of a meditation cell, only larger and with a few bits of extra furniture. A writing desk stood along one wall, although she had never seen a bigfoot write anything before.

She recognized the standard issue cot and bare lamps that lit the dull gray floor and walls. A wall hanging appeared to be the only other concession to his status as a council member. It depicted an idyllic scene of a stream coursing beneath trees. Lush grass grew along the banks, and a six-legged creature leaned its head down to drink.

Notchy sat on his cot and studied his trainer. When Breyona walked in, his eyes snapped up. "What brings you here, Breyona? I thought you went after Danny."

"Tog discovered Hanameesovenama speaking with Bronson. They've struck a deal to secure Bronson's vote for First Contact. Shiv will vote against, so the human's vote will be canceled."

Notchy set aside his trainer and smoothed the hair on his arms.

"This is grave news. I'll do my best to sway the members of the conclave, but we will not prevail without the human vote."

"That's why I stayed behind," Breyona said. "Grizz and Em left over an hour ago."

"A difficult decision for you, Breyona. I understand you have some affection for Danny." He motioned for her to take a seat on the floor before him.

But she didn't sit. Instead, she hugged her elbows and struggled against sudden tears.

"I love him," she said, feeling the full impact of the words as she spoke them. She'd known it but had never said it before. Not even to Danny.

Yes, she'd known it. But she hadn't realized how much she loved him until the words fell from her lips, as though her subconscious had spilled a wonderful secret to her waking mind.

She took a few deep breaths and gained control over the turmoil inside her. "Danny understands that we have to make sacrifices sometimes. He's always supported my work to help those who need it." She did sit then, crossing her legs to mirror Notchy's posture. "That's a big part of why I love him."

Notchy chuckled. "Again you demonstrate Hanameesovenama wrong. He believes humans are a race of children. But a child would have followed her heart without regard to the consequences." He pointed a big finger at her. "Yet *you* place the greater good ahead of your personal desire. You are not only wise but brave."

Breyona didn't feel brave. If anything, she felt uncertain. "Hanameesovenama must be confident he's going to win," she said. "I noticed a new building going up in the city. It's obviously designed for humans."

Notchy nodded. "There was nothing I could do to stop that, short of invoking *okchen*. One cannot invoke the right of conclave too frequently, and I wanted to preserve it for a very important reason." He chuckled then and took several deep breaths. "Someday, hopefully far in the future, humans will enjoy those appropriately sized living arrangements."

"So you think it's inevitable that at some point the human race will be indoctrinated into the Oath?" Breyona was disappointed in Notchy. She'd assumed he was different.

Notchy chuckled and reached forward to pat her shoulder. "You misunderstand me, child. I hope that the human race can, as you might say, 'get its act together,' and then indoctrination won't be necessary."

The councilor leaned against the wall and folded his hands over his paunch. "I don't agree with Hanameesovenama's strategies. I certainly did not agree with what he did to you." He considered her for a moment with his wide eyes. Unlike Shaggy, his face had a look of compassion and curiosity.

"Hanameesovenama," Notchy said, with a laugh, "certainly had no idea what effect his intense calming would have on you. Tell me, have you used your ability much among the humans?"

"On occasion," Breyona said. "I've tried to be responsible."

She didn't want to admit she had used it on her parents more than once in order to get something she wanted. "As you may know, I've been working with troubled teens. Sometimes it's more efficient to use a little bit of calming. It helps them focus, takes away some of the anger, fear, and anxiety that gets in the way."

"Understandable," Notchy said. "It's a quandary, isn't it? Deciding how much calming to use. Among the People, calming is very much necessary. Has anyone told you about *grot*, the passage from adolescence to adulthood?"

"Danny mentioned it to me once. Grizz had said something to him about it, but Danny didn't really get it."

Notchy closed his eyes, and his voice fell into a rhythmic cadence. He'd obviously spoken these words a thousand times. "The

People are extremely violent by nature. Whatever our past was, survival required great strength and aggression." He held his hands out to either side, flexed his muscles. "But because Voo showed us the way to the Oath, we no longer need this physical strength. We have the power of peace. Somewhere along the way, we developed the ability to pass calm from one individual to the other, just as you have learned to do."

Breyona sighed. "I had to use it pretty hard a couple of days ago. I was helping a friend who was threatening to commit suicide. I wanted to talk him through it, but I ran out of time. I calmed him senseless to save his life. But it won't have fixed his anxiety, his fear, whatever it was that led him to that point."

Notchy nodded sagely, but then he chuckled and sighed.

A flutter of discomfort, like the beginnings of a cold sweat, tickled the edges of Breyona's calm. "And yet it felt good to be seen as a hero," she said. "Maybe I'm more like Shaggy than you think."

Notchy's lips curled back, and a rumble sounded from deep within his chest. Breyona couldn't tell whether it was laughter or disgust. "Strive for perfection, but do not expect to attain it. That truly is the best anyone can do."

Breyona frowned. "That's a wonderful philosophy. But I don't see Shaggy striving to perfect himself. How did he get into a place of such power anyway?"

Notchy raised both hands in a shrug. "How does anyone get into a position of power? Some are born to it, like me, and others have great ambition. The Oath is not a law. It's not a rule like the tangoga follow. Hanameesovenama has his interpretation. I have mine."

"I don't think Shaggy is going to give up on First Contact, even if he loses the vote in the conclave," Breyona said. "What's to stop him from working on the other members of the conclave and calling for a new vote after we're gone?"

"Some condition would have to change substantially for that to happen," Notchy said. "Once the conclave has spoken on an issue, it can't be voted again just because Hanameesovenama didn't like the outcome. No, something dramatic would have to happen."

"Like what?"

"I don't know. But I would if I saw it." That struck the old councilor as hilarious, and he bellowed for a few minutes, eventually having to cover both ears with his hands.

Breyona closed her eyes and took deep breaths, waiting for her own anxiety and Notchy's laughter to subside. "I have a question about the Gift of Peace," she said. "Do you always have to be touching the subject to pass it?"

"There have been acolytes of extreme dedication who have been able to influence others by their mere presence. I believe the effect is more from the awe the individual inspires than any ability to actually push calm through thin air. Why do you ask?"

"No reason," Breyona said quickly. "There's one other thing–" She cut herself off, not knowing how to proceed.

"Go on," Notchy said.

"I was wondering if the ability to pass calm means that something else could be transferred, some other emotion."

For the first time in Breyona's experience, Notchy stiffened. His ears stood erect, and he leaned forward, eyes narrow. "Have you done this? Tell me, have you passed fear or anger to another individual?" His voice left no doubt as to what he thought of this.

Breyona paused for a moment, thinking, trying to remember what had happened with Bronson. "I–I don't know."

She told Notchy about the confrontation with Bronson and about how he had shrunk away from her.

Notchy relaxed, even chuckled. "I see. Since you weren't touching him, I'm quite confident you did not pass those feelings. More likely Bronson shrank from the expression on your face."

Breyona relaxed, relieved. "Thank you," she said. "I'll leave you alone now. I'm going to get some rest and prepare myself for the vote."

"I will see you in the Hall of the Strict."

23

FINISH THE KILL

Danny and Wa woke early and headed out of the palace to explore the city. Danny reasoned that if the Asht had hidden a weapon, it wouldn't be out in the open. But it also wouldn't be inside anything that looked Egyptian, since all those monuments were relatively new. Relatively, being the operative word.

"But what if the queen built something up around it?" Wa asked. "Like that." He pointed to the huge pyramid in the distance.

Danny conceded the possibility with a nod. "We'll have to look everywhere."

They headed to the wall and found a stairway leading up. The stairs were sized for humans, probably on the orders of Nefertiti.

The wall curved east and west across the valley to butt against the sheer cliffs on both ends. They turned to look back at the city. The waterfall descended in the distance, disappearing in a shroud of mist behind the palace.

Danny pointed to the cliffs on either side of the falls. "Do you see that? There are structures built into the cliffs." He could just make out a few unnatural, rectangular protrusions.

"I think I see windows," Wa said.

"Let's see if we can get in."

They descended and headed back up the thoroughfare toward the palace, which sat at the very back of the city. Something sped toward them. It appeared to be a carriage pulled by a great, black bug.

"That's nothing," Wa said. "Just your Egyptian queen driving a run-of-the-mill chariot drawn by a giant, alien ant."

Nefer reined the beast in. It gnashed its pincers and stamped its feet. A smell like burnt plastic wafted from it.

"I'm glad to see you so eager," Nefer said. "I didn't expect you to be waiting at the gates."

Danny walked past her toward the palace. Wa looked nervously over his shoulder. "Um, Danny?"

"Forget her. She's a spoiled brat."

"That's not the problem."

Danny turned to find four meezu trotting after them, swords and axes drawn. Moments later, they blocked Danny and Wa from continuing up the thoroughfare.

"Come," said the leader, a wide meezu wearing black breastplate. His muscles flexed as he pointed toward Nefer.

Danny ground his teeth and turned around. Nefer eyed him, one eyebrow raised, and an amused smile on her lips.

"I'm not a hunter," Danny said. "I told you."

She turned her back on him. "You will be."

Anger boiled in Danny's stomach, but he followed along as the chariot rolled toward the gate. They arrived in the courtyard where two more golden chariots stood side-by-side, weird bug things harnessed before them.

"Have a care," Nefer said. "Skopa are fast, but they cannot stop quickly."

Complicated harnesses wrapped around the skopa's thorax, and a strange crown of blinders adorned its head. A meezu handed Danny the reins. "Pull left. Pull right. Pull both to stop. Don't turn too sharply." A vertical tube inside the chariot held several long spears.

Wa jumped into his chariot, eyes gleaming.

The gate opened and Nefer led them out. Danny flicked the reins and the skopa darted forward, nearly throwing him out the back.

The skopa accelerated as they passed through the gate and onto the plain. Ahead, Nefer lashed her reins, urging her skopa to go faster. Her hair blew behind her, and her delighted laughter drifted back to Danny.

Nefer headed for the river, which she followed for several kilometers. The morning sun glinted orange on the water, and birds startled by the chariots rose in multicolored flocks, squawking in irritation.

Danny felt like he was flying over the plain as the grass blurred under the chariot's wheels. The vehicle's suspension absorbed every bump in the terrain.

Nefer swung her chariot away from the river toward a thick splotch of blackness on the grass ahead. Danny squinted and made out the shapes of an animal herd. As they drew nearer, Danny recognized them as more skopa.

Nefer streaked out ahead, spear held aloft in one hand. The herd flowed away from her, but she locked onto a straggler. She hurled the spear, skewering the bug through its abdomen. A splutter of black ichor geysered from the wound.

Danny kept his chariot on a line to intercept the herd as it reformed. He eyed a large skopa in the middle. If he was going to hunt, he was going to make it count. The herd parted as he approached, but instead of running, the bull skopa stood its ground. Danny pulled back on the reins, planning to slow just enough to get a good shot. He raised his spear and tested its balance.

The skopa lifted from its front feet, pincers trembling with fury. Danny cocked his arm back and hurled straight for the creature's face.

The spear missed, knocked aside by a flailing leg as the skopa jumped like a cheetah. Danny dropped to the floor of the chariot and felt it begin to tip as the weight of the skopa came down atop it.

He didn't understand what was happening until the sky stopped spinning. He lay in the grass, spitting out bits of turf. He sat up. Nothing seemed broken. His chariot shrank away as his skopa dragged it, wheels to the sky.

Danny stood and looked for Nefer or Wa, but his eyes fell on the bull skopa bearing down on him. From ground level, the creature seemed to be the size of a half-ton pickup.

Danny ran. A few steps later he spotted a spear in the grass, fallen from his chariot.

He grabbed it and spun, planting the butt end into the ground and aiming the tip at the skopa. All around him, the herd circled in a stampede, making a continuous roar in the grass.

The bull skopa kicked up clods of dirt and grass with every step and lowered its head for its final approach. With its pincers spread, it lunged the last few meters.

Danny intended to place the tip of the spear between the pincers, but saw a dark fleshy area just under the head. At the last moment, he dropped the spear a few inches, and the bull's momentum pushed the spear in deep. The shaft broke with a loud report and Danny flew back. He pulled himself into a ball and rolled, expecting the weight of the skopa to crush him.

It didn't, so he sprang up and looked back, ready to run for his life. The skopa stood on its four hind legs and pulled the spear from its throat with its front two. Then it ran straight at

Danny, passed him, and headed for a fringe of jungle in the distance.

Nefer and Wa rode up, Nefer's face shining with delight, Wa's pale with terror.

"You are brave, Danny," Nefer said. "Stupid, but brave. Very few things in this valley are more dangerous than a bull skopa."

"What could be more dangerous than that?"

"A horgodon," she said and smiled. "And me."

Danny couldn't tell if she was joking about that last part or not.

"A pity you failed," she said, then lashed her skopa forward and continued her hunt.

"Failed?" He looked back to the jungle where the bull had fled. "I stabbed it in the neck."

Wa rubbed the back of his head and made a pained expression. "Yeah. The one that got away. It never impresses anyone but the person who didn't catch it."

Danny pursed his lips and searched for his chariot. His skopa had given up dragging it and stood idly in the grass, chomping at something with its pincers. Danny headed for it.

"Do you want a ride?" Wa asked.

"No." Danny stomped through the grass, recovering two more spears along the way. He got to his chariot, managed to lever it onto one side, and pushed it onto its wheels. He got in and mushed the skopa toward the jungle.

Once he got to the trees, he pulled to stop and continued on foot. Splotches of black goo marked the bull's path. He followed the blood trail under the canopy, thankful the wide palm fronds blocked most of the sunlight. With little undergrowth, the way was easy and cooler. He soon discovered the dying skopa, its body a black mound in the shadows.

Its pincers clasped and released slowly. One leg twitched. Danny placed his spear between the thorax and abdomen and shoved. The skopa didn't even flinch, but its leg stopped moving.

"One that got away, huh?" He pulled the spear, and it slid out with a wet sucking noise. "How am I going to get this thing to my cart?"

"You can't. You must come with me now." Nefer stood in a patch of sunlight, eyes shining. She beckoned to him. "Now."

Something in her voice stopped his reply about how she wasn't his queen. She looked afraid. She kept darting her eyes to the jungle behind Danny.

"Quick," she said. "Before they come. They can smell skopa blood from far away."

A chill passed across Danny's skin. "What can?"

The ground shook. Trees rattled in the distance. The ground shook again, followed by a long hooting call.

"Danny, you must come." Nefer ran to him and pulled on his arm.

He gave one last look at the bull skopa and started after her. The crashes were louder and came from the south.

Nefer licked her lips and looked over her shoulder. "Hopefully it will take the skopa and be satisfied." She didn't sound very optimistic.

The crashing drew nearer as they passed out of the jungle and onto the grass where their chariots waited. Danny looked back to see tree tops swinging wildly as something massive passed among them. New urgency sped him to his chariot.

A horrific crack sounded behind him, and out of the jungle stepped a nightmare.

"Horgodon!" Nefertiti cried.

Danny thought the bigfeet were large. He thought the bull skopa was huge. But as his grandfather used to say, this was beyond the beyond. It looked like a bigfoot, but it stood at least twice as tall. Maybe twenty-five feet.

Danny and Nefer leapt into their chariots and urged their skopa to move. Danny pled with himself not to look back. He never wanted to see a horgodon again. But suddenly the sun went out as the long shadow of the beast overtook him. Danny did look over his shoulder then. The creature ran right behind him. It carried a tree trunk in one hand and swung it at him.

Danny's hair ruffled as the massive club passed over his head, just feet from decapitating him.

Danny whipped the reins against the skopa's chitinous body. Ahead of him, the skopa herd dispersed like a flock of birds, juking this way and that as though controlled by a single mind.

Danny guided his chariot among them, hoping the horgodon would choose another target. He looked back in time to see the club launch a skopa high into the air. The horgodon roared but did not stop pursuing Danny.

Danny turned the chariot to weave across the stream of the herd, hoping the bug creatures might trip up the beast. One leapt directly over his head. Its black body crunched as the horgodon's club connected with it. Flecks of hot, black skopa blood spattered Danny's face and clothes.

A small cry sounded nearby. Nefertiti rode in, hair flying. She raised her spear and threw it at the horgodon. Danny didn't see it strike, but a moment later, a high-pitched howl erupted behind him.

The wound sent the horgodon into a berserk rage, and it turned to go after Nefertiti. Without thinking, Danny turned his chariot, lifted a spear, and gave chase.

"It *is* a bigfoot," he said to himself. "The biggest frickin' bigfoot ever."

The shape of the body and limbs were identical to the bigfeet Danny knew. From the back, even the ears seemed the same. Except this creature towered twice the height of any bigfoot Danny had ever seen.

Nefer turned her chariot so sharply one wheel lifted. The horgodon slipped trying to make the same cut. As it fell, it swung the club, just catching the side of Nefer's car. The side wall exploded in splinters and Nefer disappeared.

Danny searched the air, sure the horgodon's swipe had sent her flying, but a moment later, her head popped up from the chariot. She cried out in triumph and pumped a fist in the air.

The horgodon threw its club.

"Watch out!" Danny shouted. But he was too far away, and the horgodon's roars drowned his voice.

The club, as long as a car, twirled end over end. The throw went long, but the club fell in the chariot's path, sending up gouts of turf where it struck. Nefer's skopa hurdled the log, but the chariot bounced roughly over it and started to careen wildly, tipping from wheel to wheel. Nefer's head whipped from side to side until a wheel popped off and rolled away. The bare axle ground into the soft turf and sent Nefer flying.

The horgodon got to its feet and stomped toward the fallen queen.

"Stay away from her!" Danny cried. He hefted a spear and guided the chariot forward. The horgodon turned to look at him. The head was nearly identical to a bigfoot's. The brows were heavier, the eyes were sunk a little deeper, but it had the same bear-like snout. It wore a large hide over one shoulder.

Nefertiti lay still, just a small, white mound in an ocean of greenish-blue grass. The chariot lay on its side, the remaining wheel spinning idly in the air. The horgodon ignored Danny and lumbered toward Nefer.

Danny lashed the skopa for more speed, eyeing the horgodon in search of a weakness. He circled behind it as it neared the queen. He hoisted his spear and threw it with everything he had, aiming for the horgodon's back. The spear arced out but fell short. Danny already held another, which he threw, aiming even higher to compensate for the distance. This one also fell short of his intended mark, but lanced deep into the tendon above the horgodon's left foot.

The cry that followed nearly split Danny's head in half. The horgodon fell to the ground, holding its foot and howling. It pulled the spear free and flung it away, sending it straight over Danny's head.

Danny raced past the downed beast and jumped out of the chariot. "Nefer!"

He touched her cautiously, fearing her neck might be broken. She stirred, straightened her legs, and gripped the grass in one hand. Her breath rattled as she drew it in. Since she was able to move, he picked her up and carried her to his chariot. He set her down as gently as he could. The horgodon crawled toward them, lips pulled back in a hideous growl.

He was about to send the skopa forward when Nefer spoke. "You must finish the kill."

"Are you insane?"

"You must honor the prey. If you do not, its brethren will take great joy in tormenting the poor creature. They do not tolerate weakness among their own."

"Poor creature?" he said weakly.

Nefer looked up at him, eyes serious. "You must kill it. And quick." She pointed to the forest. Trees swayed all along the verge of the jungle.

"Can't we do something to help it escape until it heals?"

Nefer gave him a queer look, as though he were the insane one.

"I suppose not." He grabbed the spear and stepped out of the chariot.

Wa steered his chariot close, eyes wide. "What are you doing?"

Danny ignored his friend and headed straight for the horgodon. He held up the spear. "The heart is to the left," Nefer called. "You must throw it hard to pierce deeply enough. Unless you think you can make an eye shot."

The horgodon struggled to stand as Danny approached. But with its Achilles tendon severed, it fell over and howled with pain.

Roars sounded in the distance, and a pack of horgodons emerged from the jungle a half-kilometer away. They stood tall, scanning the plain. At the sight of Danny, they started forward at full speed.

The fallen horgodon looked up and spotted his brethren approaching. It howled again, this time in fear. It got to its knees despite the agony in its foot and desperately crawled away, knocking Danny aside.

Danny followed it, unsure of what to do. The beast didn't go far before collapsing and grabbing its ankle. The ground shook with the approaching horgodons, at least ten of them now barreled across the plain.

As if sensing the futility of flight, Danny's victim turned to face him. Danny went close. "I'm supposed to put you out of your misery."

The horgodon locked eyes with him. It grunted and growled and covered its ears with its hands. Then it shook its head and tapped a huge fur-covered fist against its chest. It dropped its arms to its side and closed its eyes. Danny realized what it wanted.

He stepped forward, gritted his teeth. The hot smell of the creature nearly overwhelmed him. Rancid plumes billowed out of it with every breath. It opened its eyes again and pounded its chest, right over its heart.

Danny walked close to it. Nefertiti called from behind him, but he couldn't tell what she said.

Danny raised the spear, positioning the point just inches from the beast's heart. He swore and thrust the point in deep. The horgodon's hands came up reflexively and pulled the spear free. But its lifeblood, black and thick, welled out in a pulsing stream. Wide, dark eyes stared at Danny. The beast shoved him aside and tilted like a falling tree, finally crashing to the ground.

"Danny!" Nefertiti's voice came to his attention as if someone had unmuted the world. He became aware of the pounding of feet and the horrific cries of the horgodon pack bearing down on him. He dashed to the chariot and lashed the skopa forward. Nefertiti had managed to stand, though she favored one arm.

As they rode, Wa fell in beside him. "Show off!"

Danny didn't have the energy to respond. He focused on driving the chariot and supporting Nefer's weight, such as it was. Her slight body leaned against his, and her good arm wrapped around his waist. He looked back to see the pack of horgodons tearing their fallen brother to pieces. One ran off, carrying an arm.

They entered the city too fast, and meezu had to grab the skopa's halters to slow them. A priest rushed forward to assist the queen. She batted his hands away and pulled Danny's face toward hers. Her eyes searched his, as if trying to remember where she'd seen him before. The meezu priest grew more persistent and eventually scooped her up.

"You are worthy," she said as the priest started toward the palace.

Danny's hands trembled, and he couldn't make them release the reins. The shaking spread to his gut, then his knees. He slumped to the floor of the chariot, heart racing, until huge furry hands picked him up and carried him away.

24

____

SOMETHING DARK AND PREDATORY

Danny rolled out of his comfy bed, rubbed his eyes, and stretched. Every muscle in his body ached. He splashed water on his face from a washbasin and used the mirror to study the scrapes that covered his neck and cheeks. Only then did he notice Nefer standing at the door.

His face went hot as she slinked in. He ripped a blanket from the bed and covered himself. "Have you been there the whole time?"

She wore a light blue, sleeveless gown belted at the waist with a silver tasseled sash. Her hair was again drawn up, wider at the top. "I came to show you the city."

"Oh." He wrapped the blanket around himself more securely. "How's your arm?"

"It's fine." She held out her hand. "Come."

"I think I'll get dressed first."

"Of course," she said and stood there watching him, eyes twinkling.

"Uh, if you don't mind waiting outside."

She shrugged and gave a little smirk–half smile, half appraisal–before turning to go out.

Danny hastily pulled on his jeans, t-shirt, and shoes. He found Nefer waiting impatiently outside. She led him through long galleries, past brightly painted statues of meezu and of herself. Frescos decorated many walls with jungle scenes and vistas of the grassy plain in the valley.

Danny's sneakers squeaked on the polished tile floors, but Nefer glided so smoothly she made no sound. They emerged at the front steps leading onto the plaza. Ahead, the main thoroughfare led to the city wall, but Nefer took him to the left and across a bridge shiny with mist from the waterfall.

They stopped on the far side of the falls and surveyed the array of monuments and pyramids that stood beyond. In a flat field many square kilometers in size, marched row upon row of short pyramids. Between the pyramids ran paved roadways bordered by columns and statuary. One structure dominated the array. The golden pyramid. Danny had no idea how this pyramid compared with the great pyramids of Giza, but his gut told him this was larger–by a lot.

As if reading his thoughts, Nefertiti spoke about the structures. "I once visited the great pyramids of Khufu and Khafre. I was greatly impressed by their size and majesty. Since I was chosen by Aten, I declared an even greater pyramid be built in my glory."

"Can we go inside?" Danny asked.

Nefer paled. "Absolutely not."

"Ah," Danny said knowingly, "like walking on your own grave, eh?"

She didn't reply. Sensing her discomfort at the topic of her own tomb, Danny turned his attention to the smaller pyramids. There had to be more than fifty of them. "I thought all pyramids were tombs."

"Yes, they are," she replied grimly.

Danny realized that in the thousands of years she had managed to live here, she must have buried many meezu servants, and maybe a few favored tangoga. He thought of how sad it must have been.

They strolled among the pyramids for a while, stopping every so often for her to describe the meaning of one of the statues, or to wander through a temple and admire the artwork and architecture. She seemed to grow weary of it and soon guided him back to the palace. "There is something else I want to show you, a private area."

He followed her to the back of the palace and through a tall gate that opened into a lush garden. Flowers of all varieties grew in neat rows. Bushes heavy with blossoms and fruit divided the garden into sections. Tall palm trees provided shady areas through which water tumbled down carefully constructed falls. Danny remembered seeing something similar at a Japanese garden exhibit at a fair in Nashville once, except this was twenty times larger.

As they walked along, she held his arm. He couldn't help but notice her exotic perfume and the warmth of her closeness. He cleared his throat and tried to separate from her a little, but she held on tightly.

She had stopped speaking, but frequently glanced up at him with expressions so sultry he had to force himself not to meet her eyes.

They passed by a low gate which barred a walkway leading off among the foliage near the cliff.

"What's through there?" he asked

"Nothing," she said, making eye contact with him again.

The path seemed to lead toward the cliff. He looked up and saw again the protrusions in the rock and the dark openings of windows. He pointed to them. "Is there a way in there from ground level?"

"No," Nefer said. She stiffened, obviously irritated by his curiosity. Which made him even more curious.

Danny opened the gate and started along the walkway.

Nefer pulled at him, but he pried her fingers from his arm. "There must be something to see, or there wouldn't be a gate and a path."

Nefer's lips thinned, and she threw up a hand. "Go then." The fact that he could hear her footsteps following him told of her displeasure.

The path wound through more gardens and emerged at a wide, flat patio of black paving stones. Flush with the face of the cliff stood a massive black, steel gate.

Wa sat there staring at the gate as though his eyes alone could bore through and expose the secrets that lay beyond.

Wa glanced up at Danny. "While you were off on your date, I decided to work on the task of finding the weapon you're so worried about."

"It wasn't a date. And you should be worried too."

"I am."

"Then why are you just sitting here? Let's go in."

"The gate is locked."

Nefer ambled to a bench at the edge of the patio and sat, like a mother waiting patiently while children played in the park.

Danny studied the door. There were no latches, knobs, or hinges, no obvious way to open it. He pushed on the door, knocked on it with his knuckles, hoping to find some hidden panel. It occurred to him that Asht technology probably worked the same way bigfoot technology did.

He stood back and cleared his throat. "*Hoffharr.*"

Nothing happened.

"Don't you think I already tried that?" Wa and Nefer said simultaneously in two different languages.

Wa stood and looked up the cliff. "I think we're going to have to climb it."

Danny followed Wa's gaze. Vines clung to the rock, just like on the cliff they had descended into the valley. The thought of climbing it made his insides quaver. "There must be some other way in. One that's not so risky."

Nefer snorted. "Not any way you'd want to take."

"What does that mean? I thought you said there was no way in."

She looked down at her hands and studied her nails. "There isn't. The gate cannot be opened. It might as well not be there at all."

Wa went to the cliff and tested his weight on the vines before starting up.

"Tell your friend not to do that," Nefer said. She continued to inspect her nails.

"Why not?" Danny asked.

"Because SulKit will be along momentarily to shoot him down."

"He'll do what?"

"He'll shoot him down. With one of those projectile throwers I told you about. He claims the Asht do not want anyone going inside the complex. One of his many, many rules." Her tone made it clear what she thought about tangoga policies.

"How do you know this?" Danny asked.

She just looked at him.

He realized then that she had tried to climb this before, probably more than once. He called up to Wa and warned him about SulKit.

Wa craned his neck and peered over the gardens. "They're not here now," he said and continued up. He ascended quickly, pausing only to test a vine or locate a suitable spot for his foot.

Danny backed up to get a better view. "There's a ledge straight above you," he called. "Maybe you can find a door or window on top."

Wa was only a few meters below the ledge when SulKit clicked into view. Their necks stood erect, and their cape fluttered behind them. "Come down immediately," Sul shouted in Footese. The tangoga held a shiny, rifle-like object in its golden claws. The rifle came up, and Kit sighted down the barrel. "Kit will fire in three seconds," Sul shouted up. "Begin your descent immediately."

"Stop, Wa," Danny shouted. "He's going to kill you."

Wa froze and looked down over his shoulder.

Sul said, "Three, two . . ."

"Fire a warning shot first," Danny said.

". . . one." SulKit pulled the trigger and a flash of projectiles arrowed toward Wa, striking just inches to the right of his hand, throwing up flakes of rock. The vine Wa held burst into fibrous strands, which made it peel away from the cliff. Wa started to fall. He flailed out with a hand, barely catching himself. He screamed curses down at SulKit.

"I think he got the message," Danny said to Sul. "Give him a moment to climb down."

Wa didn't waste any time and in minutes had reached the ground. He marched up to SulKit, fists clenched, and began reaming the tangoga out in English, and much to Danny's surprise, a considerable bit of Spanish.

Danny hadn't done very well in Spanish in high school, but he knew all of the curse words. Or at least he thought he had until he heard Wa's diatribe.

Sul eyed Wa placidly, said something to Kit, turned around, and marched away.

Still steaming, Wa watched the tangoga leave. He glanced back at the cliff face and gave one final curse. "I was so close," he said, holding up his finger and thumb to show just how close. "How did he even know I was up there?"

Nefer stood and strolled to Danny. "Your friend is very fortunate. I was not given such lenient treatment."

A meezu rushed down the path and burst in, breathless. He

prostrated himself on the black paving stones. "My queen. Forgive my intrusion into your private gardens, but there is a human approaching the city accompanied by a strange meezu."

"A human?" Danny said in English.

"What about a human?" Wa asked. "What's going on?"

"What do they look like?" Danny demanded, this time in Footese.

The meezu looked at him and then looked to Nefer for permission to speak. She nodded.

"I believe it is a human female. Its hair," he said, pointing to his head and making a motion of long curls, "comes to here." He pointed at Danny's shoulder. "It wears similar clothing. This fabric." He pointed to Danny's jeans.

"And the meezu?" he asked, hope rising.

"Black fur and strange garb."

"A black bigfoot and a human female with curly hair," he said to Wa. "It's Breyona. And probably Grizz!"

"There is more," the meezu said. "They are pursued by skopa. Many, many skopa."

Fear seized Danny's heart. A herd of those giant ant things would tear Breyona and Grizz to pieces.

Nefer stood, chin lifting with an air of supreme authority. "Run ahead and prepare my chariot," she said to the meezu. "We will meet this human and meezu at the gates, if they get that far."

By the time they got to the plaza in front of the palace, a single chariot awaited them.

They crowded aboard, and Nefer took up the reins. She clicked her tongue and lashed the skopa down the main thoroughfare. In minutes, they were to the gate. Danny leapt out and raced up the stairs to the top of the wall and looked out over the grassy plain.

Less than a kilometer away, two figures ran toward the city, one obviously much larger and covered with fur. The smaller struggled to keep up, slowed by the thick grass.

Wa shaded his eyes with a hand. "That's not Breyona. It's Em."

A short distance beyond Grizz and Em tromped a black mass of skopa. The herd didn't seem to be running full out, but they steadily gained on the two lone figures.

"That's how they hunt," Nefer said. "They wear down their prey, and then sweep in for the kill. It will be over soon."

"We can't let them die," Danny said. "That's my sister!"

Nefer arched an eyebrow but didn't say anything.

"Let's take the chariot and pick them up," Wa said.

Danny and Wa started for the steps. "Tell the meezu to open the gate."

"I will not," Nefer said.

Danny stopped. "But they'll be killed."

"If Aten wills it."

Danny realized what was happening. Nefer didn't want Em to come into the city. She still believed he was married to her or something, as disgusting as that idea was. She'd made her designs on Danny very clear, and she didn't welcome competition.

"She's not my wife!" he said. "Open the gates."

Nefer frowned, eyebrows knitting.

Danny's mind raced and latched upon a new argument. "If they are here, it is Aten's will. Look, the skopa don't pursue at full speed. They're just herding them to the city. That is Aten's will."

Nefer clenched her teeth, her lips tight. He could tell his argument had power. He also saw she did not like it. She turned her gaze on the approaching figures.

The skopa picked up speed and started to close the distance.

"We must save them," Danny said. "Tell your meezu to open the gate."

Nefer's gaze flashed from Em and Grizz to the gate, clearly gauging their likelihood of survival.

"Please," Danny said.

He couldn't read her expression, but it changed from passive disinterest to something else. Something dark and predatory.

She nodded to a meezu, who barked an order down to the gate. The two meezu stationed there began the strenuous effort of cranking it open.

Danny and Wa raced down the steps, jumped into the chariot, and whipped the reins, sending the skopa steed out of the city.

By the time they reached Em and Grizz, the herd tramped only a few dozen meters away. Danny swept between his friends and the skopa, spear raised. The skopa shied away. He stabbed out with his spear, prodding them back. With a hard yank on the reins, he turned the chariot toward Em and Grizz.

"Em!" Wa shouted. "Get in."

Fear showed stark on her face as they approached, but then she recognized them and cried out with relief. Grizz's wide, green eyes flashed in the sunlight. He picked up Em and set her in the chariot. "Go, I will run alongside."

Danny lashed his skopa and sped away. The thunder of the herd sounded behind, and he feared that his steed wouldn't be able to outpace it while pulling the weight of the chariot and the three humans.

Danny was happy to see his sister, yet he couldn't help but feel a terrible weight of disappointment that it wasn't Breyona.

They didn't have opportunity to speak, for the skopa herd started to catch up. Danny zigged and zagged the chariot trying to throw the herd off, but they were too smart for that and stayed close at their heels. Wa chucked spears behind them. Danny kept his eyes on the gate, but Wa's shouts told of a few direct hits.

As they approached the gate, Danny noticed a number of tangoga on the city wall. They aimed down with their rifles and began firing into the herd, which stopped it short. Danny and Grizz plowed through the gate into the city.

They came to a stop in the plaza. Danny hugged his sister

briefly, greeted Grizz with a "*donovthosameezu*," and turned to face Nefertiti, who stood flanked by two priests.

SulKit stood off to one side, clearly displeased by the prospect of even more visitors entering his city. Despite this, he stepped forward and sketched a slight bow. "Welcome to the Golden City."

25

ATEN PROVIDES A PATH

Nefertiti stood regally in the sunlight, jewelry glittering. She stared at Em, eyes narrow, and then turned her gaze to Grizz. She grunted at him. "You may join the other meezu. Perhaps I will allow you to join the Chosen."

Danny stepped forward. "Grizz is not–"

"It's okay, Danny," Grizz said. "I have many questions to ask the People here. I'm quite confused by what I'm seeing. They're holding weapons." His tone suggested it was the most horrific thing he had ever seen. Grizz strode away with a meezu priest, already deep in conversation with him.

Nefer clapped her hands. "SulKit! Take Danny's guest to the palace and see to her needs. Later we shall enjoy an informal meal in my quarters." With that, she hopped into the chariot and drove off, leaving Danny and his companions to walk.

As they made their way up the thoroughfare to the palace, Em filled Danny in on what had happened after his abduction at Grandma's house. Danny grumbled when she told him about the vote for First Contact and how Breyona had decided she must stay behind. "She wanted to come," Em said, "but we found out that Shaggy made a deal for Bronson's vote."

Danny understood Breyona's choice, but he still couldn't shake the feeling that she always found a cause more important than their relationship. And though it was good to see his sister, her presence added to his worries. She and Grizz became two more things he needed to see safely off this planet. And he still had to find whatever weapon the Asht had hidden here. Which reminded him of GorVit. The fact that the tangoga boss hadn't made an appearance yet bothered Danny greatly.

SulKit showed Em to a suite of her own. She gaped at it, amazed. "Everything here is Egyptian. That woman, who is she?"

"Nefertiti," Danny said. "I don't know many of the details, but she's been here for thousands of years."

Em grunted. "That explains her bad attitude. She's forgotten basic social skills."

"I don't think she ever had to be very polite," Wa said. "She was married to a pharaoh."

"Why are you defending her?" Em said suspiciously.

Wa held his hands up. "I'm not. I'm just trying to explain. Besides, I think she's got a thing for Danny."

"Never mind," Em said. She ran a finger along the gold details on the edge of a table. "She seems pretty skanky to me."

Danny thought he'd seen all of his sister's many moods, but he had never seen her jealous before. In fact, she was the one who made other people jealous. Most recently, Nefertiti herself.

To lower the tension in the room, Danny explained the Asht complex in the cliff and how they had failed to get in.

"Did you try '*hoffhar*?'" Em asked.

Danny grimaced, and Wa laughed. It seemed everyone knew the Footese word for "open."

"Yeah, we tried it," Danny said.

"And where's GorVit?" Em asked. "We had a meeting with Shiv

and a bigfoot called Luon. He knew everything there was to know about the Spheroid and about how it was lost. He was very concerned about what might happen if GorVit got access to it."

Danny explained that he hadn't seen GorVit since they had escaped, but it was just a matter of time before he showed up.

He went to a veranda overlooking the city and beyond to the valley. "It's not like Gor to be this quiet for so long."

"Are you sure about that?" Wa said. "He must have planned for a long time to set up that assault on Undermountain."

Wa had a good point. GorVit had hidden in plain view, posing as a boss among the tangoga in the sub-city. "But what could he be planning out there in the jungle?"

"Who knows? Maybe a horgodon already killed him."

"We can hope."

"What the hell is a horgodon?" Em asked.

Wa's eyes lit up, and he started telling her the story of the skopa hunt and Danny's encounter with the giants.

Em yawned and raised her eyebrows skeptically at his description of the horgodons.

"You think I'm making it up," Wa said, crestfallen. "I can't believe it."

"You can't blame her," Danny said. "I was there, and I can hardly believe it."

"I just want to sleep," Em said. She collapsed onto an elaborately embroidered chaise lounge and closed her eyes.

SulKit clattered in, golden claws daintily clasped. "The queen awaits you in her private dining hall. No need to dress for dinner."

Em covered her face with her hands. "Can't you just bring me a piece of fruit or something?"

"Yeah," Wa said, "she's tired. You know, from nearly being killed by a herd of skopa."

Sul tilted his head to one side and turned his gaze on Danny. "Shall you explain the situation to your new guest, or shall I?"

Danny sighed and turned to his sister. "Dinner isn't exactly optional here."

Em opened her eyes and stared at him. "Who does that girl think she is? She doesn't really believe she's a queen, does she?"

"She has meezu guards who believe it. So . . ."

Em held up a hand. "I got it. Just give me a moment to freshen up." She found a full-length mirror and gave herself a once over. "I can't go out looking like this."

"Yeah," Wa agreed sadly.

Em turned and gave Wa a glare.

"What? I just meant that you make us all look bad."

Danny rolled his eyes. "Come on. Let's get this over with."

They followed SulKit through several passages and into the queen's quarters. Walls covered in bas-relief murals surrounded a long, low table laden with food. Nefer stood by one of the windows and stared up at the cliffs rising over the palace gardens.

"Be careful what you say to Nefertiti," Danny warned Em in a whisper. "She's prickly."

Em nodded and covered a yawn with her hand. "Whatever."

But Nefer greeted them warmly and smiled at Em. She spread her arms and invited them to sit and enjoy their dinner. She even decanted a pale, yellow liquid into delicate goblets for each of them. Once everyone had settled in, she took her position at the head of the table and gazed to the ceiling. "Aten's blessings be upon us."

Danny set his trainer on the table, relieved to have it out of his possession. "This device can translate our conversation so Em and Wa can understand you."

Nefer raised an eyebrow at the device, but she didn't object. She sat, speared a piece of fruit with a narrow blade, and took a delicate bite. She chewed it thoughtfully, all the while scrutinizing Em.

"So," she said, "why do you refuse to marry your brother?"

Em's face went pale with horror as the trainer translated. "What?"

Wa burst into laughter mid gulp and set a spew of mist across the table.

"I told you," Danny said to Nefer, "we don't marry our sisters. It's gross."

Nefer frowned while she considered this. "But you're a man. She's a woman. What's disgusting about a marriage? Especially a suitable one?" Her head tilted thoughtfully, and she glanced at Wa. "Or do you prefer men? It would explain much."

"That's not it," Danny said flatly. Wa turned bright red, and Em whispered something in his ear, which made him snicker.

Nefer dismissed the topic with a shrug. "So she is not your wife." This fact seemed to give Nefer a certain amount of satisfaction, and it became clear that Em had fallen in her esteem.

Wa cleared his throat and changed the subject. "I don't think we're going to be able to get into the Asht complex through the black gate. And if we can't get in, neither can GorVit. Why don't we climb the cliff and go back through the portal?"

"No," Nefer said.

Wa smiled insincerely. "I wasn't asking."

She mirrored his smile and waved with her eating utensil. "I wasn't suggesting."

She returned to her food, giving a bit of black meat a vicious stab. "It's too dangerous for you to venture out of the city at this time. Not only is there this GorVit you seem so worried about, but there are skopa, horgodons, and many other things happy to kill you. So you shall stay." She raised her hand in a gesture that took in the whole city. "There's plenty of room for all of you."

Danny opened his mouth to argue, but SulKit bustled in. "Excuse me, my queen," Sul said. "I thought you should know the new meezu has jumped to his death from the city wall."

Nefer sighed. "Pity. Send a runner to the cliffs to inform Mother." She pushed her plate away and grabbed her goblet.

"Not Grizz!" Danny said, horrified, picturing his friend leaping from the wall.

"No," Sul said. "It was the one that came with you when you first entered the city. Jostosh."

Danny felt little relief. He had liked Jostosh, who had seemed so calm and wise, almost like one of the bigfeet from Undermountain.

"I have other news," Sul said, and Kit chuckled with anticipation. "The tangoga this human has been talking about has arrived. GorVit."

"Tell me you didn't let them in," Danny said.

"Of course not. GorVit claims to be a *frellk*. Can you believe it?"

Kit chuckled and said *frellk* over and over until Sul hissed at him.

Nefer took a sip of her wine, a bored expression on her face. "What is the significance of being a *frellk*?"

Sul took on a teacher's air, raising a golden finger. "The *frellk* are among the highest in the tangoga hierarchy. Because of our isolation here on this planet, we have not had contact with any of the *frellk* for thousands of years. But I guarantee you, no *frellk* would conduct themselves in such a base manner as this GorVit. He demands that you turn over these humans. He claims they are his property."

Nefer raised an eyebrow at Danny. "Ah! So you are escaped slaves of this tangoga. No wonder you slander his name and create tall stories about him."

"I'm not making up stories, and you know it," Danny said. "Tangoga don't possess slaves."

"You may leave," Nefer told SulKit. "Inform me if GorVit returns. I would like to see them with my own eyes." The tangoga nodded both heads and strode out of the room.

Nefer turned her gaze back to Danny. "Are you satisfied now? Nothing comes into the city without my permission."

Danny had seen the wall from the outside. It appeared to be insurmountable. But still . . .

"As long as GorVit are on this planet," he said, "I'm not going to be satisfied. Unless I can secure the weapon and make sure Gor never gets it."

"There is no weapon."

"There is."

Nefer pursed her lips and looked away.

Em yawned and slumped back in her chair. "I need to lie down."

The gracious Nefer returned in a flash. She stood and smiled. "Of course. You've had a very trying day. I'm sure Wa would be happy to escort you back to your quarters."

Danny got up to go too, but Nefer stopped him. "I need to discuss something with you. Please sit."

Nefer watched Em and Wa walk out and then glided around the table to sit next to Danny. He sat still, nearly a statue. He moved only his eyes, trying to catch a glimpse of her in his peripheral vision. She placed a warm hand on his arm.

"Shall we discuss my request now?" Nefer asked, her voice light and airy.

"W–what request?" he ask, trying to keep his voice hard, though his throat betrayed him by cracking.

"I opened the gate to admit your sister and her meezu."

Danny swallowed. He didn't like where this was going. At all. "And?"

"I do not grant favors and expect nothing in return."

"What do you want?" Danny said, though he had suspicions. He tried to picture Breyona's face, tried to find the resolve to resist.

Nefer pressed hard into him. He couldn't help but turn toward her then. Her slight smile and intense gaze pulled at him, devoured him. He found himself leaning closer.

Her breath, laced with spicy liqueur, intoxicated him.

"Marry me," she said.

Danny inhaled sharply. "What? That's crazy."

She ignored his comment and pressed closer. Her eyes seemed to bore into his. She was serious.

"You shall be my king," she said. "You'll rule by my side."

Danny pulled away from her and stood. "Rule what?" He spun around and looked pointedly at the empty room. "You have no empire here, you're alone."

Nefer's face went cold. "Then why have you enticed me with your eyes and your shoulders? Why did you kill skopa and horgodons for me? You led me to believe you loved me!"

Danny's jaw worked for several moments. "I did?"

Nefer turned away from him and hugged her arms to her chest. "You have no honor." She walked to the veranda and stared out over the gardens. "I lost everyone I loved when I came here. I left behind my children, my people, my world. I have waited so long for Aten to send me a mate."

He felt himself softening. He never wanted to hurt her feelings. "I think you've been alone so long you forgot how to get along with people."

She turned back to him, tears standing out in her eyes but not quite falling. "That may be." In three steps, she stood face to face with him, her arms pulling him close. "Remind me how to get along with people." She reached up with her hands, drew his face close to hers, and stared into his eyes. Her sudden vulnerability made her that much harder to resist.

Danny cleared his throat. "You could start by being more respectful and not ordering me around."

She blinked and tilted her head, obviously confused. "But I'm your queen," she said.

He gently pulled her hands away from his face and stepped back. "That may be true for the meezu, but you are not *my* queen."

"I have the throne," she said. "I have priests who worship me, and through me, Aten. If I am not your queen, what am I?"

Danny sighed. "You are a lonely girl."

Tears did fall then, and she wiped her wrist across her eyes. "I hate crying," she said. "It's weak."

Not knowing what else to do, Danny put his hands in his pockets. "Listen. Why don't you go back through the portal with us? The world has changed so much, you won't even recognize it."

"And that is supposed to entice me? No. Aten brought me here for a reason. And he brought you to me for the same reason. To bring forth a new race of men in this world."

"But I love someone else."

"And does she love you?"

The question pierced Danny's heart like an arrow. He'd been asking himself the same question for weeks. He'd asked it every time Breyona had been late for a video chat or when she'd been late for their reunion at Grandma's. He'd asked himself that question when he found out she'd chosen to stay in Undermountain instead of coming after him. Each time, she'd had legitimate reasons, but it still hurt. He'd prioritized her above everything else, but she hadn't done the same for him.

He knew he wasn't being fair, but there it was. He wanted Breyona to himself, and she wasn't willing to give herself to him.

Nefer still looked up at him, face questioning. "From your long pause, can I conclude that this woman's love for you is in doubt?"

"No," he said, though it tasted like a lie. Of course he doubted Breyona's love. Danny wondered if that was why Nefer tempted him. Because he wanted to punish Breyona for being less than completely dedicated.

He laughed at the idea. He wasn't going to fool himself or make up excuses. Nefer tempted him because she was desirable.

Nefer collected herself with a shuddering breath and wiped the remaining wetness from her eyes. "You could come to love me, I think. I was once considered the most beautiful woman in the world."

"You are very beautiful." *More so right now than ever before*, he thought.

"And you are acceptable to me. It's why I chose you over Wa."

"Gee, thanks. I think many women would question that choice. It just shows that your time here has affected your judgment."

Nefer laughed, a genuine laugh. She held out her hand. "Come."

He looked down at her outstretched hand. He wanted to take it. Oh, how he ached to take it and follow her wherever she wanted to go. But he didn't. He couldn't.

Nefer lowered her hand and sighed. "I was married once, long ago. I know what passions course in a man's blood. You cannot deny you desire me. And you cannot convince yourself this other woman desires you. Aten provides a path for you; all you must do is take it."

In the quiet that followed, Nefer glided out.

26

BREYONA DAY

Breyona had never seen so many bigfeet in the great Hall of the Strict. The twenty acolytes of the conclave gathered around the dais, upon which the three councilors sat, bathed in a pool of light.

Even though the chamber could hold ten times their number, the already muggy air of Undermountain grew even warmer in the presence of so many large, hairy beasts.

Breyona sat next to Shiv and Bronson. Shiv looked composed, interested in the proceedings. Bronson, smug.

Shaggy opened his eyes and studied the faces in the room. "Filinesama has invoked *okchen*, the conclave of senior acolytes, to vote on my motion to make First Contact with the human population of Earth. The council is not unanimous. Therefore, in this matter of such great import to the People, I have conceded to the necessity of a conclave vote. Let history show that in this hour, we deliberated with care, mindfulness, and particular attention to the teachings of the Oath."

Breyona could barely keep herself from snorting in disgust. Shaggy's ego knew no limits.

"We will begin with an argument against First Contact," Shaggy said, voice betraying contempt for that side of the argument. He gave a stiff nod to Notchy who stood and looked around the room.

"I have spoken with all of you individually. You know my arguments. I will offer only this, the words of the great Voo: 'I do not ask you to believe in the Oath, merely to follow it.'" Notchy sat and closed his eyes.

Breyona's jaw fell open. She glanced at Shiv. "That's it?"

Shiv frowned but didn't respond.

Notchy's speech had been utterly uninspiring, to the point of being an argument for the wrong side.

"Terrenora?" Shaggy said.

The gaunt councilor stood and spread his hands. "I shall make the argument in favor of First Contact," he said. He paused to collect his thoughts, then strode among the crowd. "The humans have a word, *humane*. It means to be compassionate. Making First Contact is our only humane option." He came to a stop behind Breyona. "We will take temporary control of their governments and eliminate all scarcity, disease, and hunger, any lack at all. That way, every individual on Earth will be free to devote themselves to the study and practice of the Oath. That is the epitome of compassion."

Breyona twisted in her seat to see Terrenora. He gestured dramatically with his hands. "It is time for the People to pass on the gift that Voo gave us. The humans have shown themselves to be capable and intelligent. I would like to echo Filinesama's statement, his most apt quotation of Voo. 'I do not ask you to believe in the Oath, merely to follow it.'" Terrenora returned to the dais and took his seat.

Breyona wondered why Notchy hadn't been able to come up with something as moving as that. She disagreed completely with the sentiment, but at least Terrenora had made an argument.

She started to stand, ready to speak out, but Shaggy locked eyes with her, freezing her momentarily. Before she could open her mouth, he spoke. "I've generously granted the human contingent a vote in the conclave. I've instructed them to discuss their vote amongst themselves and that their consensus will count as one vote. We shall allow one of them to speak. I have chosen my acolyte, Breyona, for that honor."

Breyona bit her tongue, torn between the desire to speak out and her desire to say nothing just to spite Shaggy. Realizing that petulance didn't serve her cause, she stepped onto the dais. Shaggy's eyes narrowed, and Terrenora's jaw fell open at her breach of protocol. Notchy chuckled and scratched an ear.

Breyona turned her back on Shaggy and addressed the conclave. "Last summer I was subjected to Hanameesovenama's indoctrination methods. The treatment was cruel and," she turned to Terrenora, "*grossly* inhumane. I was kept apart from my friends, fed tasteless mush, and allowed no form of intellectual diversion besides what Hanameesovenama decided to dole out. Humans treat pets more humanely than that."

Taking a play from Terrenora's book, Breyona strode around the dais, coming to a stop behind Shaggy so that all eyes would be on him. Even though he sat cross-legged, his head was nearly even with hers.

"What Hanameesovenama proposes to do, to take over our world for our greater good, sounds fine on the surface. I'll even admit it would ease a lot of suffering among the human race in the short term. But at what cost?

"The loss of our free will and the subjugation of our species to yours would rob us of our identity as a race. It would change us fundamentally from who and what we are and interrupt the course of human history. I submit that we humans own our future, and the choices we make are ours, not yours. Wresting these choices from us is nothing less than the theft of our future, no matter what your intentions are."

"Are you quite finished?" Shaggy asked.

"No." Breyona stepped past him and gazed down at the acolytes.

"The Oath says 'do no harm.' What a magnificent concept. Honor it by voting against First Contact."

"Terrenora," Shaggy said and tilted his head at Breyona.

Terrenora stood and placed a hand on Breyona's head. She felt his attempt to calm her and fended it off as easily as she would swat a mosquito. Terrenora fell onto his side, grunting in pain as his elbow struck the hard rock of the dais.

"Unbelievable," he said.

A murmur of conversation rose in the room. Breyona stepped from the dais, disgusted that Shaggy had tried to have her calmed. Perhaps her argument had been too convincing for his taste.

"Silence!" Shaggy shouted.

He stood. His ten-foot height loomed over Breyona.

She looked up at his face but did not find the anger she expected. Instead, she saw glee.

"I ask the conclave to note my acolyte's extreme facility with the Gift of Peace. You all know that Terrenora has one of the most powerful abilities among the People to pass the Gift of Peace. He has broken the most savage of you in *klindeensen*." Shaggy turned to Terrenora, who sat rubbing his injured elbow. "Did you give her all the calming you had?"

"Yes, Hanameesovenama. Everything."

More murmurs arose. Breyona wasn't sure what the big deal was. Compared to her experience with Shaggy, Terrenora's calming attack had seemed like nothing. But maybe her ability to resist had grown since then.

Shaggy continued, waving a huge, furry hand at Breyona. "I

would also like to note the work that my acolyte has done amongst her people since she left here. Reaching out to those who are disadvantaged, those filled with anxiety and fear, she helps them straighten out their lives, continue their education, and become productive citizens.

"We have seen these reports in the human news media. We have seen the following she has cultivated on the human Internet. She is truly a great example of what humans are capable of when brought to the Oath. I would also like the conclave to note her very articulate and beautiful argument, as mistaken as it was. She has not yet taken the Oath, and yet she embodies it in her daily practice and her ability to maintain her center of calm amidst unbelievably difficult circumstances. She stands as the primary evidence that First Contact should be made. No, *must* be made."

Shaggy sat and settled his robes about him. "Let us begin the vote."

Breyona fell heavily next to Bronson and Shiv. It had all been a trick. Shaggy had known what Breyona would say. Somehow he had known her capabilities, and he had used her as an example to make his case.

Shaggy began calling names. The yeas and the nays stayed equal all the way through to the end and Breyona felt a great sense of relief. It came down to the humans.

Shaggy turned to Bronson. "And how do you vote?"

"I vote yes for First Contact," Bronson said. He had a strange smirk on his face. And he looked at Breyona as though he'd won something, as though he was already the King of Texas.

What an idiot, she thought. He doesn't even realize his side lost.

"And Breyona, your vote."

"Nay." She relaxed and took a deep breath. This sealed it. And if Notchy was right, Shaggy would not be able to bring this issue to a vote unless something significant changed.

But a flicker of concern grew in the back of Breyona's mind.

Shaggy wasn't acting like someone who'd just suffered a humiliating public loss. He had an air of victory about him.

"And you, Shiv, Acolyte of Filinesama."

Breyona gasped, and her eyes flashed to Shiv, suddenly remembering the moment in Luon's chamber when Shiv first greeted her. He'd try to calm her then. . . . And she'd deflected it.

Shiv stared at the floor, face pale. In a bare whisper, he spoke. "I vote yea for First Contact."

For the first time ever, Breyona heard Shaggy laugh, deep and menacing. "The humans voted two for and one against; therefore their vote shall be counted as yea. The motion to make First Contact with the human race has passed. We must make arrangements now for a most significant moment. The first *donovthosameezu!*"

Breyona stared at Shiv. He kept his eyes closed.

Bronson leaned back, a smile splitting his fat face. He winked at her. "Come to Texas sometime. I'll create a holiday in your name. Breyona Day!"

27

SACRIFICING ONE TO BREAK THROUGH

Anger flared in Breyona, as hot as nuclear fusion. She caught herself in that moment and hung there suspended. She wanted to turn her fury against all assembled in the Hall. They were insignificant. They could do nothing to stop her.

The bigfeet of the conclave continued to discuss the next steps of making First Contact. But their voices seemed muffled, as if a sphere of water enclosed her. Except the sphere that surrounded her contained all of the energy of a million suns, and all she had to do was release it.

She stood, though her legs trembled. Every fiber of her body pulsed with electrical energy. She closed her eyes and took deep breaths. She felt a hand on her arm and glanced down to see Shiv. Involuntarily, she sent a jolt of anger through the contact, and he recoiled. He clutched his hand as if he'd placed it on a hot stove. Fear and speculation crossed his face, but she ignored him and fled for the exit.

Shaggy bellowed something behind her, arguing with Notchy.

She ignored him and continued forward. Part of her wished that some bigfoot would try to stop her. She would show them. She would burn them to cinders with her anger. But they didn't see her as important. They didn't notice her any more than they would notice Tog.

She stepped out of the Hall, her decision made. There was nothing left to do here. No. There was nothing she was *willing* to do to stop the bigfeet from making First Contact. The course of human events was about to change, and not for the better.

At least she was free to go after Danny. She had stayed and done her duty. She had followed her conscience. But now she could do as she wished, and all she wanted was to be with Danny.

She strode through the hallways, quickly picking up speed as she crossed the Hall of Statues. A short monorail ride took her to the apartment where she collected her backpack. As she started toward the elevator, a familiar figure clattered out of Em's room.

"Tog?"

"I thought you might be back to collect your things. I thought you might be going after Danny."

"Then you knew this would happen," she said. "Did you know Shiv was going to change his vote?"

"After we exposed Hanameesovenama's deal with Bronson, it only made sense he'd strike one with Shiv."

"What did he offer him?"

"The implant," Tog said. "Shiv has always wanted it, and Hanameesovenama granted it to him, though technically it isn't his to give."

"Of course." Breyona remembered Danny talking about how jealous Shiv was of Danny's tangoga implant. All Shiv ever wanted was knowledge and more knowledge. And the implant could provide that.

Danny never liked talking about the procedure, always gave her vague answers about the experience. Breyona had talked to Wa about it once. He had seen it happen from hiding. Based on what he described, Shiv would pay the price in pain.

"Come on, Tog. Let's go."

Tog's feathers ruffled from teal to gray to teal. "You're going to let me go with you?"

"We've both been kept from what we really want for too long. Let's go find Danny. I had hoped that Em and Grizz would be back by now."

Together they ascended to the teleportation atrium. Breyona had never teleported before, but she understood the principle of it. They entered one of the tiny rooms that circled the periphery of the atrium.

"Sahara," Breyona said.

The world flashed to blue and gravity went away. The world came back with a rush, and she found herself in what appeared to be the same room.

A quick peek out of the window showed a much different scenario. Instead of the brightly lit teleportation atrium of Under-mountain, the exterior was dim. She and Tog walked into a vast and silent area. Teleportation rooms circled the space, each window dark as an empty eye socket. Footprints led away through a thick layer of dust covering the floor. A dome ceiling, like a football stadium, stretched into the distance overhead.

"Do you know the way, Tog?"

"I have a map of the complex in my implant. I can get us as far as the caves that supposedly connect to Amarna. The rest is unmapped."

Breyona found it hard to believe she had just teleported across the world. "I don't feel like I'm in Egypt," she said.

She tried to remember the details Shiv and Luon had mentioned during their history lesson. About how the bigfeet had settled here, somewhere under the Sahara Desert, thousands of years ago.

Tog took her around the periphery of the chamber and into a dark passageway.

The eerie emptiness of the settlement made the air feel heavy, even sad. According to Tog, the Sahara settlement had been mostly abandoned for hundreds of years, though GorVit had stationed some of his invasion gunners here before the attack on Undermountain the previous summer.

Tog led Breyona down a stairwell to a bank of elevators. The descent seemed to take ten minutes, but eventually the doors opened, and they exited into the old tangoga sub-city. Tog led her through a warren of passageways and rooms, all abandoned. GorVit's army had not left things in very good condition. Many lights were out, some flickered, and debris lay here and there.

Tog squawked mournfully at the sight of the mess. "This is very much against procedure. Everything should be in its place, and all refuse should be disposed of."

Breyona patted Tog and tried to impart a little compassion and cheer. But she didn't have much to give. The effort seemed to be enough, for his feathers ruffled, and he held his head a little higher.

Another elevator ride brought them to a farm cavern. A dim, artificial sun cast a bluish pallor over dead fields, the plantings dried and brown. In the bedrock across the desiccated crop were several rough openings, the entrances to the caves. They gaped like black wounds in the cavern wall, except one at the top of a ladder. A reddish glow emanated from it. "I guess they went that way," she said.

She worried Tog wouldn't be able to climb the ladder, but he managed to use his armpack to pull himself up, claw over claw.

As they started down the passageway, Tog looked back at the farm. "This is where the map in my implant leaves off."

"Keep your eyes open."

The first sign that her friends had passed that way was an apple core. Every once in a while, a new passageway split off to one side or another, or the way forked. Each time they discovered some bit evidence to guide them. "They want to make sure they can get out, so they're leaving signs the whole way."

"The People are smart," Tog said. "I wouldn't have thought of that. There is no procedure for finding your way out of a place. . . . But then, this is not the kind of environment we would go into by ourselves. And certainly not without sending some vopels in first."

Breyona shuddered, remembering the many-eyed vopels, creatures that spat paralyzing venom.

The sound of dripping water came to her just before they emerged into a black chamber. Breyona stopped short when she came to the shore of a vast, underground lake. The shoreline ran left and right. She studied the ground and saw clear evidence of footprints leading off to the right. She followed them with Tog clattering after her. Aside from their footsteps, they heard nothing but the occasional plink of water.

The footsteps ended at the water's edge. She took off her shoes, rolled up her pant legs, and waded in. It was ice cold, and she let out a little cry that echoed and reverberated.

"We should be quiet," Tog said in a whisper. "GorVit or his gunners could be anywhere."

They sloshed along, keeping close to the cavern wall. Breyona didn't know how long she could take the water. Her feet were already numb. The bottom was smooth, hard rock, though sometimes bits of gravel stabbed at her heels.

A jagged opening appeared on the right. Huge boulders lay all around, as if dynamite had blown the wall apart.

Tog sniffed at some of the rocks. "A tangeg detonated here," he said, pointing to black marks on several of the boulders. "Or a gunner." He looked at the opening. "GorVit wouldn't think twice about sacrificing one to break through this wall."

They walked through and stepped onto dry ground. Where they

had been in natural caverns before, now they entered an obviously human created and decorated environment.

"I knew we had teleported," Breyona said, gazing at an enormous stone statue. "But this really brings it home. We *are* in Egypt!"

28

TO LIFT UP

Danny wandered away from Nefer's dining room, confused about what had happened between him and the queen. He felt guilty even though he hadn't actually done anything to betray Breyona. But if she'd seen him there with Nefer, he doubted she'd ever speak to him again.

Getting off this planet was the best solution to the problem of Nefer, which led his thoughts inevitably back to the Asht complex and the black gate.

He considered going back and trying to figure out how to open it, the way he had with the Spheroid. But unlike the Spheroid, the gate gave no clues. He knew staring at it wasn't going to help, so to clear his head, he left the palace.

The sun bore down on him with its relentless fire. Sweat soaked his shirt and dripped into his eyes, but he ignored it. He had always done his best thinking when in motion, and he had a puzzle to solve.

But it wasn't about the gate. It was Breyona.

He passed one of the wooden buildings where the meezu lived.

This one stood empty. Its construction had probably been mere make-work, invented by Nefer to keep her meezu busy. A seven-meter-tall statue of the queen gazed down at him from the street corner, one of hundreds like it placed throughout the city. The statue captured Nefer's likeness, her regal bearing, but none of her seductive beauty.

He turned away from it and continued his walk. Breyona had never looked at him the way Nefer did. Never hungered for him. Instead, Breyona fed him. He wasn't sure if that even made sense, but it felt right. Breyona's smile gave him something: joy, giddiness, peace.

Nefer's pulled from him: desire, passion, lust.

Danny came to the massive city wall, happy to find a bit of relief from the heat in its growing shadows. He decided to climb the stairs to the top. Perhaps he could get some perspective there.

At the top, he scanned the grassy plain, enjoying the freshening breeze that swirled the grass in blue and green waves. Birds flocked near the river, and far out, a black splotch of skopa ambled toward the jungle.

Gray clouds roiled to the east, edging into view above the high cliffs. Epic plumes of vapor towered into the violet-blue depths of the sky. Danny imagined Breyona standing next to him. She would hold his hand, trickle calm and love into him, and they would gaze over the valley and say nothing. Yet they'd be together.

But Breyona wasn't there. She hadn't come.

Danny turned west and strolled along the wall, running his hands along the smooth, golden crenellations. He noticed a meezu standing farther down. It peered over the wall toward the ground below.

His thoughts jumped to Jostosh, the meezu who had thrown himself from this very wall just hours before. Danny refused to let another make the same choice. He ran and waved his arms. "Stop!"

The meezu turned, fixing its wide, green eyes on Danny.

"Grizz? What are you doing?"

Grizz put his great furry hands on the rampart and breathed deeply. "Just enjoying some fresh air. Join me."

"I was afraid you were going to jump."

Grizz closed his eyes and took more deep breaths. "The thought did cross my mind. But the Oath precludes suicide."

"Nefer thinks you'll become a new Chosen."

"Nefertiti's version of reality is somewhat distorted." Grizz's chuckle sounded like a deep, throaty purr. "I did go with the meezu, but only to ask them questions. It's curious to find so many of the People on an unknown planet. They know nothing of the Oath or of the People's travels throughout the galaxy."

"Why did Jostosh jump?"

"Given what the Chosen learn during their indoctrination, it's not surprising that some of them can't handle it."

"Is it about that stupid sin Jostosh was telling me about?"

Grizz huffed, eyes narrowing to slits. "If there was a sin, it wasn't the meezu who committed it. I witnessed Jostosh's indoctrination. After a considerable amount of chanting and hand waving, they recited an incredible story. I believe it to be true."

He rubbed at his ears and shifted from foot to foot, obviously disconcerted by what he'd learned.

After a long pause he continued. "Little is known of the evolution of the People. The meezu's story filled many gaps for me. Because of Ig's extremely active geology, we thought the fossil record had been lost to tectonic plate movement, volcanism, and floods." Grizz looked down at his hands, flexed them. "But the real reason we found no fossil record on Ig is because it doesn't exist there. According to meezu, Ig is not our home planet. Hoo is. The Asht came here looking for intelligent species to . . ." He paused for a moment. "I'm trying to think of the right word. To lift up, to make intelligent."

"Like turning tangeg into tangoga?"

"That's it exactly," Grizz said. "A perfect example. In fact, it was the Asht who created the tangoga. They found the tangeg, developed the implant, and then fitted them with armpack prosthetics to make them more useful."

Danny scanned his implant to see if its history of the tangoga matched Grizz's. But there was nothing there. "I never thought about it before. But I guess that makes sense."

"It's not a secret. Did you think the tangeg spontaneously created the implant for themselves?"

Danny laughed at the ridiculous suggestion. Tangeg were raving predators, incapable of abstract thought.

The wind picked up, flattening Grizz's fur against his huge body. He breathed the breeze in and spread his arms. "Ah, there's going to be a storm. I've lived so much beneath the ground that I'd forgotten how exhilarating the wind could be. Perhaps this weather has awakened some latent memory of this planet in my subconscious."

The gray clouds boiled into the valley, dragging a veil of rain beneath them. Wind whipped the canopy of the jungle along the base of the cliffs.

"The Asht weren't satisfied with the tangoga," Grizz continued. "So they searched the galaxy for another candidate species to raise. They came here, and they made the People."

A puzzle piece snapped into place in Danny's mind. "Yesterday Nefer took me on a hunt. I saw a creature that looked a lot like . . . you guys, but bigger. Way bigger."

"The Asht began with horgodons," Grizz said, nodding. "Their size made them impractical servants, so the Asht genetically modified them to produce the meezu. Except those first prototypes could barely reason at all."

"So are you saying that you've got an implant in your head?"

"No!" Grizz said. "This is where it gets very strange. Once the Asht had sized their new creation to their satisfaction, they genetically engineered a hybrid brain: part meezu, part Asht. All at once, they had meezu with the same intelligence as theirs, or nearly so. But no matter what they did, they couldn't breed out the horgodon's extreme aggression, a character trait we retain to this day. The Asht burned through many generations of meezu to figure out how to deal with it."

The bitterness in Grizz's voice startled Danny. Not because he felt it was unjustified, but because it was so unlike Grizz to express that kind of emotion.

"The Asht developed a device that could affect brainwaves, that could calm the rage until the individual could get control over its temper."

"But you can do that without a device," Danny said. "You calm others just by using your hands."

Grizz nodded. "The meezu's story did not get that far in the history of the People. At some point, we must have developed the capacity. Maybe due to extreme exposure to the device."

"I don't understand why the Asht would go to all that trouble. What did they need you for?"

Grizz shook his head and raised his hands in a shrug. "I have no idea."

"Do you think Jostosh killed himself because he couldn't handle the idea he was descended from horgodons?"

"It is not so simple. I think Jostosh could handle that. He was surprisingly calm, considering his lack of training in the Oath. Jostosh's problem was that this new information conflicts with the mythology the Mothers teach.

"The cliff meezu believe they were cast out of the city due to some great sin. They think that if they can redeem themselves, the Asht will return. But the truth is that the cast-outs were simply the last batch of meezu created. When the Asht decided to leave, they turned the meezu out of the city."

"Why?"

"They were young. They weren't tamed yet. The Asht figured the meezu would destroy everything if left unattended. Apparently, the Asht had some idea they might return. They didn't want the meezu making a mess of things while they were gone. When a new Chosen meezu learns the truth, he must face the fact his entire life is based upon a lie. There never was a great sin. There is no way to be redeemed. Like many before him, Jostosh felt immense anger and shame because the meezu are nothing but leftovers."

"But not all of them commit suicide."

"They put their faith in Nefertiti. They think she speaks for an Asht named Aten, who they believe will return some day and bring them into the city." Grizz heaved a great sigh and shook his arms, an attempt to snap himself out of his melancholy mood. "There is good news in all this, Danny."

"By all means, tell me."

Grizz turned away from the grassy plain and pointed across the city to the Asht complex built into the cliff. He had to raise his voice to be heard over the wind. "The Asht didn't make things that decay. Whatever they left inside there still functions. That will certainly include a teleportation platform. All we need is to get inside."

Danny rubbed his temples as he turned his mind back to the problem at hand. "The gate is locked, and SulKit shoots anyone who tries to climb through a window."

Grizz scratched at his chin and glanced at the sky. "We'd better get to shelter. The storm will be upon us soon."

They climbed down the steps and out of the wind. They hustled up the thoroughfare in silence, chased by distant rumbles of thunder. The first fat raindrops splattered behind them as they ducked into the safety of the palace.

Danny had a sudden thought. "Sul says it's forbidden to go into the Asht complex. But he never said why."

"And I won't," said Sul as he strode into view, flanked by two meezu priests and two guards bearing swords. "That the Asht forbid it should be enough for both of you." He turned to Danny. "Nefertiti says it is time for you to satisfy your debt."

The two meezu priests stepped forward and beckoned Danny to approach them.

"What is this?" Grizz asked.

Sul cocked his head. "Nefertiti has declared that Danny will marry her."

Grizz squinted down at Danny, who held his hands up. "You said yourself her version of reality is different." He squeezed past the meezu priests, but the guards intercepted him.

"You will come," the one to Danny's right said. "Willingly . . . or unwillingly."

29

______

I WAS MANHANDLED

A crack of thunder shook the palace like the footfall of a titan. Rain blasted onto the plaza outside in sheets so dense it appeared the falls had suddenly grown to cover the world.

At a word from one of the meezu priests, the two guards retreated a few steps. The priest stepped forward and bowed to Danny. "The queen wishes me to convey a message." He unfolded a sheet of paper so large it would have been a poster in Danny's hands. He read:

"I, Nefertiti, Queen of the Golden City, declare my union and marriage to Danny the Horgodon Killer. At three hours before sunset, let all loyal subjects gather at the Temple of Aten to witness the joining."

The priest solemnly folded the paper and handed it to Danny. "The queen included a personal note as well."

"Did she confess her undying love for me?" He shouldered past the priests. "Come on, Grizz," he said in English. "We've got to get out of the city."

The meezu priests followed him, heavy staves clicking on the polished tile floor with every stride. Danny glared back at them. "Leave me alone."

The priests said nothing, but they continued to follow him, as did SulKit and the two guards. The tangoga seemed agitated, golden fingers waggling. "Do you remember what you said the night before the hunt?" Sul asked.

"No."

"You said you weren't going on the hunt."

"This is different." But a rising fear made Danny pick up his pace. He meant to find Wa and Em and go. They'd risk the dangers outside the walls and hope whatever weapon was hidden here would stay hidden.

Sul gave up and stopped following Danny. "I'll see you three hours before sunset."

No you won't, Danny thought. He'd be to the meezu's cliff dwellings, or farther, by then.

Thunder rumbled, reminding him of the storm raging outside. He didn't relish the thought of heading into it, but he didn't see any alternative. "This changes everything, Grizz. We're getting out of the city and heading for the portal."

He marched into Em's suite. She lay on a chaise lounge, dressed in a beautiful, peach gown, her curly hair swept up into a loose bun. Wa sat on the floor beside her, feeding her bits of fruit.

Wa winked at Danny. "I think I'm starting to like it here. No school, free food, and beautiful women."

"Where did you get that?" Danny asked Em, stabbing a finger at her outfit.

"A gift from the queen," she said. "I thought it would be rude not to at least try it on."

"Take it off. We're leaving." Danny threw Nefer's announcement in Em's general direction, but it fluttered away and slid under a table. "Pack up some supplies. I want to be out of here in fifteen minutes."

"I don't think those guys are going to let you go," she said, pointing at the two guards stationed at the doorway. The priests hovered just inside the door, conferring in low voices.

"We'll sneak out somehow. I'm sure Wa knows a secret way out of the city by now."

Wa smiled. "As a matter of fact, I do." He eyed the priests, and put a conspiratorial hand to his mouth. "Are you sure they don't understand English?"

Danny made rude gesture at the priests. "Get lost, monkey-clowns!"

The priests blinked at him. "I beg your pardon?" one said in Footese.

Satisfied, Wa took Danny to a window overlooking the city. Rain still pummeled the world, making it hard to see anything beyond the city wall.

"You see the river there?" Wa asked. "It goes under the wall to flow out into the valley. If you can hold your breath for a minute or so, you can swim out."

"There'll be a grate," Danny said. "Otherwise anyone could get in."

"Of course there's a grate. But I'm pretty sure it's sized to keep out horgodons and meezu, not us wee humans."

"Pretty sure?"

Em hovered behind them. "Guys, there's no way I'm going out in that storm. I'll get soaked."

Danny turned a flat stare on his sister. "And you won't get soaked swimming in the river?"

"Danny," Grizz said, "you need to see this." He held out Nefer's marriage declaration.

Danny slapped it away. "I already know what it says."

"No, you don't."

Danny took it and read the neat black script. In addition to the announcement the meezu priest had read, Nefer had written a note.

As a wedding gift, I shall tell you how to enter the Asht complex.

He pursed and lips as he reread the sentence a few more times. "I thought there was no way in," he said to himself.

"What is it?" Em asked, trying to read over his shoulder.

He handed the paper to his sister and turned back to the window.

"This is in Footese," Em complained. "What does it say?"

The rain was lessening; already beams of sun shone on the grass beyond the wall. The wind had settled, and the thunder rumbled far away.

Grizz's massive hand touched Danny's shoulder. No calm passed into Danny, but it comforted him all the same. He knew what Grizz was thinking. If they could get into the Asht complex, they'd be able to secure the weapon and eliminate any risk of GorVit getting it. And they'd be able to teleport home without facing the dangers of skopa herds, horgodons, and the difficult climb up to the portal.

He nodded to Grizz and summoned the meezu priests. They approached and bowed low.

"Let's get this over with," Danny said.

One priest nodded. "Follow me."

The other priest faced Em and Wa. "Please. Your ceremonial garments await you."

"What's going on, Danny?" Em asked, voice rising in concern.

"Grizz can explain. I've got to go put on my own dress right now."

Another meezu waited in Danny's suite next to a steaming copper bathtub. After Danny had washed, the meezu slathered oil onto Danny's limbs and dressed him in a loose skirt with a wide, golden belt. A priest strode in bearing a broad, golden necklace that he solemnly placed over Danny's head. From the necklace hung the disc of Aten. The metal chilled the bare skin of Danny's chest. Cuffs of gold were placed around the biceps of both his arms. He stepped into sandals that laced up his calves. The meezu attacked Danny's hair, slicking it back so that he could place something heavy on Danny's head–a crown with a golden serpent standing erect at the brow, its tongue extended, eyes of red jewels.

"Danny, where are you?" Em called.

"In here."

Em stomped into the room, waving a rolled up document. "That brat Nefertiti sent me a message commanding me to 'get with child.' Grizz had to read it to me. Do you know how embarrassing that–"

She stopped cold when she saw him standing there in his ridiculous costume. "You're not going through with this," she said. She put her hands on her hips just like their mother did when she was upset.

"I don't really have a choice," Danny said.

"Of course you do. Just say no."

Danny looked at himself in a tall mirror. Despite the fact he wore a skirt and had no shirt on, he decided he didn't look too bad. He adjusted the sash around his waist and flexed his abs. "Do you think a spear would make this get-up look more masculine?"

"You're not old enough to get married. Hell, that . . . that . . . *child* is not old enough to get married."

Danny met Em's eyes in the mirror. "She's older than all of us combined times one hundred."

Em grabbed his shoulder and spun him around. "And what about Breyona?"

"What about her?" he said, unable to keep his voice light. "I don't see her anywhere. I haven't seen her for months. When we arrange to see each other through video chat or at Grandma's house, she never shows up."

"But she did show up," Em said. "She's the one who helped us get to Undermountain to come after you. She would have come, but–"

Danny turned back to the mirror. "I don't want to hear excuses about why she stayed behind. I understand that there was a vote for First Contact. I know that it's important, but Breyona always finds things that are more important than me."

"That's not a reason to marry someone else. Not out of spite."

Danny swallowed, realizing that maybe in some small way he did want to hurt Breyona. But it didn't matter. He had to go forward with the ceremony.

"All I want to do right now is go home," he said. "This wedding is just pretend. It doesn't mean anything. Didn't Grizz tell you what Nefer is offering me? A way into the Asht complex. There's a tele-portation hub in there."

Wa stormed in, forehead furrowed. "This is your fault," he said, bare-chested except for a white skirt, embroidered belt, and sandals. With Wa's darker coloring, he looked far more Egyptian than Danny ever would. "I was manhandled!" He caught Em staring at him. "What?"

A smile played on her lips, and her eyes flashed. "Nothing," she said innocently, though her eyes looked him up and down. "It's just that I never expected to see you in a dress."

Wa gritted his teeth, turned around, and marched out. "I'm not coming to your wedding, Daniel!"

"I'd better go after him," Em said. "And if we're going to go through with this, I'd better get myself put together." The prospect of getting dressed up seemed to excite her far more than it had Danny.

After chanting over him and anointing him with various smelly waters, oils, and perfumes, the priests started to lead Danny out of his suite. But Danny stopped and dug in the pocket of his discarded jeans. He pulled free a silver necklace bearing two charms: the letter 'B' and a heart with a little keyhole in it. He put it around his neck.

"I'm ready now."

30

DANNYDANNYDANNY

Danny boarded an elaborately decorated chariot pulled by two meezu guards rather than a skopa.

They joined up with a procession of meezu and tangoga. Another chariot carried a huge statue of Nefer. Strings of giant yellow blossoms hung from its neck. They drove down the thoroughfare toward the gate and crossed a bridge over the river into the pyramid field. They came to a temple set on a wide, open courtyard in front of the Golden Pyramid.

The temple consisted of ornate columns surrounding a central square open to the sky. Inside, a granite altar stood in the middle. One of the meezu priests strode to the altar holding his staff aloft. Danny was directed to stand in front of the altar. He noticed then that Wa, Em, and Grizz had already arrived.

Em wore the raiment of a princess, a silver-blue gown, detailed with beads and thread of gold. Her hair had been swept up into a tower and bound with a golden tiara that sparkled with jewels. Chains of gems hung from her neck. Still more laced around her wrists. A ruby ring flashed on one hand, diamonds on the other.

Wa stood beside her uncomfortably, clearly displeased with the whole proceeding. And if the priests had tried to dress Grizz in something, they had failed, for he stood in his normal bigfoot attire, a long tunic belted at the waist and short pants. His wide, green eyes scanned the procession with great interest.

More meezu entered the temple, taking position along the periphery. Danny was surprised to see cliff-dwellers in their rough skins. They carried drums and began beating an intricate rhythm.

Danny realized that SulKit must have allowed them in temporarily as part of the ceremony. Four meezu guards, clad in shiny breastplate and with axes slung over their backs, marched in carrying a palanquin.

They set it down nearby and opened the curtains. Mother rested inside, surrounded by pillows, her massive body almost indistinguishable from the skins and cushions around her. She waved a careless hand at the guards, and they departed.

The drumming built to a crescendo and then stopped. Danny heard the approach of another chariot and the sharp clatter of tangoga just outside the temple.

Five minutes passed. Then ten.

Leave it to Nefer to make everyone wait. The heat of the day grew more intense and sweat trickled down his forehead from beneath the headdress. He felt like he carried at least seventy pounds of gold on his head.

She appeared in the doorway, backlit by the sun. Her silhouette appeared alien, topped by a towering headdress.

With soft, cat-like steps, she glided through the throng. She wore pure white robes with a golden sash across one shoulder. A jeweled headdress fell down over her shoulders like hair.

She came forward, chin slightly lifted, commanding all eyes in the room. She passed by Danny to be lifted onto the altar by a priest. She gazed down at all assembled with supreme confidence.

To Danny she looked almost ethereal, like some strange elf

queen out of lore. He met her gaze, and his breath nearly went out of him.

"I claim this man as my husband," she announced, holding a hand over Danny's head.

The priest nodded, raised his staff, touched Danny's forehead just under the serpent on the headdress, and intoned in Footese, "The Queen of the Golden City, the eternal NeferNeferNefer, claims thee as her husband. In her name and in the presence of Aten, I anoint thee king."

The priest stepped back, knelt, and bowed his head. All the meezu in the temple followed suit. "Hail the great DannyDanny-Danny," they said in unison.

Nefer stared at him, clearly expecting him to say something. He improvised. "I take this woman, NeferNeferNefer, as my wife."

A gasp sounded in the room. The priest looked up at Nefer uncertainly. Her jaw went slack for a moment, and Danny realized he had goofed. He smiled and winked at her, which seemed to disarm her anger a little bit, and she laughed. She held out her hand. Danny took it, and a priest quickly stooped to lift him onto the altar next to her.

"Hail, the Queen and King of the Golden City. NeferNeferNefer! DannyDannyDanny!" They repeated it over and over. At some signal Danny didn't see, the meezu started drumming, this time the rhythm celebratory and wild. The crowd parted, and Danny and Nefer were lowered from the altar. They walked hand in hand from the temple and stepped into a chariot.

"Now what?" Danny asked her. "How do we get into the Asht complex?"

She glanced up at him coyly. "I'll explain, but I want to show you something first."

She took the reins and guided the chariot away from the temple and toward the Golden Pyramid. They pulled in front of it, and Danny saw a great block pushed aside, revealing a dark entrance.

Nefer led him into the cool belly of the pyramid. At the end of a sloping passageway, they came into a wide room. It contained nothing but a sarcophagus, one unlike any Danny had seen on the Discovery Channel.

On top of a stone platform stood a rectangular box of glass. Danny peered inside where the perfectly preserved body of an ancient woman lay in repose.

He glanced at the figure and back at Nefer. "Who is this? I thought you were going to be buried here."

Nefer glanced down at the dead figure. "I am buried here."

The revelation made Danny blink and step away from the sarcophagus. "That's you." It was half question, half statement.

Nefer's voice fell to just above a whisper as she gazed at the body. "This is what the tangoga call 'instance zero.'"

"But that's an old . . . but you're . . ." Sudden understanding, a mix of wonder and horror, filled Danny.

Nefer nodded slightly and ran a finger along the glass top of the sarcophagus. "I don't feel like this woman," she said. "I remember her life, and yet I feel like a different person. It's hard to believe I once had a husband and children. But I did. I lived a full life and died of old age." She circled to stand next to Danny and took his hand. "And I've lived it again and again and again."

"So all of those pyramids . . . ?"

She nodded. "My tombs."

Danny couldn't believe it. He had assumed they were monuments to favored meezu or tangoga. "How does it work? How do the tangoga reincarnate you?"

"They will not tell me. But they serve the will of Aten that I might live forever. And now," she said to Danny, "that will be your destiny as well."

"But–"

She put a finger to his lips and led him back to the chariot.

SulKit waited nearby. "Are you ready, Queen?" Sul asked.

She nodded. "Proceed."

SulKit led them to the palace and down dark stairways to a basement. The corridors reminded Danny of the sub-city of Undermountain.

They came into a laboratory. Nefer removed her headdress and lay on a bare steel table in the center of the room. SulKit opened a cabinet and rolled out a familiar apparatus, one that Danny had experienced when he had received his implant in Antarctica. SulKit lowered it over Nefer's head, and Danny watched as the long fingers of the apparatus probed her ears, nose, and the corners of her eyes. She shuddered a moment, and the probes lifted.

"This is what they call a backup," Nefer said as she stood and lifted her headdress back into place. "When something important happens, I make sure to save it."

Danny understood. Nefer backed up her mind in case she was killed, so when the tangoga restored her to a new body, she would keep her memories.

Sul patted the table with his golden claw. "If you please, King Danny, we need to perform a procedure to prepare you for your backups."

Danny laughed. "I'm not doing that procedure again. I already have an implant."

Kit squawked. Sul's eyes went wide, and the feathers of his body flashed from teal to gray to teal again. "How is this possible?"

Nefer stared at him as though seeing him for the first time. "You truly were sent by Aten," she said, a tinge of awe in her voice.

Danny took off his headdress and lay on the table, not sure why he was subjecting himself to the backup procedure. He just hoped it didn't hurt as much as the implant procedure had.

He didn't feel a thing. In a moment, it was over, and SulKit rolled the device back to the cabinet.

"Now that the official business is over," Nefer said, "it is time for a more personal thing."

Danny wondered what could be more personal than showing someone the tomb where the first of your many bodies had been buried.

They ascended to the main level of the palace and found the halls empty and quiet. Nefer led Danny to her quarters, which occupied the entire west wing of the palace.

She removed her jewelry, laying it casually on a table, and turned to face him. He knew that look in her eye, knew he had to stop her.

"How do I get into the Asht—?" he started to ask, but something in her face dried the words in his mouth.

She took slow steps toward him, strides soft, cat-like. She curled her arms around his neck. He resisted, tried to pull back, but she held him firmly, forcing him to support half her weight. Her eyes seemed to hover before his, dark and unblinking. They conveyed more than mere hunger. Starvation.

She pressed her mouth on his, drawing a reflexive response from his lips. The kiss never ended. He didn't want it to. He couldn't think at all, his brain overloaded by Nefer's presence. The warmth of her lips and the press of her slim body against his overpowered his resolve. He pulled her close.

She started to lead him to the bed, but he broke away. He pulled the charm necklace from around his neck. He stroked the glittering 'B' with his thumb for a moment before setting the necklace in a dish.

Nefer's delicate fingers lifted the circle of Aten from his shoulders. He continued to stare at the charm necklace until Nefer slipped in front of him. She kissed him again, and he forgot everything else.

31

YOU HAVE TO DIE

Danny closed his eyes and surrendered to the moment as they fell onto the bed. Nefer filled his senses—her perfume, the feel of her skin, the sound of her breath, which suddenly seemed too labored and heavy to come from her small body.

He opened his eyes and discovered he was right. The breathing came from a meezu who stood over the bed looking down at them. It held its hands over its ears.

"What is the meaning of this intrusion?" Nefer demanded.

Danny disentangled himself from her and sat up, felt his face burning with embarrassment.

"My queen, an army approaches the wall."

SulKit clattered in, cape flapping behind him in his rush. "This is most serious," Sul said. "You must come see."

"What kind of army?" Nefer asked, curiosity replacing anger in her tone. Her disheveled gown hung off one smooth shoulder as she jumped from the bed.

Danny followed her to the balcony. They looked out over the

city, past the temples, to the high wall. A great, black mass stained the grassy plain beyond.

Danny squinted against the setting sun. "It's just a skopa herd."

"No, it is not," Sul said. "It's a great host of horgodons."

Nefer's face went pale. "Send your tangoga weapons to the wall."

"We shall," Sul said. "But they'll do little good against a force so large."

She turned to the meezu. "How many meezu from the cliff-dwellings remain in the city?"

"I don't know," the meezu said.

"Find out!"

The meezu fled.

"I thought the walls were impregnable," Danny said.

"To meezu, yes. To tangoga, certainly. But against so many horgodons . . . I'm not sure we can fight them off. We must get to the wall to oversee the defense."

Danny ran to his room and changed into his normal clothes. Apparently, SulKit had alerted Wa and Em, for he found them in the plaza in front of the palace. They wore their normal clothes, though the ruby ring still flashed on Em's hand.

Nefer had changed into a simple blue dress, belted with a thin cord. Her hair hung free. They jumped into chariots and raced down the thoroughfare to the wall.

Grizz was already there, along with a number of the Chosen and cliff meezu.

"What could make so many horgodons come to the city," Nefer wondered as they arrived at the top of the wall.

Danny had his suspicions. Grizz confirmed them with a nod. "GorVit."

The horde was still too far off to make out the hateful tangoga, but the approaching host smelled of GorVit's scheming.

"That's why he waited so long," Danny said. "He was rounding up every horgodon in the valley."

"But why would those savage animals obey a tangoga?" Nefertiti asked.

"Savage, maybe. I'm not so sure they're merely animals," Danny said, remembering his experience with the one he'd killed. Remembering how it had recognized and accepted the mercy Danny offered. "I don't think you give them enough credit."

"It's possible they've noticed the tangoga in the city," Grizz said. "Perhaps they felt honored by Gor's attention. Perhaps he promised them something."

"That would be Gor's style," Danny said.

Em shaded her eyes and cocked her head. "What are they carrying?"

Danny squinted. Many of the horgodons bore huge clubs over their shoulders. Each one appeared to be a tree trunk.

"They bear hidle trees," one of the meezu said. "Strong, but brittle. Not their usual choice for weapons."

Each flank held over three hundred horgodons. Even with guns, Danny didn't think SulKit and his tangoga would be effective against so many.

"I never dreamed there were so many of those horrible beasts in the whole valley," Nefer said. "They usually stick to packs of four or five."

Danny caught a glimpse of a red shirt flashing against the grass. "There's GorVit. SulKit, shoot them!"

"They're not in range," Kit said, though he held the rifle at the ready. Sul observed the advancing horde with great displeasure. "The Asht will not be pleased," he said. "Not at all."

GorVit slipped momentarily out of view behind the line of horgodons. When he appeared again, he trailed a group of small figures. Meezu. They walked sullenly ahead, feet bound together by thick ropes, a living shield for the tangoga boss to hide behind.

A low growl sounded from the meezu on the wall. The priests pounded their staves and roared, teeth bared with fury.

Danny could see the horgodons' faces now. Their breath heaved in and out like bellows. Like the bigfeet, they were of all different colors: some black, some beige, some striped. They wore crude skins over their bodies, harvested from some monstrous animal Danny hadn't seen yet and hoped he never would.

"They do look just like bigfeet," Em said. She turned to Wa, placed a hand on his arm. "I'm sorry I doubted you, honey."

"I'm sorry I didn't make it up," Wa said somberly.

The horgodons halted just out of range of the tangoga guns. GorVit rushed around, squawking orders. Many of the horgodons dropped their great clubs in a pile, which the meezu set about arranging. Using huge coils of rope, they bound the trunks together.

"They're constructing ladders," Sul said quietly.

The scene repeated to the east and west. Team after team of meezu lashed together crude siege ladders, which the horgodons then hoisted overhead. Even with their great size, they strained under the weight of the ladders, muscles rippling across their chests as they came forward.

A tangoga shriek floated up to Danny. Other cries echoed it and tangoga gunners on the plain raced out, guns blazing. But they did not attack the wall. Their own meezu laborers in the field fell before the assault, caught utterly by surprise.

The meezu on the wall howled, pounded their fists on their chests, and hurled unintelligible curses down at the tangoga.

"It's murder!" Sul cried.

Grizz covered his ears with his hands and looked away, eyes squeezed shut. Em put a hand to her mouth, eyebrows knit with horror. Wa's jaw clamped shut and his body tensed, as if he might leap over the wall and personally take revenge on GorVit.

Nefer lifted her chin, and her eyes blazed. "Take up your arms.

Defend your city. Avenge the meezu of the cliffs. Let these interlopers feel the full force of Aten's wrath!"

The horgodon ladder teams started toward the wall. SulKit's tangoga opened fire. Bullet impacts knocked some of the creatures sideways, blew off chunks of flesh and fur. The beasts screamed and howled with unrestrained fury, but they did not stop.

Behind the first wave, more horgodons lowered huge, lumpy sacks from their shoulders. They pulled out boulders and hurled them with great force. The rocks flew high into the air and crashed down on top of the wall. One caught a nearby tangoga, knocking its crushed body to the stone plaza behind the wall.

There simply weren't enough tangoga to cover the entire length of the assault. Long stretches remained undefended. Horgodons collected there, climbing their crude ladders until the first one topped the wall.

That was enough for Danny. He grabbed Nefer and pulled her down the steps, though she resisted, beating at his arm with her small fists.

Wa, Em, and Grizz followed. "Where can we go?" Em cried as they reached the plaza.

A horgodon appeared on the wall directly overhead. It shook a meezu priest in its hands like a doll before throwing the body down. The priest struck the paving stones of the plaza with a horrific crunch.

Nefer no longer resisted Danny. Instead, she raced to the nearest chariot, barely waiting for Danny, Wa, and Em to join her. She took the reins. "To the palace!"

Danny doubted that the palace would be able to withstand an attack from the horgodons. He looked back. Hundreds of them wreaked havoc behind them. Monuments toppled and trees flew aside as the raging beasts tore through the gardens and temples.

Shrieks of tangoga cut through the din of horgodon roars. GorVit appeared, straight down the thoroughfare, flanked by several gunners. The tangoga boss and his minions chased after the chariots racing toward the palace.

Nefer reined in and leapt from the chariot before it stopped. "This way," she said and ascended the front steps to the entry foyer.

"GorVit's almost here," Wa said, looking back through the door.

"We must go to the black gate," Grizz said. "It's our only hope."

"Then there is no hope," Nefer said.

"We must try," Grizz said. "Come."

Nefer didn't argue, though it may have been the shrieks of GorVit and his gunners that convinced her to move.

"I'll see if I can slow them down," Wa said. He darted down a side passage.

Em cried out. "Wa! Come back!" She started to follow, but an unmistakable clattering sounded on the steps just outside.

"Quick!" Grizz said. "To the gardens."

Danny grabbed his sister's hand and dragged her along. "We can't fight GorVit."

Em stumbled after him. Tears streamed down her cheeks. Danny didn't know what Wa could do, but his friend had made his decision.

A crash sounded from a high window in the palace. Shrieks answered it.

"It's working," Danny said. "Wa's leading them upstairs."

"Let's not waste the chance," Grizz said. "To the black gate."

They followed Nefer through the private gardens and along the walkway to the gate. They stopped on the stone patio before the inscrutable door. Danny turned to face Nefer. "Okay, dear wife. Time to fulfill your end of the deal."

Nefer stared at him blankly.

"Tell me how to get in."

She burst out laughing and turned away. "You fool."

He grabbed her arm and spun her back around. "Tell me. How do we get in?"

Her laughter cut off, replaced with a humorless smile. "You have to die."

The statement was so unexpected he couldn't process it. "Huh?"

"The only way in is to die." She stared at him until he got it.

And when he did, he swore and slapped his forehead. "That's where they resurrect you, isn't it?"

Grizz growled and covered his ears, realizing their last hope had vanished. His eyes snapped to the door, and he collected himself with a deep breath. He approached the gate, arms held wide. "*Electonus! Yolistar! Effelvur!*"

Danny recognized the Footese words for *activate*, *commence*, and *feces*. Grizz was guessing, saying anything that might cause the gate to open.

An explosion sounded from the palace, and a column of smoke rose high overhead from somewhere in the city. Footsteps pounded on the path behind them. Danny stepped in front of Nefer and clenched his fists, ready to fight.

Wa burst into view, panting and laughing. A gash in one leg bled freely, but he didn't seem to notice. "I've got them tearing the palace apart, and I think I got one of them with a little booby trap."

Em rushed to Wa and hugged him. She pressed her face into his shoulder, swore at him, and berated him for risking his life.

Danny looked up at the dark windows in the cliff face. "We have to climb, Wa. Are you up for it?"

"Let's go," Wa said. He disengaged from Em and started up the vines.

"The tangoga will shoot you," Nefer warned.

"SulKit and his tangoga are probably all dead," Danny said. He watched the path Wa chose and started climbing after.

"Get down from there, Danny," Em said. "Let Wa go."

She shouted something else, but he ignored her. A plan formed as he ascended. He reasoned that SulKit kept tangeg bodies inside the complex, probably growing in whatever kind of vat they used to make new iterations of Nefer. It made perfect sense, since they had to have a source of tangeg in order to make replacement tangoga.

From that, it followed logically that there was an implant lab, which is what Danny needed.

He continued up, keeping his focus on the vines. Sweat poured from his forehead, and his hands burned. He made the mistake of looking down and his head swam. He had to stop and pull himself tight against the cliff and wait for the vertigo to pass. Not trusting his grip, he wound the vine around one wrist.

"Come on, you're almost there," Wa said from above. His head poked out from a ledge. Wa waved, beckoning Danny to climb. "There's a window–"

A cry rose from below. It sounded like Nefer's voice. A bit of vine exploded next to Danny, startling him so badly he slipped. Only the vine around his wrist saved him. He looked down to see SulKit standing below, rifle pointed straight at him. Kit had gotten one shot off and was about to loose another.

Grizz stepped behind the tangoga and placed his hands on both heads. SulKit collapsed in a heap, calmed into unconsciousness.

Danny didn't pause to enjoy his relief. Adrenaline fueled him as he pulled himself up the vine. He threw his leg over the ledge and felt Wa's hands drag him to safety beneath a wide-open window in the cliff face.

They stood on a balcony, which gave them a panoramic view of the city. Horgodons ran amok in the streets, toppling every statue and temple. Great orange gouts of flame shot skyward as the meezu apartments burned.

Below, the tiny figures of Nefer, Em, and Grizz stared up at him. Danny scanned the gardens for signs of pursuit but didn't see anything. Smoke billowed from the palace.

He followed Wa through the window and into an empty room.

Danny accessed his implant, hoping to find some layout, some plan for this type of facility. If the Asht created the tangoga to be their servants, the tangoga had to have a wealth of data about Asht architecture. He didn't find anything for the specific facility he was in, but there were some generic plans. Interestingly, they matched up with bigfoot settlements well.

"There's got to be a tangoga area in here someplace," he told Wa and explained how the tangoga resurrected Nefertiti every time she died. "I think we should head to the lowest levels."

They went through the door and continued along the corridor until they found an elevator. "*Hoffhar*," Danny said.

The door slid open.

"I thought this was an Asht facility," Wa said as they stepped in. "Why would Footese work to open the door?"

"Because the Asht language *is* Footese. Actually, it's the other way around." He told the elevator to go down.

The two boys' breaths came in loud gasps as they waited. "Come on, come on," Danny said. He worried GorVit and his gunners would find the gate before Danny could open it. Grizz, Em, and Nefer would be helpless against them.

The elevator stopped, the door slid open, and Danny stepped through into darkness.

32

THE SPHERE OF HER AWARENESS

Breyona took a long drink from her water bottle and wiped her mouth on her sleeve. They stood in a large chamber with a plinth at one end. The bones of a bigfoot lay to one side.

"I'm guessing that's our old friend Choolenama," she said, remembering Luon's story of the bigfoot who disappeared with the Spheroid thousands of years before. "And that makes this the Spheroid." A thin stalk protruded from the Spheroid, topped with a glowing bulb that projected an image against a far wall.

"It's a jungle," she said. Trees swayed under a strange, violet sky.

Tog clicked toward the wall, sniffing the air. The next thing Breyona knew he had walked straight into the projection.

He looked back. "It's a portal."

Breyona hoisted her pack and stepped forward, approaching the portal slowly. She reached out and touched . . . nothing. She stepped through. "This is amazing. I thought teleportation had to have a platform on both ends."

Tog tilted his head from side to side, the tangoga equivalent of a shrug. "Don't ask me. Tangoga aren't allowed to know anything about teleportation."

Stray weeds grew in patches in an otherwise bare stretch of rocky ground beyond the portal. If she was to go any farther, she would have to go into the thick of the jungle. She noticed a few bent plants, some snapped in half. On a thorny stalk, a tuft of black fur waved like a flag.

"Grizz went this way," she said and stepped into the jungle.

The bigfoot's path took her to the edge of a cliff overlooking a magnificent valley. She saw a city to her left. Smoke obscured most of it, but the tip of some golden monument flashed in the sun. The path led along the ledge, eventually coming to the top of a rough stair carved directly into the cliff face. The narrow path switched back and wound out of view, disappearing into the jungle far below. She took a moment to find her center of calm and started down.

Tog took the steps with no concern whatsoever, but he was a more stable platform, having four legs. They descended, making occasional stops for Breyona to rest and drink. As they approached the base of the cliff, they descended into dense jungle. The pathway was clear though, and soon they came out onto a grassy plain.

Ahead lay an area of trampled grass. Gouges in the ground exposed turned up black dirt. It looked like a large herd of heavy animals had passed recently.

Breyona exchanged a glance with Tog, who scanned across the valley, neck extended as high as it would go. A flash of his feathers showed his trepidation. His head swung to and fro as he tried to see everywhere at once. With a pang of pity, Breyona realized he had once had Yip to help keep watch.

A terrible howl sounded in the jungle and echoed from the cliffs. Tog's head snapped down. "We should distance ourselves from the source of that sound," he said, as though reading from a wilderness survival guide.

The only choice was to go forward.

As they walked along the beaten trail, more howls came from the jungle. Breyona took a few deep breaths and observed her fear, acknowledged it, and set it aside. There was no point worrying over things she–

A sharp crack came from the trees. She spun.

"Uh oh."

The creature that stepped from the jungle was the most massive bigfoot she'd ever seen, standing over twice as high. Tog let out an unintelligible shriek, followed by a string of Footese curses.

Another giant emerged, followed by two more.

The closest stood tall, searching the plain with squinted eyes. In seconds, it locked its gaze on Breyona and Tog. It bellowed and loped toward her, waving to its companions. The other three stomped into the open and circled around.

A rustling off to her left told of Tog's flight through the grass. She followed, driving her legs as hard as she could.

Ground shaking thumps pursued her as the incredible weight of the creatures pounded down. Realizing she had no chance to outrun the monsters, she collapsed and instinctively curled into a ball. She covered her head, sure she was about to be squished by a massive foot.

A moment passed. Then another. She peeked up and found the giant standing right over her. Its eyes bore into hers, as wide and green as any bigfoot's. It whacked the shaft of its club in its palm. Without thought, Breyona leapt up and threw herself at the monster's leg. It grunted in surprise and tried to backpedal, but its movements were slow. She dug her fingers into its fur and delivered a dose of calm.

The creature stumbled wildly, shaking Breyona loose. She fell and landed on her back, wind blowing out of her lungs, and a hot pain shooting through her left leg.

She let out a cry so shrill she shocked herself. The tip of a narrow black spike stood out from the top of her thigh. Her trembling hands found where the shaft entered the back of her leg. If she had landed a little differently, it might have thrust into her back. Another spike stuck up from the turf half a meter to her left. It could have gone in her skull.

The giant stumbled side to side, fighting the numbness she had poured into it. It swung its club toward her.

Like a stone dropped in a pond, Breyona slipped into the center of calm. Peace surrounded her like a force field, though fear and agony raged just above the surface.

Without knowing how she did it, she pushed and widened her sphere of peace until it encompassed the giant. She marveled as one infinitesimal instant of time stretched and inflated. Her mind slid over the rough wooden club that sought to destroy her; she felt the roughness of the bark and the wetness of its pithy center. Her consciousness penetrated the beast's hand, arm, and shoulder. She worked her way to its brain and doused it with utter calm.

The club continued in its inexorable trajectory toward her head. No amount of calm could fight its inertia. Breyona relaxed her own body and flopped back, trying to draw herself into the ground.

The club fell hard to her left, the wind of it blowing her hair across her face. The ground shook, jarring the spike in her leg. The pain nearly broke her peace.

Seconds inflated again. She was aware of the light breeze that swept across the plain, stirring the grass. Sun glanced from the tip of the spike in her leg, glared off drops of blood that trickled from it. Behind her, heavy steps of more giants concussed the ground. She reached out to the creatures, spreading the sphere of her awareness to encompass them. Grunts, deep and rough, like a slowed down recording, sounded from somewhere behind her, followed by great thumps and moans as the weight of three more giants crashed to the ground.

With a cry, she lifted herself up. The spike slid out of the wound. And this time the bubble of peace did shatter, and in its place was nothing but her own scream.

She rolled away, exposing a horrific black thorn at least a foot tall jutting up from a black dome embedded in the soil.

Blood poured freely from her wounded leg and soaked her jeans. The giants stirred in the grass.

"Tog?" she shouted. "Where are you?"

A honking shriek replied.

"Come here."

Tog shuffled forward, head held low. His eyes caught sight of her wound. "Can you walk?"

"No."

The first giant sat up and shook its head. Its eyes darted around, plainly confused. Breyona managed to regain a measure of her calm.

"Help me up."

Tog offered a metal claw and lifted her to her feet. The wounded leg gave way immediately, and Tog had to steady her.

The giant stared dumbly at her and Tog.

Breyona held a hand out. "*Donovthosameezu.*"

The giant grunted.

"We're friendly," Breyona said, pointing first to herself then to Tog. "No more fighting."

It cocked its head and blinked its eyes, then leaned forward to sniff the air around Breyona and Tog. In a voice like tumbling rocks, it said something. The words didn't sound like Footese. It snatched up the club and raised it.

Reflex kicked in, and Breyona smothered the creature with a sphere of calm. Both the giant and Tog fell over, unconscious. Without Tog's support she, too, fell, sharp jabs ripping at her leg.

"Dammit."

But this time she kept the sphere in place. She analyzed it, felt it, stretched it out and in again. Control came easier this time, like muscle memory, though she still didn't know how it worked. She shrank the sphere until it encompassed only her own mind. Anything smaller and she knew it would pop away like a soap bubble.

She spread it out again, this time seeking to bend it in order to keep Tog out of its influence, but it didn't work. He'd no sooner raised his head and squawked than she hit him with it by mistake. He flopped over.

"Sorry."

She brought the sphere in again and waited for Tog to regain his feet.

"Go to the jungle and bring back a vine for a tourniquet."

Without a word, Tog sprinted away, though he zigged and zagged drunkenly.

Breyona maintained a wide, but low-intensity calming sphere around her. By the time Tog returned, she had four giants sitting around her, calmly stripping stalks of wrist-thick weeds and eating the soft innards. She tried a bite and found it sweet and mushy, almost like a banana.

Tog helped her tighten the vine around her leg and tie it off. He cut the long remainder away with one of his arm blades.

"Now what?" he asked.

"We go to the city."

"Can you walk now?"

She looked at the lead giant. "No, but I think I've got a ride."

Tog helped her hobble close to the giant, who looked up with placid eyes. It whuffed a greeting, or maybe a weak warning.

She stretched out a hand and stroked its arm. "I never thought you were a bad monster," she said. "You just needed a little love."

At her touch, the giant lowered its head toward hers. For a second she thought he was going to try to bite her in half, but he kept lowering it until his eyes were beneath hers, a clear gesture of submission.

She patted and rubbed his nose, which was as warm and soft as a horse's. "Would you carry me?" she asked.

The giant straightened and blinked.

"Carry me," she said again, pretending to pick something up and hold it in her arms. She pointed to the city and rocked her arms. "Carry me to the city."

The giant grunted and scratched an ear.

She repeated her mime four more times before the giant shot to its feet and mimicked her.

"Yes! Yes! Carry me." She held her arms up, like a toddler asking to be carried. Tog kept a steadying claw on her back.

The giant's hands cupped her, ever so gently, as if picking up a baby bird, then lifted her into his arms. He started toward the city, and the other three jumped up to trail after. Tog sped out front, careful to stay out from under their crushing feet.

The grass swept by below Breyona, and she snuggled deep into the soft but somewhat stinky fur of her escort.

33

DEESHA, DEESHA, DEESHA

Danny and Wa stepped off the elevator, took a hard right, and ran down the dark hall. Dim bulbs spaced every ten meters along the wall gave just enough illumination for Danny to navigate by.

"So how are we going to open the gate?" Wa asked.

"I need to get the code first. This is it." He turned into a room on his right; a steel table stood in the middle. He spotted the cabinet he knew would be there and flung open the door. Inside stood a familiar apparatus on wheels.

He dragged it out and shoved it toward the table. "There should be download spheres around here somewhere."

"I think I found them," Wa said. He stood by a glass cylinder filled with silver balls. "That, or it's a bingo machine."

While rolling the apparatus to the table, Danny asked the cylinder for a ball. Seconds later, one rolled out of a hole at the bottom, ran down a short track, and came to rest on a little black stand. "Toss it over, Wa."

Danny caught the ball and slipped it into the apparatus. "I need you to put it in position." He jumped onto the steel table and waited for Wa to wheel the apparatus into the place over his face.

"*Yolistar*," he said. The machine's steel fingers started to spin and lower toward his face.

"Why are you doing this?" Wa asked.

"It's a standard tangoga download. It should contain everything about this complex."

Danny closed his eyes and prepared himself. He felt pressure in his nostrils, in his ears, and at the corners of his eyes. He heard Wa swearing, but he couldn't pay attention to it because the flashes started in his brain, like twenty movies playing at once.

And then it was over. He opened his eyes. "I've got it."

"Got what?" Wa demanded.

"The unlock phrase for the black gate."

They raced to the elevator, and Danny gave a command for the main floor. The doors opened a moment later, and they piled out.

Danny scanned his implant and the new download information. And there it was, the layout of the entire complex. "This way," he said and raced forward.

They ran past side passages and rooms. Danny ducked into one and gave a curt command, causing a bank of cabinet doors to slide open, reveals racks of sizzleguns. He tossed one to Wa and took one for himself.

"The gate's not far," he said and headed the opposite way. His footfalls echoed hollowly in the eerily abandoned halls.

They came to a great room filled with statuary. A railing in the center overlooked a large atrium below. They spotted stairs leading down.

"Down there," Danny said. "It's the entry foyer."

They clambered down the steps and crossed the atrium to the black gate.

"Wait!" Wa said. "How do I fire this thing?"

"Say '*deesha*.'"

Danny stood before the gate, sizzlegun at the ready. The unlock command appeared before his eyes. "*Funeshen elecfun reffernum hoffhar.*"

A hiss of pressurized air came from the door, followed by clanks, clatters, and a low hum. The door slowly slid into a pocket in the bedrock.

Sunlight glared through, blinding him. He held up a hand to block it. Grizz, Nefer, and Em stood motionless, facing away from him. Beyond were a row of tangoga gunners, a horgodon, and GorVit.

Grizz spun. "Close the door. Don't let–"

But Danny rushed forward. "Get down!"

Em and Grizz dropped, but Nefer turned, confused by the command. Em grabbed a handful of the queen's gown and yanked her to the ground.

"*Deesha, deesha, deesha,*" Danny said. The sizzleshots slammed into GorVit and his gunners, stunning their heads. Next to Danny, Wa fired over and over, "*Deesha, deesha, deesha, deesha.*" His sizzleshots struck the horgodon again and again. It stumbled back, dazed and confused.

"Get in!" Danny called.

Grizz, Em, and Nefer scampered through the doorway on hands and knees. Wa kept up the sizzlefire, but the horgodon would not fall. Danny commanded the door to close. For a moment, nothing happened except for more hissing and clanks. Then with painful slowness, the heavy door started to close, pinching off the sunlight.

The horgodon stumbled toward the door, and Danny added his sizzleshots to Wa's. The great beast roared, fell forward, and with one last effort lunged at the shrinking opening. Its head and shoulders shot through, blocking the door, which ground to a stop as it squeezed against the beast's massive ribcage. The horgodon howled in pain and pounded a fist on the floor. The other arm lay pinned against the doorjamb.

Danny backed away as the horgodon struggled. Its great wide eyes locked on Nefer, and it lashed out with its arm, thick as a tree trunk. The blow caught the queen square in the chest and sent her flying across the smooth, black floor. She landed hard and did not rise.

The door thumped and pulsed, still trying to close. A horrific crack came from the horgodon's body as ribs snapped. It shrieked, long and piercing, before cutting off with a final, weak exhale. Trickles of blood ran from its nose, and its eyes fell shut.

A shriek and clatter came from beyond the door. Above the dead horgodon sunlight beamed through.

Danny went to Nefer. Though unconscious, she still breathed. Purple bruises marred one side of her face, and one eye had already swollen shut. "Grizz, can you carry her? We've got to run," he said. "The teleportation hub is that way." He pointed down a passage.

"No," Grizz said as he got to his feet. "We must secure the weapon before GorVit gets it."

Danny scanned his implant and the new download. While there was no specific record of a weapon, he knew where it would be. An entire level of the facility served as an archive.

"It's on a lower level," he said. "Take Nefer to the teleportation hub. I'll go after the weapon."

Grizz nodded and scooped up Nefer. Danny started for the elevator.

Wa followed. "I'm coming with."

"Me too," Em said.

Gouts of blood, fur, and flesh blasted from the dead horgodon. A tangoga leapt through the newly widened gap at the door. It fired wildly, and Em dropped to the ground. For a moment, Danny thought she'd been hit, but then she moved, crawling away from the gunner and toward Grizz.

"Go with Grizz," Danny said. "This'll only take a few minutes."

Em looked like she was going to argue, but the gunner swung its weapons toward her. Only a sizzleshot from Wa stopped it from shooting her dead. The tangoga slumped back, stunned, though it didn't stop firing. Bullets flew across the foyer in random directions.

Em darted for cover in the far passage. Grizz followed with Nefer in his arms.

Danny and Wa jumped into the relative safety of the elevator, and Danny gave the command to go down.

THAT WHICH IS ABHORRENT

"What kind of bulbs are these?" Wa asked as they stepped from the elevator and into the dim archive. "One watt?"

The ceiling lights barely glowed, leaving most of the room in shadow. A white banner with black Footese characters on it hung over the room. Loosely interpreted it read, "The acquisition and preservation of knowledge is the first virtue. Let nothing learned be lost."

Danny understood from the implant that many of the extremely ancient items here were sensitive to light. Shelf after shelf held strange objects: bowls, bones, boxes, jars of preserved animal specimens. Most things he didn't recognize. He searched his implant and cursed. The tangoga didn't know what any of this stuff was, either.

"What am I looking for?" Wa asked as they ran down the aisles of shelving.

"I don't know."

They hadn't gotten far when they heard shrieks behind them.

"GorVit," Danny said. He looked up and down the aisle at a complete loss. "It could be anything."

"What's that say?" Wa pointed to another sign hanging over the entrance to a side room.

"'For the preservation of that which is abhorrent.' Good job, Wa. That's gotta be it."

The room was small, circular, and dark. In the center, a tiny sphere sat on a low stand. A dusty glass case surrounded it.

"What is it with the Asht and spheres?" Wa asked.

Danny tried to lift the glass, but it wouldn't budge. He smashed the butt of his sizzlegun against it, and it shattered.

They heard sounds of GorVit and his gunners rummaging through the shelves in the main archive. Danny knew they were looking for an actual weapon, like a bomb or a gun. Even so, it wouldn't take long before they found him and Wa.

He reached for the sphere. "We'll have to find a way around GorVit. If we can get to the teleportation hub, he'll never get his claws on it."

The sphere didn't move. In fact, as soon as his hand touched it, his mind flooded with knowledge.

"A binding sphere," he said.

It didn't contain much, just a strange sequence of formulae, mathematical statements he didn't understand and didn't have time to ponder. He pulled on the sphere again, but even using both hands, he couldn't lift it.

"How can this be so heavy? Maybe it's attached to the stand."

"Let me try," Wa said. He tugged and pushed, but it didn't budge. In a fit of frustration, he swung his sizzlegun at it like a bat. The gun bounced off the sphere and flew from Wa's hands. He rubbed his forearms.

The shrieks grew louder. A clatter sounded just outside the room. Danny brought up his sizzlegun and nearly shot SulKit.

Danny's breath went out of him. "Oh my God," he said. "I

thought you were GorVit." He pointed at the sphere. "How do I get that thing off the stand? I need to take it out of here."

"You're not going anywhere," Sul said. The tangoga lifted a rifle to Kit's eyes and aimed it at Danny's head. Outside, squawks came more frequently and sounded more desperate.

"I'm not the enemy," Danny said. "GorVit is."

"According to you," Sul said. "But it's against procedure for anyone to be in these rooms."

"We've got to get out of here. GorVit will kill us all."

Sul didn't move.

"Look," Danny said, "the Asht didn't say to kill anyone who had the knowledge from this binding sphere, but to prevent access to it in the first place. You failed with us, but you can still keep GorVit from getting it."

Sul blinked at him, and Kit whispered something. Sul nodded, acknowledging Danny's point. He lowered the rifle.

"I'm going to leave," Danny said. "But you've got to fight GorVit off. I don't know what this information is. I don't know what it's for. But if the Asht worked so hard to keep it from every-one, GorVit must not get it."

"He will not," Sul said. He pulled a device from a belt beneath his armpack.

Danny recognized the detonator and he reached for it. "I have GorVit's code! I can end this right here!"

Sul pulled the detonator back, obviously shocked at the idea.

"Handing over the detonator is entirely against procedure. I would never, not even for an instant, consider doing such a thing."

"What's going on?" Wa demanded. He stood by the door, peering out. "Shouldn't we be getting out of here?"

Danny swore. "Sul won't let me use the detonator."

"Don't you think Gor changed his code by now anyway? I would have. Let's just go."

Danny took a step toward SulKit. "If you don't have GorVit's code, what use is the detonator?" But as soon as the words left his mouth, he realized what SulKit meant to do.

"At least try GorVit's code first," Danny said. He accessed his implant and read off the sequence. Sul's golden fingers clicked away on the detonator as he entered the code. Kit drew close to Sul, his whole neck trembling.

Wa pulled on Danny. "Come on."

Danny nodded a farewell to Sul and crept out of the room with Wa.

Danny wanted to take a different elevator, one that would bring him closer to the teleportation platform. But clatters and squawks from that direction stopped him.

"We've got to go back the way we came," he whispered. They skirted the edge of the archives, keeping low and peering down each aisle before sneaking to the next row.

Sul shouted out, "GorVit! I'm in here."

"What's he doing?" Wa hissed.

"He's luring GorVit in."

"But–"

"Shhh," Danny said, grabbing Wa's arm and pointing down the aisle.

They froze as a gunner passed the end of their row of shelves. Once it disappeared, they picked up speed and headed toward the elevator. Shrieks came from behind them.

"SulKit!" came Gor's voice. "Put it down!"

Several shrieks pierced the air, followed by a clattering of pointed feet on the stone floor. An explosion shook the room, knocking shelving sideways. Wa and Danny threw themselves to the ground, and Danny lost his grip on his sizzlegun. It slid under a row of shelves. Smoke poured down the aisles of the archive.

Wa lifted his head and tried to see through the black cloud. "Sul got him!"

"No," Danny said, surprised at the sadness that filled him.

Wa turned to Danny, obviously confused. "But the explosion . . ."

"Sul tried GorVit's code as soon as I gave it to him. It failed."

"But . . ."

"SulKit blew themselves up," Danny said.

"Oh my God."

Gor's voice called out in fury. "The boy was here. He has it in his head now. We *must* find him."

The clattering came fast. Danny and Wa sprinted for the elevator. Danny shouted for it to open. A tangoga gunner fired wildly, blinded by smoke. Bullets struck the wall over Danny's head. Danny and Wa threw themselves down.

"There he is," Gor said as he emerged from the swirling black cloud. He clattered forward, bladed arms waving. Wa crawled away and disappeared into the shadows.

Danny pushed himself back on his hands and tried to get away as GorVit rose over him, blades raised high. Steel claws grasped Danny's shoulders and lifted him in the air.

Danny kicked out and landed a solid blow on Gor's torso, hard enough that Vit squawked. A second later, one of GorVit's blades pressed against Danny's neck.

Danny went limp. If he moved at all, the knife would draw blood.

"If it's in his head," Vit said, "it will be simple enough to extract, especially since he's already been implanted."

Gor summoned his gunners, but only one came into view. One of its heads hung unconscious, mangled and dangling. Black wires jutted from the remains of its right arm. It stumbled drunkenly and waved its head side to side, navigating by sound rather than sight.

"Is that all you've got left?" Danny said.

"Those idiots SulKit blew themselves to *chulk* and took my gunners with them. But no matter. What I want is in your head. Soon it will be in mine."

"And mine," Vit said.

"Shut up, Vit," Gor barked. He carried Danny toward the elevator. "Let's take him to the implant lab."

Wa rolled from the shadows. He had found Danny's sizzlegun.

"*Deesha, deesha.*" Sizzleshots slammed into Gor's head and then Vit's. GorVit fell and dropped Danny hard onto the stone floor. Danny pulled himself free of GorVit's claws and backed into the elevator.

Wa leaned into a sprint to follow. "Let's get out of here," he shouted.

The injured gunner snapped its head around at the sound of Wa's voice and footfalls. It lifted the gun in its remaining claw and fired. Bullets tracked Wa's steps.

Wa screamed and fell forward, arms out, sizzlegun flying. The gunner stumbled forward, obviously disoriented but drawn to the sound of the clattering sizzlegun.

Danny darted forward, skirting GorVit, and snatched up the sizzlegun. He backpedaled as the gunner approached and fired pointblank into its face. It fell to the floor.

Wa moaned and lifted his head. Danny let out a breath, relieved his friend still lived. He stooped to help Wa wrap an arm around his shoulder. Together they stumbled for the elevator.

35

A CAT AMONG A HERD OF ELEPHANTS

"I said what is your name?" Breyona asked again.

The giant carrying her didn't respond. She knew it had a name of some sort because one of the other two giants escorting her had gotten its attention with a relatively articulate grunt. It might have been the giant equivalent of, "hey you," but Breyona didn't think so.

"Fine," she said and folded her arms. "I'm calling you Tiny until you come up with something better." She lay back into Tiny's arms but couldn't really enjoy the lulling rise and fall of his steps. Tendrils of smoke crawled up to the sky and hung in a heavy, black cloud over the city. She hoped Danny wasn't there, despite the sickening certainty in her gut that he was.

To distract herself, she studied the valley. From her perch in Tiny's arms, she could easily see over the grassy plain, which stretched to a ribbon of water running through the center of the valley. Light from the massive, orange sun glanced off its ripples, which blurred in the hot and humid air.

Breyona shoed away another of the reptilian birds swarming

them. They skimmed all around, drawn to the feast of insects kicked up by the giants' steps. Waves of blue-green grasshoppers, pencil thin and as long as her forearm, boinged like flying fish. Tiny occasionally snatched them out of the air and popped them into his mouth.

Tog spidered farther ahead, making a path through the grass, occasionally throwing back glances and letting out low squawks. He hadn't been very enthusiastic about Breyona's decision to bring the giant bigfeet along. But with the wound in her leg, she was in no condition to walk. She tugged at the tourniquet and wondered if Tog had made it too tight. The wound didn't bleed any more, but her whole leg ached. It felt like it was being crushed in a vice.

The smell of smoke brought her gaze back to the city. She remembered her grandmother's old saying. *A worrier is a fool pretending to be wise.* Breyona hadn't understood it then, but it resonated with her at the moment.

She didn't think she was a fool, though. Even her grandmother would have to admit that Danny was likely in danger. And never mind the mess Shiv had made back on Earth.

As she got closer, she saw bonfires all around the city. Giant bigfeet dragged bodies of other giants and threw them on the flames. As Breyona and her companions approached, Tiny howled and shook his club in the air. The three closest giants answered with howls, which drew the attention of those farther off. In moments, several dozen stood before Breyona and her guards. Tog circled to cower somewhere behind Tiny.

Breyona sensed a fight brewing, so she spread out a gentle wave of calm.

"Hello," she said.

One giant, a good deal taller and thicker than the others, with charcoal fur and wearing ragged skins across one shoulder, stepped forward and reached out a long, fat finger to touch her. Tiny knocked the hand away and swung his club with braining force.

The blow connected with a crunch, sending the beast sideways into the trampled grass.

"No!" Breyona said. "I won't have any fighting." She closed her eyes and deepened the calm, and without thinking about how she did it, added a tinge of fear.

When she opened her eyes, she found all the giants crouching low. Some had their hands over their ears. Others twisted their bodies away, lifting arms above their heads to ward off invisible blows.

Perhaps she'd sent a bit more than a tinge.

She released it, immediately feeling sorry about her actions. But at least it got the result she wanted. She would not tolerate violence. While she was around, people—or at least giant bigfeet—were going to behave themselves.

She pointed to the gate. "Let's go there." Tiny started forward, and the others trailed after.

Breyona pitied Tog, who must have felt like a cat among a herd of elephants. He darted ahead to keep from being trampled.

The city gate hung askew. Breyona wondered at the force that had left it dangling from one hinge. She didn't think even the giants had that much strength. Once through the main wall, she found more giant bigfeet lounging around.

The surrounding districts looked like a tornado had swept through them. A fiery tornado. Areas that had obviously once been parks and gardens lay stripped to bare soil. The charred wrecks of wooden buildings leaned precariously next to tangled piles of rubble. Nearby, a stone roof lay flat on the ground, surrounded by a sprawl of stone pillars resting atop each other like a fallen domino chain.

The city wall blocked the breeze, locking in the heat and smell. Breyona covered her nose with her sleeve to block the over-whelming stench of burnt fur, dung, and smoke.

Tiny snuffled and grunted. Breyona wasn't sure whether it was at the smell or because another group of giants approached. This time she didn't wait for a confrontation, she pulsed the newcomers with fear and watched them sink to their knees. She had Tiny carry her close to them.

"While I am here, there will be no violence." She knew they didn't understand her words, but she thought they got her meaning because they bobbed their heads low. To reinforce their state, she sent a flash of goodwill and affection to them.

She realized she'd overdone it when four of them crawled forward and prostrated themselves before her. Even her guards eyed her with adoration. Breyona glanced up at Tiny but didn't find the same look there. Maybe being this close to her had sheltered him from it, like standing in the eye of a storm.

Breyona tried to even out the feelings in the crowd with a boost of confidence and cheer. Those who lay on their bellies jumped up and clasped each other's arms, laughing in surprisingly high-pitched hyena chuckles.

"Are you quite finished?" Tog asked.

She could have sworn Tog smiled, if tangoga were capable of such an expression. His neck stood erect and his feathers vibrated a nearly permanent blue. "I think I prefer being knocked unconscious to these emotional gyrations you're putting me through."

"Sorry." She dropped all of her sendings and watched the surrounding giants slump, worn out.

Tog's feathers settled back to their normal gray. "Let's get away from this smell. I suspect Danny and the others went there." He pointed a bladed arm up a wide thoroughfare leading to a palace in the distance. Breyona urged Tiny ahead, and they left behind the worst of the smells.

Judging from the size of the structures, Breyona knew that the city wasn't intended for these brutish giants. They passed a temple, and she caught her breath. Standing to either side of the entrance stood statues as tall as Tiny. But in the form of a beautiful human woman, unmistakably Egyptian.

"It can't be," she said, craning to see past Tiny's massive shoulders as he passed them. "I've seen her before. In a book."

The thoroughfare ended in a broad plaza in front of the palace. Walls of hewn stone blocks stood mostly intact, though charred black. Areas of brightly colored friezes showed through in spots, hinting at the structure's lost magnificence.

Shallow steps led up to an entryway guarded by black statues of giant bigfeet. The doorway was nearly too low for Tiny, who wrapped her in his arms like a football before stooping to go through.

They emerged into what would surely have been a grand entrance hall. Statuary lay around the perimeter, bodies fractured; decapitated heads stared blankly into the sky. Soot caked the floor, the walls, and the half-burned timbers littering the floor. Tiny stepped forward, sending up swirls of ash that filled the air with salt and pepper snowflakes.

A tangoga stood in the center of the room, its white cape stark against the destruction all around. The fabric draped along the tangoga's back and swept to the floor behind its four pointed legs. It held its golden claws clenched in tight fists. The eyes of its two heads stared at her, unblinking. The right head leaned almost imperceptibly closer to the left and whispered something. The left head snapped a rebuke, which caused the right head to lower an inch. The tangoga took a step back.

"Hello," Breyona said. "Is Danny here?"

The tangoga didn't respond.

"Who are you?" she asked, sending out a touch of calm. They didn't answer.

Tog spoke to them in Footese.

The white-robed tangoga didn't respond, but its left head turned by a degree to glance at him.

Tog stepped forward and spoke again.

A response came this time, hot and loud. Tog shrank back, head nearly to the floor.

Reflexively, Breyona flashed them with peace and goodwill.

The tangoga's demeanor changed instantly. The necks relaxed and the heads swayed. It spoke to Tog, who turned to Breyona and interpreted.

"This is JieBik. Jie welcomes the great NeferNeferNefer and apologizes for the state of the city. He just arrived from the Verfes outpost to replace the former primary here, a tangoga called SulKit."

"Who is NeferNeferNefer?"

Tog relayed the question.

Jie tilted his head and studied Breyona for a moment before responding.

Tog translated. "If you don't know who you are, we probably should restore from the last save." Tog stopped, feathers pulsing to teal for a second.

A rapid-fire exchange in Footese caused Tog's eyes to widen more than usual. Finally he turned to Breyona. "Jie insists that you are Nefertiti, some ancient queen that's been living here for thousands of years."

Hearing the name took Breyona's breath away. She had recognized Nefertiti's face from the statues in the city, but she hadn't really believed the long-dead queen had been here. "Tell them I'm not Nefertiti."

"I already did. Jie thinks your brain is corrupted. . . . And that I'm a worthless single-head."

"Tell them my name is Breyona, and I'm looking for my friends. What happened to them? Does he know where they are?"

Again, the two tangoga conferred; this time it ended with a frustrated squawk from Tog.

"Jie says the meezu insist that you are Nefertiti. He says if you don't remember, then the download must have become corrupted. He suggests they restore from the previous save. He's quite impatient to proceed. He says he has other things to do, like getting the horgodons out of the city."

"I have no idea what he's talking about."

"I think the horgodons are these things." Tog pointed at Tiny.

"Put me down, Tiny." She motioned to the floor, and the beast gently lowered her to her feet. Tog swept forward to offer a supporting claw. "Ask where Danny is. That's all I want to know."

Tog relayed her question but apparently wasn't satisfied with the answer. He continued to make the same sounds over and over, showing increasing anxiety with each of Jie's responses. His knife arms started to wave erratically. Between Tog and JieBik, three heads spoke all at once. Breyona started to think Shiv was right about getting the implant, if just to understand Footese.

Tog broke off and turned to her. "Danny, Em, Wa, and Grizz were all here at the time of the attack, but they escaped into a restricted area. But–"

"Let's go find them!"

"The area is off limits. We are not allowed to go there. But there's something–"

"Restricted? You've got to be kidding. The tangoga don't have to go in. Just have them show us where it is."

"It's against procedure," Tog said.

"That's stupid. Tell them . . ." Breyona felt the room spin.

She was on her back looking up at the sky. Tog's head came into view and gazed down at her. He spoke to JieBik, who also leaned in to inspect her.

"JieBik believes you've lost too much blood. He's called for a meezu to assist."

"A what–?"

A normal-sized bigfoot appeared and lifted her. Tiny howled, so she sent out calm and the room fell silent. She blinked, trying to clear the dark edges of her vision.

At the edge of consciousness, she heard Tog speaking Footese. He sounded so urgent, so upset she wanted to help him, send him some calm. But she could barely keep her own center of calm, just enough to hold the pain in her leg at bay.

Time passed in flashes of sensation. First came a chill across her skin as she was laid naked on a bare metal surface. Then came a sharp, chemical smell, followed by a pressure around her wounded leg. She felt herself falling, twisting, weightless. She couldn't move, couldn't swim for the blurry surface of consciousness just out of reach.

An explosion of pain blasted away the last vestiges of her sheltering peace. Electric shocks wove into her brain. Pressure built, threatening to break her skull open from within. She wanted nothing more than the relief that eruption would bring. Death. Oblivion.

Something snapped. Like a guitar string tightened a quarter-turn too far. The pain washed out, leaving behind nothing but a barren plain of awareness.

Breath followed breath. Heartbeat followed heartbeat.

And all was silent.

36

A BOY FOR A BOY

Danny staggered down the hall, heart racing, breath coming in ragged gulps. He carried almost all of Wa's weight.

"Keep your eyes open, Wa."

His friend gasped and mumbled unintelligibly. Danny propped Wa against a wall and lifted his friend's bloody shirt. A pencil-thin bullet hole puckered the skin just under his right shoulder blade. Blood welled from it, dark and red.

Danny pounded his fist against the wall in frustration. Gritting his teeth, he picked Wa up and shuffled toward the teleportation hub down the hallway.

A shriek sounded ahead, and Danny swore. It had to be one of GorVit's gunners. Probably sent after Em and Grizz. Danny slowed, at a loss for what to do. He'd dropped his sizzlegun back in the elevator, finding it too hard to hold onto Wa and the weapon at the same time.

The anger in his heart propelled him forward. If a gunner lay ahead, he'd find a way around, or he'd find a way through.

He turned a corner and nearly ran into a meezu priest. Beyond it stood a gunner surrounded by dead meezu. The tangoga limped slightly, and Danny saw one of its spindly legs had split just above the pointed end.

The priest held up a hand to keep Danny back. He crouched into a *deshuk* form. His white robes billowed as he darted forward. The ceremonial staff in his hands became a weapon as he twirled it over his head.

The tangoga tried to dance back, but the staff cracked into the side of one of its heads. The head wobbled for a moment then fell toward the ground. The other head shrieked. The tangoga's claws ripped the staff from the priest's hands. With a loud pop, it snapped it in half.

The priest ducked low, spun, and kicked the tangoga's injured leg. He rolled in, grabbed the tangoga by the neck, and twisted. The two creatures collapsed into a ball of fur, white robes, steel claws, and sharp, pointed legs.

The tangoga gave a final shriek before falling still. The meezu priest struggled wearily to his feet, panting. "My king," he said, "do you know where the queen is?"

"Straight ahead, I hope. At the teleportation platform."

The meezu priest looked at him blankly, clearly not under-standing what Danny referred to.

"Straight," Danny said, commanding the priest to move.

It blinked then gave a quick bow. Danny passed the dead tangoga and followed the priest through more hallways, eventually coming to a wide, circular room that Danny immediately recog-nized as a teleportation hub, just like the one in Antarctica.

What he discovered there made him gasp in horror.

GorVit stood between Danny and the platform, facing Grizz and Em. Grizz was in the process of setting Nefer's unconscious form on the floor. His wide, green eyes never left GorVit, who held a gunner's weapon in one claw. His bladed arms swished as he stalked toward the platform.

Danny cursed, realizing GorVit had taken the shortcut to the hub Danny had wanted to take. But since Grizz and Em still lived, GorVit must have just arrived.

Danny lowered Wa to the floor. Wa gave a little cry, though he didn't appear to be awake. There was nothing more Danny could do to help his friend. Not until he'd dealt with GorVit. The meezu priest started to creep toward the tangoga boss, but Danny waved him back. Danny had already seen too many meezu killed.

"Gor!" he called.

The tangoga turned, casually, as though he'd been waiting for Danny's arrival. Gor cackled and waved the gun at Danny. "I don't need you alive to get what I want from your head," he said. "In fact, all I need is your head." One of his blades made a slicing motion across Vit's neck.

Danny sidestepped, trying to lead GorVit away from the platform and from Wa. Gor was bluffing. Not about needing Danny's head, for that much was true. No. The gun was a bluff. It had to be empty, or he would have already killed Em and Grizz.

"I didn't get anything from the binding sphere," Danny said. "SulKit stopped me."

"Liar! The glass was smashed. I saw that much before those idiots blew themselves up."

Grizz silently moved toward GorVit. Vit spotted him, though, and gave Gor a warning shriek. The gun came around and Grizz froze, apparently not as positive it was empty as Danny was.

The priest edged to the left, staying close to the wall. Gor ignored the meezu entirely, though Vit did not. He swung his eyes from the priest and back to Grizz like a security camera.

"Get Em and Nefer out of here, Grizz."

His bigfoot friend seemed to want to say something but didn't want Gor to overhear. He made no effort to teleport away, either.

In a flash, Gor made his move. The sudden motion startled Danny because it wasn't toward him at all. The tangoga sprinted to Wa, scooped him up, and slung him over a steel arm.

"Wa!" Em screamed. She ran to the edge of the platform and started to swing down, but Grizz caught her and pulled her back up.

GorVit put the tip of a blade to Wa's spine. "Let's discuss a trade."

Like a falling man watching the ledge disappear above him, Danny felt hope slip away.

GorVit stepped forward and lifted Wa on his arm, the same way a man might show off a fish. "This pathetic creature," Gor said, "in exchange for you." The free blade pointed at Danny.

The meezu priest leapt forward. Gor spun, both blades poised over Wa's body. "Hold! Hold, or I'll gut him like a vopel!"

Em's screams echoed Danny's shouts. The priest froze.

"Move back," Danny ordered. He pointed to the platform. "See to the queen." The meezu bowed and sprinted to the platform, where he crouched to hover protectively over Nefer's body.

"Wa," Em cried, her voice choked with sobs. Tears poured down her cheeks as she strained in Grizz's hands. "Wa!"

Danny held up his hands and took a step toward GorVit. Then another.

"You can't, Danny," Grizz said, voice low.

Danny took another step.

"Danny!" Grizz shouted. The bite in his voice stopped Danny.

Folded over Gor's arm as he was, Wa's face hung just above the floor. Blood ran from his wound and down his neck to where it dripped from his nose.

"Gor must not get whatever terrible knowledge you've uncovered," Grizz said. "The Asht tried to keep it from the tangoga for a reason."

Danny's jaw trembled. With rage, with fear. With hate.

"Wa's dead, Danny," Grizz said.

Em moaned and covered her face. Sobs shook her body.

With a cry of frustration, Danny fled toward the platform. Grizz took his hand and hauled him up.

Gor shrieked. "Does a dead human body breathe?"

Vit swung his head low to peer at the side of Wa's face. "He still breathes."

"He's lying," Grizz said. "Teleport us away if you can."

Danny stared at Wa's limp body, trying to see any rise and fall of his breath. But Gor stood too far away. "You do it, Grizz."

"I've tried. The platform doesn't recognize any destinations I know."

"Does a dead body feel pain?" Gor mused. He pressed the point of a blade into Wa's back. The boy's arms flailed and he let out a moan.

"Oh my God!" Em shrieked, though it was half whisper. Her eyes flashed to Danny. "Do something."

"It doesn't matter," Grizz said. "You cannot let Gor–"

"Shut up!" Danny covered his ears and squatted. The room seemed to swirl around him as the reality of his choice sank in. "There's no way out of this," he said in disbelief.

Gor raged. "A simple trade! A boy for a boy!"

Behind him, Grizz uttered destination after destination, trying to find one the teleportation platform would recognize.

Em pulled at Grizz's leg. "No, no, no, no."

Danny scanned his implant and realized what he had to do. He dropped next to his sister and wrapped his arms around her. "Hold your breath."

Em pushed him away. "No!" She stood and staggered for the edge of the platform.

Danny caught her and pulled her back. She kicked and screamed. Her fingernails tore at his arms, drawing long, bloody scrapes across his skin.

"Hold your breath," Danny said again.

Gor shrieked and raised his knives high overhead. Eyes locked on Danny's, he drove the blades hard into Wa's back. Wa's legs kicked convulsively and then fell still.

Danny closed his eyes against an infinite flood of tears. "*Hothenshon!*"

Em screamed, a long, continuous wail, which cut off suddenly as the world turned blue.

37

A TERRIBLE, TERRIBLE THING

Danny's weight seemed to triple as he collapsed onto his back. The air went out of his lungs, and he struggled to inhale. Em slumped on top of him, wheezing, gasping, and sobbing. Her eyes went wide, and her hands went to her throat.

A strange, yellow sky arced above, and impossibly tall mountains, crowned in black, stood all around. Danny glanced at Grizz and the meezu priest who also struggled under the weight of this hell world. Danny inhaled, not caring about oxygen, only hoping the atmosphere would move his vocal chords. "*Vishenquia!*"

Again the world went blue, and his weight disappeared. They materialized moments later on Ig, the central planet of the bigfeet. Danny's weight returned, not as heavy as before, but still too much. He took a breath and enjoyed the sweet relief of breathable air. An enormous crescent moon filled half of the sky.

A quick scan of his implant gave him the serial number for Earth. The Ig teleportation hub he rested on did not know English, so spoke the words in Footese. They teleported again, this time home.

Tangoga and bigfeet stood around the periphery of the inter-planetary hub in Antarctica. Their eyes bugged and jaws dropped, surprised at the unexpected arrival of such a strange group.

The meezu priest looked around, confused and afraid. "Is this the afterlife?"

"We're on Earth," Grizz said, "Nefertiti's homeworld."

Em lay on her back, gasping and sobbing. She held her hands over her face as her body shook. At the sight of her grief, Danny could no longer hold back his own. He knelt next to her. "I'm so sorry. I'm so sorry. I'm so sorry." He took his sister's hand and pulled her into his arms. She clung to him. They huddled there, faces buried in each other's shoulders, the only two people on Earth who understood the other's pain.

"Aten be praised!" the meezu priest said. He fell to his knees and began uttering a long prayer.

"We must continue on to Undermountain," Grizz said. "Nefer needs medical attention, and we must report to the council."

Danny felt the bigfoot's hand on his head and expected a wash of calm. But none came. "Danny. Em. We need to go."

Grizz spoke a long string of numbers and then the command, "*Roodenosh.*"

The world went blue yet again, and moments later they arrived in a small room. A window looked into the teleportation atrium of Undermountain.

Em followed Danny out of the room, sniffling and wiping at her eyes. "We should go back for him."

"Someday," Danny said. He took some of the breaths Breyona had taught him, tried to clear his mind. He had business to take care of.

"We need to get Nefer to the infirmary," Danny said. He looked up at Grizz. "Quickly."

Grizz nodded, understanding Danny's point. He strode to a service closet, donned a backpack, and took Nefer from the priest.

A few long strides carried him to the central railing and he leapt over, plummeting down the central shaft toward Undermountain.

The priest roared in horror and ran after, nearly throwing himself over the railing too. He must have spotted the parachute then, for he barked in surprise. "Strange magic," he said. "Wondrous magic."

Danny and Em guided the meezu priest down a hallway to the tangoga service elevators, and they began their long descent to Undermountain.

Em leaned on Danny. Her tears still flowed, and she stared at nothing. Danny had never seen her look so terrible. "I'll take you to our old apartment, then I'll go to the temple. I need to talk to Shiv."

She didn't say anything for a long while. But when they got to the monorail, she looked at him with a fierce expression. "It's over now, isn't it?" she asked. "We can go home. Forget all of this."

"I hope so."

"I'm going to the temple with you. They need to know that Wa died because of them." Danny knew who she meant. The Strict. And he agreed with her. The bigfeet had brought the whole mess to Earth in the first place.

The meezu sat looking out the window during the monorail ride, mouth working but saying nothing. When they arrived at the Temple of the Strict, the priest asked where the Altar of Aten was, but Danny didn't even try to answer. He figured the bigfeet could explain themselves.

An acolyte stopped them as soon as they entered the Hall of Statues. He asked the meezu what his business was at the temple and why was he in the company of humans. The meezu looked at Danny, obviously out of his depth.

"Can you take him to the infirmary?" Danny asked. "One of his loved ones was just admitted."

Before the acolyte could answer, Danny stepped past him, dragging Em along. He glanced back at the meezu. "This acolyte will take you to Nefertiti. I'll come to check on her later."

They left the Hall of Statues and walked through the grand corridors of the temple. He waved down another acolyte and sent them to alert the council.

"This ought to be interesting," he said under his breath.

They came into the vast Hall of the Strict. They made their way to the dais. The adrenaline that fueled him ran out the moment he sat on the stone floor. He sagged, nearly fell. But Em slid close to him and put her arm around him. She rested her head on his shoulder.

"I'm sorry," he said.

She sniffed and wiped her nose on the back of her hand. "I loved him."

Sharp pain squeezed Danny's throat. What could he say to that? Nothing.

A side door swung open to admit Shiv. He trotted forward, breathless. "You're back!" He wore the white robes of an acolyte, tied at the waist with a red belt embroidered with simple patterns. He'd changed little since Danny had last seen him in person, six months prior. Shiv still had those dark, sad eyes. Still cared little for social graces.

"How did you find us so fast?" Danny asked.

"I set my trainer to alert me if yours reappeared in the city." Shiv took a seat and leaned forward, eyes bright. "Did GorVit really find the Spheroid?"

"Yes. And I activated it."

Shiv smiled and motioned greedily with his fingers. "What happened?"

"Remember how we studied one-sided teleportation for a while in the trainer?"

"Pseudoscience. And it wrecked my academic reputation for a month."

"The trainer's wrong. The Spheroid *is* a one-sided teleportation device."

Shiv's mouth dropped open, and he blinked rapidly. Danny thought he could see the boy's brain recalibrating to incorporate this new information. "That's amazing. Very useful. So the Spheroid didn't contain anything dangerous after all?"

"I didn't say that. It opened a portal to a world called Hoo. There is an abandoned Asht complex there containing an archive of all kinds of stuff."

Shiv's eyes lit up at the idea of an Asht archive—of a whole library filled with lost technology and knowledge.

"Don't get too excited," Danny said. "I didn't get to see much of it. But I suspected the weapon was there somewhere. And I found it in the form of a binding sphere."

Shiv's eyes hungered for more, and he leaned forward. If he hadn't trained as an acolyte of the Strict, Danny was sure Shiv would have tried to shake the story out of him.

"Give me your journal," Danny said.

Shiv hastily dug his journal out of his pocket and handed it over.

Danny slipped the pencil from under the flap and sketched out a series of long equations. "This is what was in the binding sphere." He turned the pages for Shiv to see. The boy took it and studied the math, eyebrows furrowed.

"You're not going to tell him about Wa?" Em asked quietly.

"What about Wa?" Shiv asked absently as he scribbled some calculations on the page.

"He's dead."

Shiv paused and looked up, meeting Em's eyes for the first time. "He's what?"

"He's dead. GorVit killed him."

Shiv's face was unreadable, dispassionate even. "I'm sorry." He dropped his attention to the journal.

Em made a disgusted sound and looked away.

And then Shiv swore, an occurrence that always presaged very bad news. He looked up, face filled with worry. "You're sure GorVit didn't get this?"

"Yes. The room the binding sphere was in got destroyed. Why?"

Shiv lifted his head and closed his eyes. He took long, deep breaths.

"What is it, Shiv?"

"Yes," boomed a voice behind Danny, "what is it, acolyte?"

Danny recognized Shaggy's voice, but he didn't turn to face the bigfoot. He didn't want to give him that much respect.

Shiv wasn't in a position to ignore Hanameesovenama. He cleared his throat and pointed to the journal. "Danny got these equations from a binding sphere in an Asht complex on an unknown world that he accessed through a portal created by the Spheroid."

A chuckle came at that point, and Danny did turn, happy to see Notchy.

"That's quite a story," Notchy said. He nodded a greeting to Danny and Em. "And what do these equations tell you, my former acolyte?"

Shiv winced at the stress Notchy placed on *former*. But he pointed to a squiggle on the page. "This variable here is the Footese word *forsoom*. In Asht mathematics, this is a constant, like the speed of light. What the first equation says is that one-sided teleportation is possible. You can instantaneously travel by opening a portal using a single device. A device that is portable, no less. The Spheroid, for instance. Two-sided teleportation, on the other hand, requires two permanent platforms to be linked together by–"

"I know how teleportation works," Shaggy snapped.

Shiv shook his head violently. "There's far more here than that. The Spheroid is just one application of this technology. These other equations describe a destructive application." Shiv swallowed and met Danny's eyes. "It's a recipe for a star-striker."

Cold seeped into Danny's muscles and bones. Long after Shiv's words had faded into the silence of the Hall, the reverberations continued in Danny's mind.

Star-striker.

The breath of the bigfeet seemed to grow louder. "Explain yourself, acolyte," Shaggy said.

"The math is very complicated," Shiv said, "but I will simplify the concept for you."

Notchy chuckled quietly, and he didn't appear at all apologetic when Shaggy glared at him.

Shiv didn't notice. "If you launched the Spheroid into a star and activated it . . ."

Shiv seemed to forget his concerns and got excited about the concept. He drew a simple diagram on a blank sheet of his journal. A circle for the sun, and a dot for the device. He drew an arrow to the center of the sun and tapped it. "Once the device gets into the star and activates, it would open a teleportation portal. A big one, many thousands of kilometers in diameter. It would be like someone poking a hole in a bucket of water. The star plasma would start to drain through the portal, and the mass of the sun would drop until its nuclear fires burned out."

He scribbled in the circle, filling it with heavy black strokes. "And the star would go dark." He frowned and pursed his lips. "It wouldn't take very long at all. Perhaps a few hours if the portal was big enough."

"That's ridiculous," Shaggy said. "It would require unheard of energy to teleport that much mass away."

Shiv blinked at the bigfoot councilor. "The portal would be set to open at some random point in interstellar space. The pressure difference between the star and the void would essentially suck the star stuff out. As I said before, like water out of a hole in a bucket."

Shiv raised his eyebrows and shrugged. "But thanks to Danny, GorVit didn't get this."

Notchy grumbled, voice low and uncharacteristically serious. "And how do you know GorVit didn't get this information?"

Danny told the story of searching the archive and finding the Room of the Abhorrent. He skipped ahead to SulKit's suicide, but his voice fell off as he realized something. A terrible, terrible thing.

He remembered Wa pulling on the binding sphere, trying to get it off its stand. Wa had even hit it with his sizzlegun. Danny looked into Shiv's eyes, horrified. His voice fell to a bare whisper. "Wa touched the binding sphere."

Shiv's face paled.

"And where is your friend now?" Notchy asked, voice quiet.

Em's tears started again. Shiv pinched the bridge of his nose and breathed out. "Oh no."

Danny swallowed and buried his face in his hands. "GorVit has him."

38

YOUR LAST INSTANCE

Breyona rose from her bed and stretched her arms overhead. Her body felt good, rested, as though she'd slept for a century or more. She plucked her robe from its peg on the wall and wrapped it around her, absently wondering where her pajamas had gone. The room seemed strange. She recognized it, but it wasn't her room. . . . Certainly not the sleeping chamber of a queen.

Her stomach rumbled. She clapped her hands together sharply. A moment later, one of her meezu servants walked in and prostrated himself.

"Get up," she commanded.

The meezu stood and straightened its robe, kept its eye focused on the floor before her feet.

"Bring me food and drink at once."

The meezu backed out of the room, hands held out to either side in deference. Something about the gesture bothered Breyona.

Why is he treating me like this?

Up to this point, bigfeet had just tolerated her existence. They didn't listen to her; they didn't care about her opinions. They certainly hadn't ever shown her any deference.

Her breath caught. "The vote," she said out loud. A tsunami of memories crashed down on her then. The vote, fleeing Undermountain with Tog, meeting the giant bigfeet, the destroyed city, the palace . . . and a tangoga named JieBik.

Hastily she parted her robe and looked down at her injured leg. There was no wound at all, not even a hint of a scar.

"Ah, you're awake."

She spun to find Tog peering through the doorway. He crept in on his four pointed legs and looked around the room curiously. "They wouldn't let me see you. I had to sneak in. They said that your brain needed time to settle."

"Settle?" she asked. "From what?"

"I don't know. They won't tell me anything. I'm just a singlehead. Can you believe they tried to confiscate my boss arms?" Tog drew his knife arms behind him, tried to hide the blades. "And Jie keeps telling me that I must receive a head splice. But who could replace Yip?"

Breyona went back to the bed. It was just a simple cot, sized for a bigfoot. She sat and rubbed her temples. "I passed out. I had weird dreams." She looked around at the walls, noticing for the first time the flat, gray surface and the spartan furnishings: a cot, a lamp, and a low table against one wall. A stack of neatly folded clothes lay on the table. "Where am I?"

"You're in the tangoga facilities beneath what once was a palace."

"So who was that bigfoot that was just in here? Did Shaggy send somebody after all?"

Tog squawked with contempt. "No. That's what they call a meezu. They're some strange band of the People who have been isolated on this planet for who knows how long. From what I can tell, they don't know anything about their brethren in the rest of the galaxy. In fact, the ones who live in the city are an odd order dedicated to the service of the queen."

"I'm the queen," Breyona said. And then a moment later, her head popped up. "I am?"

Tog stepped closer, his head lowered and tilted, and he looked into her eyes. "Maybe I should find JieBik. You don't look well. You're pale. I don't think that's normal."

Breyona pushed her fingers into her cheeks, felt her nose and her jaw. They felt both familiar and wrong. "I need a mirror." Panic rose in her gut. "I need a mirror!" she cried. "Get me a mirror!"

Tog took a few hesitant steps toward the door. Breyona rose and pointed. "Now!"

What was wrong with that tangoga? Didn't it know that she was the queen and that her commands were to be obeyed instantly, without thought or hesitation?

Breyona laughed. That was ridiculous. She wasn't a queen.

The meezu came back carrying a tray. She didn't recognize any of the smells, but they made her stomach rumble nonetheless. The meezu set it down on the low table. She pulled off the cover, half fearing it might reveal the strange mush she had been fed in Undermountain. Instead, she found an array of odd fruit and a steaming bowl of stew. It smelled of spices. She lifted the bowl and sipped the hot broth eagerly, not caring if it burnt her tongue.

"Oh goodie," she said noticing a fuzzy, pink, pickle-shaped fruit. "A *bena*. My favorite." She took a bite of the juicy pickle, and inspected it in the light as she chewed. "What is this thing?"

"*Bena*," said the meezu.

She frowned at it. "Really? It looks like a p-p-pickle." The word came out slowly; it didn't seem to fit. The word was . . . English. There was no Footese word for "pickle."

But Breyona didn't know Footese. At least, she didn't think she did.

Did she?

She dropped the fruit onto the plate and stumbled to the cot and lay down, covering her eyes with her hands. "Where is that mirror?"

The meezu shuffled out and came back a moment later with Tog. The tangoga held a shard of reflective glass in one claw. "This is all I could find among the rubble in the palace." He held it up, and she stared into it.

A strange mixture of shock and relief washed through her. She was herself. Her mother always said Breyona had her father's eyes. And then horror filled her because she was not herself. And it wasn't just because her hair was crazy and matted on one side from lying down. The shape of her nose, the angle of her jaw . . . it was right, but it was wrong.

"Who am I?" she asked.

JieBik clattered in and pushed Tog aside with disgust. "You really must get that head splice. I can't bear to look at you like this." Bik twisted toward the meezu. "And neither of you should be in here. The patient hasn't settled yet."

Breyona looked up at the tangoga. "What did you do to me?" Her words came out furious, filled with accusations that she didn't actually want to make.

JieBik stood in front of her, golden claws clasped in tight fists. "Very good news. You weren't corrupt after all. It appears that whomever pulled your current body instance from cryo did not follow procedure at all. You didn't even have an implant!" Jie's feathers waved teal, and his head bobbed as if that fact was hilarious. "It's no wonder you didn't know who you were. Fortunately the damage that killed you wasn't too severe. We were able to revive and repair the body."

Breyona didn't follow half of what the tangoga said, but she did hear one thing. "I died? You repaired my body?"

"Yes. And after the repairs, we simply performed an implant, downloaded your memories, and now you are in the settling phase.

There is no reason to be alarmed. If you check your memories, you will remember that the disconcertion you currently feel happens each time you are re-instantiated. You've been through it 113 times. And there's more good news. We were able to use a very recent backup of your previous instance, taken just prior to the siege. Everything will come back to you in time."

Breyona had no idea what JieBik was talking about. . . . Except something he said sparked a question. "Where is my . . . previous instance?"

"I believe it went missing in the restricted area of the Asht complex. We're only allowed to go into the regeneration and incubation labs."

What Jie said made an odd sense to her, and yet it seemed crazy. "But, I'm not dead. I didn't die. I've died many times, but I'm not dead. I never died. Yes, I have." Breyona heard what she was saying. It all made sense. It all was true.

"Goodness me," Jie said and waved his golden claws dismissively. "Why did SulKit have to blow themselves up and leave us with this mess? Now please be careful. We have more important things to take care of than repairing you every time you get injured or killed. There's not a single competent tangoga left alive in the city, unless you count that disgusting single-head."

"Which we don't," Kit said, shooting a nasty glare at Tog, who sulked in the corner.

Jie nodded in agreement. "Now, I have to go pull some tangeg from cryo. I don't know how SulKit did things, but at the Verfes outpost, we stuck to procedure. We'll do the same here."

Breyona closed her eyes, took a deep breath, and found her center of calm. "You said you performed an implant and download on me. You called me Nefertiti. But my name is Breyona. I am the Queen of the Golden–

"No, I'm not! I'm from Chicago. I go to All Saints Academy."

Panic boiled all around her calm, threatening to seep in and take hold.

Jie glared at Tog and the meezu. "You've upset her. If her implant becomes corrupted because you—"

"Get out!" Breyona shouted. She emphasized her words with a spear of anger.

Bik squawked and ducked his head low, and Jie stumbled sideways. "Yes, my queen." The tangoga backed out of the room and clattered down the hall.

In a fit of frustration, Breyona stood and spun around, looking for something to destroy. She grasped the edge of the cot and lifted with all of her strength, sending it tumbling to the other side of the room.

She let out a frustrated cry and looked up at the ceiling. "Who am I?"

Waves of fear emanated from her, sending the meezu priest and Tog to the floor.

39

FOR WHO SHE WAS

The infirmary was tucked into a sub-basement of the Temple of the Strict. Danny had been there once, months before, to interrogate a tangoga named WadZoo. He strode the halls asking various tangoga and bigfeet where he might find the human girl. They pointed to a door down the hall. He found Nefer lying on a bed, covered with white blankets. The meezu priest lay asleep on the floor.

Nefer's eyes were closed. A great, black bruise covered one side of her face. The other side was completely untouched and as beautiful as ever. Something about the way she slept made her look child-like, innocent. So very different from the Nefertiti he knew.

He thought about all the lives she had lived. He wondered how many times she had reached eighty or one hundred years old before she died. Only to wake up the next day, a sixteen year old girl. What a blessing that would seem at first. He could only imagine the long, lonely torture she had endured over the thousands of years of her lives.

In that moment, he felt a little catch in his breath, a little pain in his throat. Despite all her impatience, bossiness, and manipulation, Danny couldn't help but feel something for her. Unlike Breyona, who had found every excuse to avoid him, Nefer had wanted him.

He put his hand on her forehead. Her skin felt too warm, and he noticed a sheen of perspiration on her face.

Nefer didn't appear to be connected to any machines; there was no IV drip. He remembered the first time they had come to Undermountain. Breyona had been injured, and a bigfoot named Ty had done something to heal her head. Apparently, they hadn't been able to do the same for Nefertiti.

He turned at the sound of steps behind him. The tangoga who entered had one unusually short neck, which placed its left head a good five centimeters below the right.

"Who are you?" Danny asked.

"Siy," said the short head. "Dil," said the tall head. SiyDil stepped around Danny and approached Nefer. They held a strange object in their claw, kind of like a trainer, but smaller with no screen. The tangoga waved the device briefly over Nefer's face.

"What is that thing?" Danny asked.

"A general diagnostics device. It's not tuned to humans, but it can detect things like brain activity, of which there is very little in this subject." Siy looked Danny up and down. He pulled a small leather pouch from a pocket and handed it to Danny. "She had this on her person when she arrived."

Danny took it and looked at it distractedly. "Why didn't you give it to the meezu."

Siy squawked quietly. "He wouldn't take it. An odd one, that one is."

Danny looked down at Nefer. "So there is some brain activity?"

"Yes. But little high level activity–thinking or even dreaming–is present in the subject."

"So do something. Heal her."

The short head swiveled to face Danny. "I'm afraid there's nothing we can do. At this point, we're just observing the course of the injury in order to learn how to diagnose this in future subjects. It is our understanding that there will be an influx of humans into the city soon."

"Can't you just put her in a new body like you've always done before?"

Dil squawked and chuckled. "Single-head."

Siy studied Danny. "What makes you think we've given a person a new body? Even if that was possible, without strong brain function, there'd be nothing to transfer."

Danny felt the weight of the situation hit him then. The Asht technology that the tangoga on Hoo possessed was beyond anything the tangoga or the bigfeet had here.

"Isn't there any chance she'll get better?"

"No. "

"But she isn't even on any life support. How is that possible?"

"Well," Siy said wearily, "one of the functions of the implant is to keep low level body functions going. If she were a tangoga that fact would be very important because, you know, to lose a head would be a travesty beyond compare. The implant keeps the head alive and ready for extraction."

Siy straightened Nefer's blanket and considered her for a moment. "We *could* perform extraction if you like."

"And that would do what? Store her on some hard drive someplace?"

Dil scoffed. "Hard drive."

Siy ignored Dil. "That's about all we could do. Store her. We could access much of her memory core and, uh, download to someone else if we needed to. It wouldn't transfer the person, you understand. But a memory dump has certainly been done many times among the tangoga. Usually only when a boss is killed and we need to pass the boss's memories to their successor."

Dil nodded in agreement. "Meet the new boss, same as the old boss."

"I don't want to store her that way," Danny said after a moment's pause. "But . . . is there a way to end this?"

"Oh, I suppose," Siy said. "If we knew her code, we could just send a shutdown command, and the implant would essentially turn off. That would–"

"Wait a minute," Danny said. "You can do that? Turn off the implant?"

"Of course."

"Does it kill tangoga when you do that without blowing them up?"

"No, no, not at all. It just turns a tangoga back into a . . . you know." SiyDil's feathers fluttered nervously.

Danny could tell that Siy didn't want to talk about it, didn't want to acknowledge the fact that every tangoga had been raised from a mere animal tangeg.

"But if we shut down her implant, she would . . . let go?"

"It would depend on the extent of the damage. But in my expert opinion, she would expire."

Danny gazed down at Nefer, focusing on the unmarred side of her face. She looked so peaceful. It seemed she could wake up at any moment and try to kiss him. And yet, she might lay there for days or months, alive but not alive. "How do we get the code?"

"We must extract it."

"Do it."

"It won't take a moment." SiyDil hustled out.

Danny took Nefer's small, delicate hand and stroked her fingers. The perfectly manicured nails were broken and chipped from her fall.

SiyDil clattered back in, rolling an implant apparatus before him. He lowered it over Nefertiti's face. Less than a minute later, the whining stopped and SiyDil shoved the cart away. "I've got it."

He pulled a device from his pocket and jabbed at it with his claws. "I've entered the code. Are you sure you want to do this?"

Danny swallowed against a hard lump in his throat and turned back to Nefer. He brushed the hair from her brow. He'd never known her for who she was, and perhaps she hadn't known who she was after all she had endured.

He held out his hand to SiyDil. "Give it to me."

SiyDil paused, then handed over the device. It looked similar to a detonator, though smaller. "This button here," Siy said.

"Can you wait outside?"

Dil was about to say something, but Siy cut him off with a squawk, and they left the room. Danny knelt next to Nefer and took her hand in his. "I'm sorry." He kissed her skin, still warm with life.

The meezu awoke with a start and stood. At the sight of Danny he bowed low. Danny met the meezu's eyes. "She's dying. Is there some last rite or prayer you want to say."

The meezu covered its ears with its hands and moaned.

"You have a duty to perform."

The meezu stopped moaning and blinked. He slowly lowered his hands and straightened. Then, after one last, long look at Nefer, he closed eyes and began to chant in a low, solemn cadence.

Danny pressed the button.

There was no sudden change, but in time her breath slowed. The meezu priest continue his chant, growing quieter with each repetition. Danny stayed with Nefer, counting the seconds between each inhalation, until with a final sigh she let go.

He waited for the change to come over him. To feel the difference between life and death. But the room felt the same. Nothing magical or mystical happened.

He got up and headed for the door, pausing once to look back at the dead queen. He remembered the pouch SiyDil had handed him. He looked down at it, wondering what she had valued so much that she took the time to grab it amidst the chaos of the siege.

He peered in, gasped, and pulled the drawstring tight with a quick jerk. With tears in his eyes, he stuffed the pouch in his pocket and strode into the hallways of the temple, a widower at sixteen.

40

SOMETHING'S AMISS

JieBik clattered into Breyona's room, golden claws clasped before him. "My queen," Jie said, "are you feeling quite well yet?"

Breyona exhaled and opened her eyes. "Much better than before. But still confused."

"The implant has had sufficient time to settle." He hesitated, obviously worried about how to behave in front of her. "My queen, we have not been successful herding the horgodons out of the city. I was wondering if perhaps you could help. We've killed several of them, but–"

"You did what?" Though she was calm inside, a storm of electric emotions crackled around the edges of her peace.

"I thought perhaps if we used force we might be able to get them out," Jie said. "They won't leave, and they're in the way. They stink and they befoul the whole city. And quite frankly, I have a lot of work to do to set things right."

Breyona thought of Tiny. "If you've killed my friends, I'll

destroy you." As soon as the words left Breyona's mouth, they sounded wrong to her. After all, her whole existence for the past six months had been about not being upset, about not being angry, certainly not threatening people.

JieBik ducked his heads deferentially. "I'm sorry if I have upset you, my queen."

"I'm not your queen," she said.

"Of course, Nefertiti."

Bik whispered something in Jie's ear.

"Shut up, Bik," Breyona said and gasped. She reached out a hand. "I'm sorry, Bik. I shouldn't have said that."

"No need to apologize," Jie said. "Bik is always talking out of turn."

Breyona closed her eyes and took deep breaths. She found the calm she sought, but she also found anger. She didn't understand how it was possible to hold both inside her at once.

"Um, Nefertiti . . . the horgodons?"

Breyona sighed and stood. "My name is not Nefertiti. It's Nefer–it's Breyona. Go on. Lead the way."

They emerged into bright, hot, humid daylight. The sky was hazy yet cloudless. Jie looked up at the sun. "The rains will be here soon. I hope we still have time."

They walked across a plaza, and Breyona found herself back in front of the destroyed palace. Collected in a rough circle were four of her giant friends.

Tiny saw her first. He leapt up and ran to her so fast she was afraid he was going to stomp her into the ground. He slowed and stooped down to look at her. She thought she saw concern in those huge, wide eyes, each one nearly the size of her head. "It's okay, Tiny," she said and passed reassurance to him and to the others.

She looked around. The city wasn't in any worse condition than when she had arrived. "I don't understand your concern, Jie. It does not look like they're causing any harm."

"It's just the principle. We can't have these beasts running amok in our city. If we try to rebuild anything, they'll just destroy it again."

"And why would you bother rebuilding? Nobody lives here except for you and some meezu. As far as I'm concerned the meezu can go back to the cliffs. I don't need servants or priests."

Just as she spoke, a procession of meezu walked into the plaza. At the front were two priests, each wearing elaborate headdresses and carrying staves. Behind them trailed ten more meezu, all dressed in white robes ornamented with gold. They stopped twenty paces away, the priests watching the horgodons uncertainly.

Breyona sighed and waved them forward. "Come here. Come here."

The priests eyed Tiny and didn't move.

Breyona pointed at Tiny. "He's not going to hurt you. Come here." And just to make sure there was no fighting, she sent out a sphere of calm and goodwill. The priests and the other meezu visibly relaxed.

"You can go home," she said to the meezu. "You don't have to serve me any longer."

The priest bowed his head. "That is not a choice that we can make. Knowing what we know, we cannot return to the cliffs."

"And what is it that you know?" she demanded.

The bigfoot paused. "Well, you know, of course."

Breyona thought for a second and realized she did know. That the meezu had been bred down from the horgodons, their intelligence uplifted as their brains had been genetically combined with those of the Asht.

"If we were to return to the cliffs," said the priest, "I fear one of us would reveal the truth to our families. Many would jump to their deaths as a result."

"Then stay. But understand that I'm leaving as soon as I can. I don't belong here. I only came back to find my friends."

"Ah," the priest said, "King Danny. It was a pity your nuptials were followed so closely by the siege. We had a week's worth of celebrations planned, and all of it came to naught."

"Why would you say Danny is the king?" she asked.

The meezu blinked at her.

JieBik stepped forward and addressed the priest. "Her last backup was restored, but sometimes it takes a while for the synaptic pathways to access all memories."

"Just stop," Breyona said to Jie. She turned to the priest. "King Danny, weddings . . . you need to fill me in because I have no idea what you're talking about."

"Why Nefertiti," the priest said. "Just a few days ago you married the human visitor, Danny."

"I am not Nefertiti." She emphasized her words with a blast of anger.

Tiny growled and pounded his fist on the ground, making it tremble. The priest growled back, and the meezu behind him crowded forward, teeth bared. JieBik shrieked like a tangeg.

Breyona cut off the anger and replaced it with numbness until they all fell silent.

"I'm sorry," she said. "I didn't mean to do that. If you have a record of this wedding, I demand to see it."

"Very well," Jie said. "This way."

"Just you and this priest here, these others should get to work cleaning up the city." As she headed back toward the tangoga quarters, she heard Tiny following along with his other horgodon companions. She turned on him and sent a reassuring wave to him. "No, you're too big to follow. You need to help them." She pointed to the meezu. "Help them clean up the city."

Tiny looked at her uncertainly.

"That's a nice idea, my queen," Jie said. "But it's fruitless to attempt to communicate with these brutes."

Breyona knew that Tiny was more intelligent than he seemed. She knew that the horgodons had a rudimentary language. She walked to a small pile of rubble nearby and picked up a loose stone. She set it into the back of a chariot. She did it again then pointed to Tiny. "You, pick up a rock, put it in here."

Tiny grabbed a boulder the size of small car, hefted it, and dropped it onto the chariot. The wheels splayed to each side and the axle snapped with a loud pop.

Jie squawked and waved his arms. Two tangoga came running, and Jie shrieked orders at them. He turned to Breyona. "We have other modes of conveyance that are better suited for clearing away debris. Will your beasts listen to tangoga?"

Breyona went to Tiny and stroked his arm and pointed to JieBik. "Do what he says. Help clean up the city." She waved her arm around. "Clean up."

Tiny didn't give any indication of whether he understood. He just grunted and looked at her sadly.

"Perhaps these meezu should model the behavior we want from the horgodons," she said. "They should be helping anyway."

"As you command," the priest said. He seemed excited for the others to have something to do. Even before he could pass along her order, they started swarming over piles of rubble, clearing it away.

"Make sure they use some logic in how they clean stuff out. Focus on clearing out all of the dead bodies and waste. That stuff carries disease. Then make sure you all have shelter. Don't worry about the palace." The priest passed along the orders and then turned to follow her and JieBik back into the tangoga quarters.

The viewing room held nothing but a wide screen. JieBik uttered a command, and a video began to play. She saw a procession of meezu, all dressed in ornate outfits. Then there was Danny, arrayed in a strange Egyptian costume. He rode in a chariot pulled by two meezu. Ahead of him in a separate chariot, rode Em and

Wa. Grizz strode next to them. They assembled in the temple, the meezu priest standing before an altar.

They waited there for a long time.

"It appears you wanted to make a grand entrance," Jie said.

In walked the most beautiful woman Breyona had ever seen. It was a strange moment, similar to watching herself on TV when she had been featured for her work with inner city kids. An odd sense of disconnect struck her because the woman didn't look like her. And yet it did.

"That's me," she said, "but I don't look like that anymore."

Jie looked from the screen and back to Breyona. "Something's amiss. That's *not* you."

"Yes, it is."

The camera zoomed in on the queen's face. She was Breyona's age, maybe slightly older. The girl held her chin high. Her eyes bore straight ahead, clearly focused on Danny. Her expression was regal, though the hint of a smile played on her lips.

"I remember this," Breyona said.

"It isn't you," Jie said, voice filled with shock.

"Yes, it is."

The camera panned back to Danny.

"I married Danny," she said, awed.

Jie stopped the video with a word and glared at the meezu priest. "You said this human," he pointed a golden finger at Brey-ona, "was Nefertiti."

The meezu priest squinted and raised his chin. "She is."

"They don't even *look* the same!" JieBik's feathers ruffled from gray to teal, and he stamped a pointed foot.

The priest waved his staff dismissively. "She returned to us in a new incarnation, this one even more powerful than the last. She bends the very emotions of her subjects." He bowed his head low. "NeferNeferNefer commands even the great horgodons."

Bik squawked and glanced at Jie. "Looks like you committed a terrible breach of procedure, Jie." He seemed somewhat delighted by it.

Jie lowered his head, feathers flashing gray, blue, gray. "I'm sorry, human. But it appears I've made a terrible mistake."

41

WISER THAN US ALL

Danny paced from the giant sofa to the huge dining table in his old Undermountain apartment. Em sat on the sofa, eyes puffy, face haggard. Next to her, sitting cross-legged, was Grizz. Shiv sat on the floor, also cross-legged, his eyes closed in meditation.

A cold decision had formed in Danny's mind since he'd left Nefer's side. At first he hadn't recognized it for what it was, thinking he'd just gone numb from exhaustion. But the numbness wasn't a lack of feeling.

It was determination. The kind that blocks out all other considerations. Nothing would turn him from his objective now, not the revelation that Breyona and Tog had gone looking for him, nor the news that Bronson and Shiv had voted for First Contact.

He glanced at Shiv. "You say Shaggy recovered the Spheroid?"

Shiv opened his eyes. "Yes. I was present when two defenders returned with it."

"Do you know where he keeps it?"

"In his quarters."

Danny took a deep breath, tried to slow his heart. Not that he was having second thoughts. "We have to steal it."

Shiv's eyes went wide, and his face paled.

"Yes," Em said, expression brightening. She stood, filled with sudden energy. "We'll go back and get Wa. And Breyona."

Danny stopped his pacing and looked down at his sister. He smiled at her sadly. "We're not going to Hoo."

Her large eyes welled up. "Then where . . .?"

Danny turned to Grizz. "Tell them what you told me."

Grizz nodded somberly. "The council just got word that Gor has withdrawn his forces from Ig. The rogue tangoga have all fled the planet via interplanetary hubs." Grizz closed his eyes and inhaled deeply. "We've received reports of similar retreats on other contested planets."

"But that's good, isn't it?" Em said. "The war is over."

Before Grizz could answer, Shiv spoke up. "No, Emma. It's bad. Very bad. The only reason Gor would withdraw his troops is because he has the star-striker technology."

Em swore and angrily wiped tears from her face. "But what about Breyona? She came after us. And what about poor Tog? And Wa might still be . . ." She broke down and covered her face.

Danny swallowed hard and looked away from his sister's suffering. No one wanted to go to Hoo more than he did. He wanted to find Breyona, wanted to hold her. He needed to explain himself and ask her for forgiveness. And he needed to tell her something else, something he realized he'd never actually said aloud.

He needed to tell her he loved her.

He went to the wall of windows that overlooked the city and stared out. "Breyona is wiser than us all," he said. "She knows that sometimes you have to sacrifice what you want most in service of the greater good. And that's what I have to do now. I can't go after Breyona . . . because I have to stop GorVit."

The reflection of Em's eyes in the window met his. "How?" she asked, so quietly Danny wouldn't have heard it if he hadn't seen her lips moving.

"I plan to use the Spheroid to go to Tangoga Prime. I'm going to find the Octz, or the Glutz, or maybe even the Supreme Primary. Either they'll order GorVit to stop, or I'll find a way to detchain the whole hierarchy. Every last one of them."

The idea of such wholesale slaughter made him queasy. As much as he hated GorVit, he didn't relish killing. But he would do it if he had to.

Em stepped next to him. Her hand found his, and she turned him to face her. "That's a suicide mission. Let the Council send defenders."

Grizz rubbed at an ear, and a long, low rumble sounded in his chest. Danny thought it might be anger. "The council has sent word to the Great Mother on Ig," Grizz said. "How the People react to the threat of the star-striker is entirely in her hands now."

"The Great Mother?" Danny said. He scanned his implant and discovered that the bigfoot society in the galaxy mirrored very closely that of the meezu on Hoo. That the females and the males lived separately, and that the true power in the society resided with a sisterhood led by the Great Mother.

He felt a surge of hope. "Will she send a delegation to the Octz? Does she have some other plan? A proactive one?"

Grizz lifted his hands in a shrug. "I don't know anything about what goes on among the sisterhood, but it seems quite unlikely. If GorVit successfully unleashes a star-striker, it may prompt her to move. It depends on factors that I don't truly understand."

"There is hope then," Em said. "We should wait. GorVit can't get the star-striker to Earth that fast anyway. He can't even get into our solar system without coming through Antarctica, right?"

Shiv blinked at her. "You haven't been listening, Emma. The star-striker is an application of one-sided teleportation. Gor can craft a teleportation spheroid as easily as he can a star-striker.

They're essentially the same device. Gor will soon be able to teleport anywhere he wants. Including to our little solar system."

Danny could tell by Em's face that she wanted to argue, wanted to deny what was plain to them all. But in the end, she just covered her face. "I'm so tired."

Danny walked with his sister to the sofa, sat with his arm around her shoulder. "I'm tired too. But I won't leave our destiny in the hands of those who will not act. It's clear the People will not shelter us. It's time for the human race to stand up for itself."

Grizz covered his ears with his hands. "It shames me to admit it, but Danny is right."

"Do you have your trainer?" Danny asked Shiv. "Can you bring up the Spheroid simulation?"

Shiv dug in the deep pocket of his acolyte robes and brought out his trainer. Danny noticed how Shiv's hands shook.

"I never knew it would be this bad," Shiv said to himself. He spoke to the trainer then turned it so everyone could see the display. "As you discovered, Danny, the top and bottom rings set up the Spheroid for teleportation. The middle ring sets the destination. I've discovered that every destination requires a slightly different setup. But unless one of these symbols on the middle ring is for Tangoga Prime, the Spheroid won't be of much use."

"Why can't we just teleport there from Antarctica?" Em asked. "I thought that's what the hub there was for?"

"Because Tangoga Prime doesn't have an interplanetary hub," Shiv said. "At least, not one known to the People." Shiv studied the simulation, spinning the middle ring and inspecting the symbols.

Danny pointed to one of the marks. "This is the one for Tangoga Prime." He squinted at Shiv, perplexed. "But you should know that now that you've had the download."

Shiv's face reddened slightly, and he cleared his throat. "Hanameesovenama is a savvy negotiator. He asked for my vote in return for the implant. I accepted. But when the time came, I only received the implant. Not the download."

Em responded with a dark laugh. "I can't tell you how happy I am to hear that, Shiv. It's nothing less than what you deserve."

Shiv lifted his chin slightly. "I'm very sorry that I misled Breyona, but I would have voted the way I voted no matter what Shaggy promised me. I voted my conscience."

Em was about to light into Shiv, but Danny placed a hand on her arm. "Not now, Em. We've got to stay focused."

Begrudgingly, she agreed and looked away from Shiv, though Danny could almost feel the prickliness radiating from her.

"So Shiv, how are you going to get the Spheroid?" Danny asked.

"What–?" Shiv looked aghast. "Me?"

Danny squatted and looked Shiv in the eye. "You betrayed everything!" His shout slapped back from the walls. Em shot upright and covered her mouth.

Shiv leaned away.

Danny realized his fists were clenched. He relaxed them and lowered his voice to a near whisper. "Maybe you voted your conscience, maybe not. I think you sold your vote for First Contact out of pure selfishness. You owe the world a huge debt."

Shiv straightened and glared back at Danny. "Everything was taken from me. Everything!" His lips trembled, and he struggled to take deep breaths, but they shuddered in his chest.

Beneath his rage, Danny felt a pang of pity for Shiv, whose parents had been killed in a car accident, leaving him to be raised by an aunt. But that was no excuse. Shiv cared only about acquiring knowledge without regard to the cost.

Danny moved even closer to his friend. "Do you truly believe First Contact by the bigfeet, and everything that means, is what's best for us?"

Shiv blinked, and tears welled in his eyes. He looked down at his hands, which shook in his lap. "No."

Danny moved to sit between Em and Grizz. "I wish First Contact was our biggest problem. But it isn't."

Shiv collected himself and looked from Grizz to Em and finally to Danny. "I can get the Spheroid. I think."

They planned deep into the night. And when they had all agreed, they went their separate ways. Shiv to his meditation cell, Grizz to make preparations, and Em to her room.

Danny stayed by the window, though he no longer saw the city before him. He gazed down at the pouch SiyDil had handed him. He opened it and dumped out its contents: a charm necklace with a sparkly B and a heart with a little keyhole in the middle.

42

ONLY ONE WAY

Breyona stood on the city wall and gazed back at the city. The sun was just rising, and it flamed off the top of the golden pyramid. Below, teams of horgodons and meezu cleared rubble from the city. The wreckage of the meezu dormitories was gone, replaced with new construction. At Breyona's orders, the remains of the palace had been disassembled, much of it salvaged for repairs of other structures.

She glanced at Tog who stood next to her, shifting uneasily from pointed foot to pointed foot. "You know what to do?" she asked.

"Yes," the tangoga said, "although I still think this is a terrible idea."

Breyona placed a calming hand on Tog's head. "You're doing a wonderful thing. I understand that no one can replace Yip."

Tog nodded and clattered away, disappearing from view. Breyona looked out over the wall into the long valley. The grass in front of the wall lay trampled and muddy from the siege.

"Do it," said a voice in her head.

But she didn't move. Instead, she gazed down at the shiny new placard that listed the names of the meezu who had thrown themselves from this point. So many names. She felt some satisfaction that the cliff meezu had learned the truth. She'd seen to that. And she had helped those who had needed it through the worst of the shock. There would be no more jumpers. And JieBik had agreed to allow all meezu to move back into the city, those who wanted to anyway.

Mother insisted that she would stay in the cliffs and keep the females apart from the males. Breyona didn't really care what decision they made as long as they didn't have to suffer so much.

Her thoughts turned to Danny. She still couldn't understand why he had agreed to marry someone he hardly knew. JieBik wasn't any help, as he had arrived in the city after Danny and the others had disappeared into the Asht complex.

The meezu priests didn't have any insights into Danny either. They just assumed that everyone should do what Nefertiti wanted and that anyone who had the opportunity to marry her was honored above all other beings in the galaxy. Breyona shook her head and sighed.

And then another memory emerged.

She had used leverage over Danny to get him to marry her. She'd promised to let him know how to get into the Asht complex.

"I would never do that," she said.

But she had. The memories had been there since she'd been healed; she just hadn't known how to access them. Watching the video of the wedding had opened a channel to them, though. Sometimes they came to her unbidden.

She couldn't blame Danny for the wedding given the circumstances. But then again . . . she remembered how he'd looked at her. The desire. The lust!

How could he be interested in someone as mean as she was?

No. As mean as *Nefertiti* was.

My name is Breyona Lewis. It had become her new mantra.

A meezu ran up the steps to join her on the wall. It bowed low. "My queen, the portal has closed."

Breyona took a deep breath of moist air and clicked her tongue. "So that's that," she said to herself. She pulsed calm into the meezu, like a ritual blessing, and dismissed him.

And now she had to put all of her trust in Tog.

The sun rose higher. Soon it would be too humid to bear being outside. She glanced back at the city to see JieBik clattering down the thoroughfare, waving his arms and shrieking.

Apparently Tog had passed his message to the tangoga boss. That was all Breyona needed to know.

Besides, JieBik had driven her to this. She'd learned that no amount of calm, trust, anger, or fear could make a tangoga break with procedure.

There is only one way in.

She pushed herself between the golden crenellations and stood on the lip of the wall.

She raised her arms to the sky.

She closed her eyes.

And she jumped.

The End of Book Two
of *Bigfoot Galaxy.*
The adventure concludes in *Star-Striker.*

Star-Striker **is the stunning final act in** ***Bigfoot Galaxy.***

While the wicked bigfoot leader Hanameesovenama plans First Contact with the human race, Danny races to stop the vile tangoga boss GorVit from using the star-striker weapon to destroy the sun.

In their search, they find an ancient king who may hold the key to preventing the apocalypse.

Star-Striker (Bigfoot Galaxy #3)